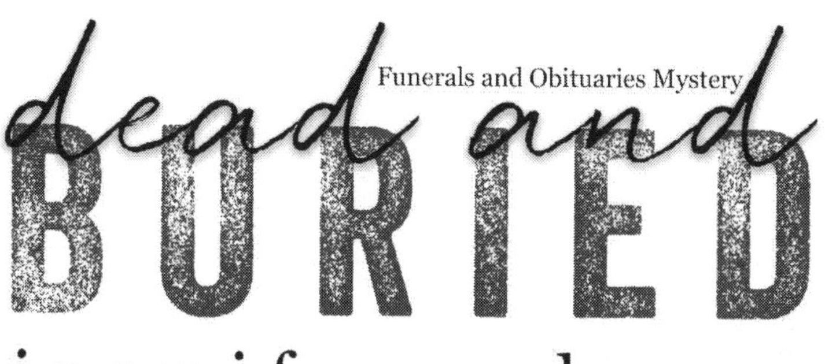

jennifer rebecca

Dead and Buried

Cover Design by
Alyssa Garcia
www.uplifting-designs.com

Photographer:
Shauna Kruse
www.kruseimagesandphotography.com

Model:
BT Urruela
www.bturruela.com

Editing by
Bethany Pennypacker
bethanyp345@ gmail.com

For more information about Jennifer Rebecca & her books, visit:
www.jenniferrebeccaauthor.com

DEDICATION

For my grandma Rita and my granny Lillian, who taught me to love, laugh, and take no prisoners. Every day I try my best to make you proud.

I love you always.

IN LOVING MEMORY OF MY GRANDFATHERS

Judge Murry Luftig

1922–2015

United States Army Air Corps

Master Chief Jones Rhineheart Pierce Jr.

1925–2015

United States Coast Guard

You are always in my heart, and I miss you every day. Not one day has gone by that I haven't thought of something I wanted to say to you, to make you smile, to make you laugh. It's then that I know you are with me.

I love you always.

Until we meet again.

prologue

TRAPPED IN THE CLOSET

Do you ever feel like you're stuck in an R. Kelly song? Because I'm definitely feeling like I'm living one. You could almost say I'm trapped in one. But not the *toot toot, beep beep* fun of "Ignition" or the motivational "I Believe I Can Fly"— I'm talking "Trapped in the Closet." All seventy-five parts. Because, you know, I am actually trapped in a closet. A utility closet to be specific.

I have no idea what happened. One minute, I'm walking up the stairs of the building my granny lives in, Peaceful Sunset Retirement Village, singing, ironically, "Ignition." I had just gotten to the good part, you know, the "hot and fresh out the kitchen" part—it's the part where I like to mime driving a car, the part after the toots when I pull down my arm like I'm honking the horn on a big rig. I'm right in the middle of my song and dance repertoire—when all of a sudden, I hear one of the doors to the stairwell open and close, which is normal since the nurses and caregivers use these halls to get around faster and not clog up the elevators that the seniors use. The next thing I know, something hits me over the head, and it's lights out. I never even saw the guy. *Or gal.* Who am I to discriminate?

Anyhoo, fast forward, however long that might be, and I find myself awake, with a killer headache. A headache a lot like the one I got when I fell out of my friend's parents' camper in the second grade. My friend who was also named Shelby. Weird, right? Anyway, we were playing after school at her house, and her mom found nothing wrong with our playing in one of those VW vans that were small campers with the part that pops up out of the roof for you to sleep in.

So there we were, playing with our Super Spy Barbies in the pop-up part, when she jumped down to get a clothing change for her doll. Shelby B., as our teachers in school called her to distinguish between us, was a lot bigger than me. I was the runt of the litter back then. When she went to pull herself back up, dress included, she grabbed the board I was sitting on, and I wasn't big enough to hold the board down, so Other Shelby pulled me and the board down on top of her. We landed in order: board, then me, then the dolls and their accoutrements. After that, I bounced off of her and out the open sliding door onto the sidewalk, face first.

Next thing I knew, I was coming to, and her mom was running down the driveway with the phone to her ear. A couple of minutes later, my mom and dad pulled up in my mom's old Jeep Cherokee, followed by a fire truck and an ambulance.

As it turned out, I had one hell of a concussion, which we found out while my dad was hanging out with all of the firemen and paramedics that he knew because they all played basketball together at the gym. I spent the night in the emergency room and the next week with the mother of all headaches, which is how I feel right now as I struggle to open my eyes and make them focus.

I look around and everything is blurry. I blink my eyes a couple of times to clear my vision. It helps a little. I take stock of what's around me—there are mops and brooms, shelves of lightbulbs and other various paraphernalia, cleaning supplies—when it dawns on me where I am, which is how I find myself trapped in a utility closet, à la R. Kelly.

I'm sitting on the floor on my butt with my back against some more shelves. My legs are straight out in front of me, and my ankles are tied together with a zip tie. Yippee! I groan out loud when I realize my hands are bound the same way behind my back.

I could lie down and wait for a psycho to come back and finish me off, but that's not how my daddy raised me. And if I did die because I was being a big baby, Granny would bring me back to life just to whoop my butt and kill me again. I wiggle around, trying to find anything I can break these zip ties on. I notice the door has hinges that look like little hooks, and I scoot over to try to hook the tie on my ankles to it. I wiggle and kick my legs and wiggle some more, all pretty thankful I keep my biweekly yoga date with my grandmother and her friends.

I hook the zip tie on the bottom door hinge and kick my feet by bending and straightening my knees. "Come on, come on," I chant under my breath as I rub the plastic against the sharp side of the door hinge. "Yes!" I shout as the tie breaks. I swing to my knees and push up to my feet. My legs shake. Impressive considering there's a polka band playing in my head and I kind of want to puke.

I lean my right shoulder against the shelves and squeeze my eyes tight, hoping to stop the room from spinning before I can find something to undo the tie at my wrists. My eyes pop open at the sudden quiet rattle of the door. I have to squint against the intrusion of the bright light that is immediately switched on. When I open them again, I am face-to-face with the vibrant jade eyes of one sexy Detective Trenton Foyle, San Diego PD.

"Jesus, Shelby, you scared the shit out of me!" he booms. I just roll my eyes, which I instantly regret, slamming them shut again.

"What?" I ask innocently.

"You just can't help yourself, can you?" he asks.

"I don't understand what you're talking about," I say coyly.

"You just have to stir up trouble, don't you?" he

asks, shaking his head.

I don't care to answer, so I don't. It's not like I find myself trapped in a closet every day. Who am I kidding? I may not find trouble, but trouble always has a way of finding me. I'd like to say this is the last time, but why lie? My name is Shelby Whitmore, and I'm sort of a reporter for the *San Diego Metro News* and most definitely trapped in a closet.

HOOKERS, VIAGRA, & GRAVEYARD DIRT

Two Weeks Earlier . . .

Today, I am a published author. Today, all of my dreams come true. Not too many, but some moons ago, my mom told me that being a literature and writing major was about as useful as a four-year degree in philosophy or underwater basket weaving. But I was sold.

I had fallen in love with Keats and Shelley, Shakespeare, and the Brownings, and of course Nora Roberts and E.L. James, too. Since then I have wanted nothing but to be a writer. It's my life's goal. Now not the White House–visiting, Nobel Prize–winning, Great American Novel–writing kind, but the bodice-ripping, Fabio-covering, down-and-dirty-but-with-a-happily-ever-after kind.

I haven't just been twiddling my thumbs since I graduated; I have been doing my romance-writing research, obviously. I've been reading as many romance books as I can. Writing as much as I can. And selling kitchen cabinet hardware at Home Depot like a boss. Hey, a girl's gotta eat.

And I can sell the shit out of some kitchen cabinets. And cut keys and thread pipe. All while hoping I would meet a shirtless contractor swinging some serious lead pipe. And maybe inspire a few books.

Sadly, that only happened in my head, but it was a recurring, long-standing affair with no one real. Well . . . there was this one guy and he was wearing a shirt, but after some quality flirting and a seriously white smile, I never saw him again. But I digress.

Today, I am a published author. Actually, I haven't published a book. *Yet.* I wrote a dandy little ditty for the *San Diego Metro News*. That's right I am a journalist. Not the roasting-in-Afghanistan-with-the-troops or hanging-out-in-Compton kinds, either. I'm not Anderson Cooper, after all. Today, I am a published author . . . in the Funerals and Obituaries section. But hey, I'm a hit with the blue hairs. Today, I am the newest reporter for the *San Diego Metro* newspaper. *Sort of.*

"Can you believe this shit show?" My granny asks from the seat next to mine in the North Park Funeral Home.

"Geez!" I hush her. I'm working, and this is my

very first paying gig for the *San Diego Metro News*.

"I mean, really . . . ," she continues as if I hadn't just shushed her. In reality, I'm lucky she didn't smack me. "Bitty Sue is sitting right next to Myra. What in the hell is that all about? If Old Man Di Francesco wasn't already dead, he sure would have a heart attack now."

I roll my eyes and squirm in my seat. It's uncomfortable to be without panties while working. Or at all. But Granny had said you could see my panty lines through the material of my black pencil skirt and that it was unbefitting of a lady. Personally, I think a lady might wear underpants to a funeral. And also, that Gran has something up her sleeve.

If I put much thought into it, I would probably be concerned that her plotting has me panty-less, but I'm trying to take in all the details of Mr. Di Francesco's funeral. Open casket, *check.* So many calla lilies I think I might suffocate, *check, check.* Along with the whole room, which is also filled with so many grieving old ladies and their copious amounts of Chanel No. 5 I fear someone might strike a match and we'll all die a fiery death, *heck, yes. Check, check, and more freaking checks!*

"By the looks of all these weepy ladies, I'd say Mr. Di Francesco really got around and could get it up regularly," I whisper to Gran, but not very quietly, as most of these old people are deaf anyway.

"That's because most of them are whores, dear," I hear my grandmother's partner in crime say from my other side.

I turn, gaping, because while these two old ladies are hell on wheels, this is a funeral, for Pete's sake. It's then that I'm caught in the sexual tractor beam of the sexiest man on the planet, and one I have met before. *Uh-oh.*

"Jesus, Nana!" he grumbles in the most gravelly voice ever. Like he drinks whiskey with broken glass in it for breakfast. When Marla just shrugs one shoulder in a *so what?* effect, he says, "I'm wearing my badge. We can't just be declaring people whores."

"Oh! Excuse me, sweetheart. I think you young people refer to them as 'crusty skanks,'" Marla replies honestly. And I cannot help myself—I bust up laughing.

"Or 'cum buckets,' I think," my granny adds.

My snickering turns to choking, which turns to gasping for breath, which I cannot seem to latch on to as black spots start to cloud my vision. I'm going to die. *At least I won't have to go far*, I mentally shrug. I am already in a funeral home . . .

"Deep breaths. I've got you," says the sexy man from beside me as his giant hand grabs the back of my neck and shoves my head between my knees. Which would be fabulous if he didn't just give me a bird's-eye view of the fact that I am not wearing any underpants. I feel the burn of my mortification slash across my face and creep over my neck and shoulders. Damn Irish skin! "It's okay, gorgeous. I've got you," he coos softly. "And my grandma is just as bad."

"Marla is your grandmother?" I ask while staring at my vagina.

"The one and only." He chuckles as he slides into the seat next to me. "When they made my Nana, they broke the mold," he tells me with all the love and reverence he has for her.

"I see you've met my Shelby, Trent," Granny declares, and I can hear the wicked glee in her voice.

"Oh, Shelby and I have already met," Trent tells my gran. "She helped me remodel my kitchen with a brilliant ruthlessness, but then I never got her number or last name. I haven't seen her since."

"Oh, you're the contractor! I should have put two and two together." Granny is practically bouncing in her seat with joy. I'm about to remind her we are at a funeral when she innocently asks, "Why were you swinging that lead pipe around the store, anyway?"

EEEERRRRRRMMMMKKKKKKK . . . There go the wheels skidding off the track. I shoot straight up in my seat, but it does me no good. This train is about to derail at one hundred miles per hour, and there is no stopping it. Shit, shit, *SHIT!*

"What lead pipe?" Trent asks.

Nope.

There it goes.

I'm a goner.

"Well, Shell said you looked to be . . . now what was it you said, dear?" she asks me, and it's then that I know she knows.

I glare at Granny, but she just smiles, that wicked twinkle in her eyes. Damn, I never should have shown her Google. I swear all she does is watch bad internet porn all day while she's not planning bank heists with Marla and Bitty Sue.

"Ah yes, she said you, and I quote, 'looked to be swinging some serious lead pipe around. In your pants!'" she finishes triumphantly.

Both Trent and I start choking and gasping again. He shoves my head back down between my knees as he bends over himself. I think his might have started as an awkward nervous laugh but quickly derailed. Dear Lord, I think we assaulted an officer of the law. We're going to jail. Or at least, I am because I am going to kill this old woman as soon as I get my job done. Which reminds me . . .

"As much as I would love to sit here and stare at my vagina all day, I have a job to do, and I'm pretty sure you two menaces have wreaked enough havoc on one funeral and one officer of the law," I say as sternly as I can—which is to say, not enough, because the old biddies probably didn't even hear me. Or don't care, which is probably closer to the truth.

"She's looking at her vagina because she's not wearing any underpants," Granny states matter-of-factly.

Yep, just flopped that little ditty right out there. Like a dead fish on a table. I sigh. Mentally I slap myself for pinning my long hair up in a tasteful chignon because I could use the curtain to hide behind. My face burns, and I know, I just know, it is as red as the hair on my head.

"Woo-hoo!" Marla hollers. "You hear that, Trent?"

I think I'm going to cry when I hear her tell my granny, "You know, I have it on good authority that the girls today don't have any hair, you know, down there." She points at her own old-lady crotch.

"Oh, I know. It's weird, right?" Granny asks. "But she's as bare as a baby. I've seen it myself." She throws her thumb over her shoulder in my direction. I can hear my growl bubble up from my throat, but there is nothing anyone can do to stop it.

I'm glad my head is between my knees because I start to see little black spots before my eyes. I'm about to faint when I feel some very large, very masculine fingers with little calluses on the ends slowly hook the hem of my skirt and start to slide it aside. I slap his oh-so-sexy man hand back and sit up. He was trying to peek. At me. *At a funeral!* I shoot him a glare, but he just smiles that toothpaste-commercial smile back at me.

"Well, I for one like it," he says for my ears only. "And I'm hoping to get a front-row seat soon. Real soon, Shelby." And then he winks at me.

I open and close my mouth like a fish on the dock while he just smiles at me and our grandmothers debate the pros and cons of a Brazilian wax. I have just about figured out what my witty retort should be when the funeral home director steps up to the podium.

"On behalf of the North Park Funeral Home, I would like to welcome you all here today. It was a great honor to prepare services for such an esteemed man. A veteran of the United States Army, he served in both Korea and Vietnam. He married his high school sweetheart, and with her, raised six sons . . ."

"Damn, with those odds, you just might be able to land a date, Shelby," my granny stage-whispers.

I hear Trent snickering, but I can't bear to look at him. Well, if he found me attractive before, I'll be lucky if he just thinks of me as a sad old spinster with a cold vagina.

"Hush! I'm not looking for a date. And this is their father's funeral."

"When was the last time you had sexual relations, Shelby?" Marla throws her grandson back in the ring. The grandson in question smiles. "I once overheard one of Trent's old girlfriends saying he's a thoroughbred, whatever that means. But I am still friendly with her parents. I could probably get you references." She smiles sweetly. Trent, on the other hand, is grinning like a loon. I start to gurgle. It's the only noise my brain will make. *Am I too young to be having a stroke?*

"I think she's having a stroke," Granny voices my worst fear

"Nah, I think she's just hoping I'm going to accept her invitation to dinner that she issued while she showed me her vagina," Trent boldly lies. At that, I snap my mouth shut, sending him my best death glare.

"I raised you better than that!" Granny shouts as she slaps the back of my head. I growl. Trent laughs. *Asshole!*

"Well, I say she's a real modern woman. Go get him, tiger!" Marla enthuses.

"Yeah, tiger, go get him," Trent whispers.

"Ok, folks, let's stop talking about genitals," I reply harshly.

Unfortunately, it was at that time the minister had called upon Mr. Di Francesco's eldest son to step up and speak about his father, so there was a break in the overall noise in the room. So I know everyone heard me. I hear Trent bark out a laugh.

"Real classy, asshole," I growl.

All six of Mr. Di Francesco's sons talked about how amazing he was as a dad, how honorable, how kind, and how funny he was. And about twenty women, including Granny and Marla's third amigo, Bitty Sue, sobbed like babies. Especially all over the sons and their wives and girlfriends. It got kind of uncomfortable from there.

"Apparently, the Di Francesco men didn't know their pops was making the old-folks rounds," I muse to

Granny, when a warm arm slithers around my shoulders like a snake. I try to shake him off, but he holds firm.

"I think it's sweet how he did his best to carry on after his wife's passing," Trent says somberly. "When you go, I'm going to feel the same way. Just going to do my best to pass the time until I can join you in the hereafter." He nods. Both grannies are audibly sniffling into their handkerchiefs and agreeing with his nonsense.

"You can't be serious?" I ask. "You don't even know me."

"I know you stole my heart the very first time I saw you." Someone coughs *bullshit.* It might have been me. Whatever. No one can prove a thing. "I know we're meant to be, Shelby." I roll my eyes as he lays it on thick. I should be wearing rubber boots and carrying a shovel for all the cow shit he's slinging around.

The minister leads the service in prayer, and we all silently bow our heads. Thank God this conversation can be over. Who knew Trent was such a looney tune?

"Okay, I know I want you, Shelby," his gravel voice whispers just for me to hear. "And I always get what I want," is what he leaves me with as he leads Marla to his car.

The rest of us file into our cars, which are marked with the bright orange FUNERAL tags that let everyone on our overcrowded highways know to leave us be as we make our way to Veterans Memorial Park to lay one of our own to rest.

Granny is uncharacteristically quiet on the drive over the bridge toward the cluster of Navy bases where the cemetery is located on the hill overlooking the ocean.

By the time we stop our cars along the curb and make our way to the gravesite, the sky is gray and misting. A storm is coming up from the coast, so we should have a few days of cooler, damp weather, but this is San Diego; it will still be beautiful.

Granny and Marla had gone forward to hold hands with a now visibly shaken Bitty Sue. According to Marla, the dirty hookers had gotten to her, so I am standing in the back near another grave that is being prepped for a funeral later this weekend. I guess Death is always in business.

I take this time alone to study the sad faces of the day. Sons left behind, the few men of their group from the Army who are still living. My own grandfather was once one of them, but he was one of the first to go. A handful of war-torn, lonely, retired women, either divorced or widowed, who had fancied themselves his lover, and one harried minister presiding over his flock. I fancy myself pretty creative, but even I'm not sure how to spin this goat rope into a sweet article for the paper. *I wonder if I can get my old job back at Home Depot . . .*

I'm lost in my own thoughts when I feel a tingle of awareness creeping up the back of my neck. I look over my shoulder, and just past the edge of all this insanity is Trent, with his arms folded across his gorgeous chest, casually leaning against a tree. His eyes are not on the burial service or even on his grandmother, Marla. They are locked on me. When he sees that I see him, Trent slowly straightens to his full height and makes his way to me.

"I can't figure you out, Red," he whispers as he bumps my shoulder with his.

"What's to figure out?"

"You really tell Miss Verna about me?" he questions.

"Yeah, but I didn't know you were Marla's grandson," I tell him. I decide to go for full disclosure. "It's been a long time since I've seen anyone. Granny was giving me a hard time about getting back out there and dating again, so I told her about how I flirted with a handsome contractor one day at work. It was true, and it got her to give me some space for a bit, but obviously that's over."

"So you liked flirting with me?" he asks honestly.

"Well, yeah," I answer as his smile widens.

"And you think I'm handsome?" Hmm . . . . Fishing for compliments is unbecoming.

"Yes." I roll my eyes, and Trent narrows his own at me.

"Did you just roll your eyes at me?" His voice has changed, a little darker, a little more demanding.

"Um, yes?" I question, not sure what the answer is.

He takes a predatory step toward me, and I take one back. I know I should stand my ground, but I can't.

"Should I teach you some manners on our date, Shelby?" he questions darkly.

"What? No, no, I'm good. I promise." Shit. This can't be good.

"Great, I'll pick you up at seven, Shelby." He steps closer and growls in my ear, "I can't wait." I shiver and step back.

"What?" I jump. "No. No date necessary. We wouldn't want to cause conflict with the grandmothers," I rationalize.

"Oh, we're going out, Shelby." *That's what he thinks.* I just won't be there when he shows up. "I'll be very disappointed if I have to hunt you down. But make no mistake, I will if I have to."

And then he nips my earlobe. I yip and jump backward, but there is no more ground to cover, and I fall into an open grave. Coughing, dirt smeared on my clothes and face, and flat on my now bruised bottom, I hang my head. My life can't get any worse.

"Jesus, Shelby, it's like you go out of your way to be this clumsy. We're at a funeral, for Pete's sake!" Granny's voice can be heard clearly, and the people at not only this funeral but at the other two funerals in the cemetery turn to stare at me as Trent reaches down and pulls me up by my arm, ridiculous smile on his face.

"This is going to be fun, Shelby," Trent whispers in my ear. I was wrong, so wrong. My life can definitely get worse, and it already has.

Aaaaaannndddd . . . I'm out. I'm going home, where there's a box of wine—yep, I'm classy—and a really hot bubble bath.

I try to hug and kiss Granny and Marla on the way out, but something about cemetery dirt doesn't appeal to them. Whatever.

"Aren't you going to kiss me good-bye, Shelby?" Trent laughs, but I'm already moving. I throw a wave over my shoulder and hop into my car.

Granny is driving Bitty Sue back to the senior center because she's too upset to drive. I make a mental note to call my mom and find out if Granny still has a driver's license. I know she doesn't have a car. Mom and I drive her everywhere. Hmm, this is concerning. Oh well, she's a survivor. They'll be fine. Now, as for the rest of the greater San Diego area, that's all in God's hands.

I drive down the hill in the now drizzling rain and think about all the gross dirt and dead people germs that are currently swirling around me. Anyone who just fell into an open grave would do the same thing.

The worst part, though, would be that it seems Dearest Trent likes a challenge. You would think chasing a girl into a grave would be the end of the chase. *Literally.* But I guess he's into that. Oh God, what if he likes graveyard sex. I am not into that. And why am I thinking about sex? With Trent! Nope, Trent and I are done. We are not compatible. There, that settles that. I mentally brush the thought away like dirt off of my hands.

I pull into the driveway of my adorable little condo that I rent just as the bottom drops out of the storm, officially meeting our yearly rain goal as Californians. Damn El Niño year.

I'm going to have to make a run for it. I drop my phone into the safety of my oversized Coach purse, which has a fun pattern of pink and red poppy flowers, obviously. I pull my keys from the ignition while tossing my bag over my shoulder and throw my door open. Slamming my door shut is like the starting shot at the Olympics. I'm off, sprinting at full speed—well, full speed for me, not Usain Bolt—and hit my front door in record time. Record time for me, that is.

I unlock the door, jump inside, and slam the door shut again. I throw the lock, drop my purse on the cute little table by the door, and immediately bend over, clutching my knees. Jesus, I need to hit a gym. Pretending to do yoga with senior citizens is no longer cutting it. Oh, shit. I think I'm having a heart attack. Fitbit, you lied!

I catch my breath and hang my Guess trench coat, with the gold buttons and the ruffle hem, on the vintage coat rack on the other side of the door. I kick my heels off on my way down the hall, finishing my quest in the master bath, where there is a giant spa tub. It's really why I live here. It's definitely not because of the creepy guy who watches me while I dress in the morning. He's creepy but harmless. He's kind of like a puppy. Only my puppy is just a fifty-year-old divorced man who watches me change and have sex.

But that doesn't really count because it hasn't happened in over a year. The sex part, that is. I change clothes and bathe regularly. He also brings me my mail. Unfortunately, it's always after he's read my Victoria's Secret catalog and circled his favorites. It's like his Christmas wish list for Santa, but for perverts. Beggars can't be choosers, and this is our normal. And it works for us.

I start the water running extra hot and add my favorite oils that I save for the worst days. They smell like oranges and vanilla, my absolute favorite. I let that go for a bit and head into the bedroom.

I toss my blouse and skirt in their own special bag for the dry cleaners. I'm going to have to add an apology note with that one. I would toss them, but, holy shit, that was a one-hundred-dollar silk blouse from Banana Republic, and mama wasn't made of money.

My stockings are ripped six ways from Sunday, so those little mistresses of torture can go right into the trash. I roll them down most of the way but am too lazy to bend over and pull them off, so I high-step up and down on them like I'm a majorette in the marching band. But when I get them to about my ankles, I get a little tangled up, fall backward, and make a grab for the long ends of my pantyhose.

I go flying onto my back on the floor with my feet scissor-kicking up in the air like a synchronized swimmer. I grasp the ends of the offending pantyhose and rip them the rest of the way off, jumping to my feet, wearing nothing but my black lace bra. I wave the pantyhose over my head in a friendly gesture in front of the sliding glass door to my patio. I don't see him, but I know Pervy Steve is out there, and hey, I'm a great neighbor.

By now my bath is probably about full, so I mosey down to the kitchen and all the way to the fridge, where I pour myself a giant glass of my favorite Moscato in my saucy, purple Pioneer Woman wineglass and throw another wave over my shoulder to Steve through the other slider in the kitchen.

My cell phone is ringing in my bag by the door, but fuck it, I'm out. I head back to my bathroom and sink into my tub, turning the spout off as I go. This definitely makes up for falling into an open grave. Tomorrow will be a new day, and I'll be ready to try again. Boom. Killing it.

My poor bruised muscles are just starting to relax, and I'm about halfway through my glass of wine when the house phone next to my bed starts ringing. *Don't you know I'm relaxing here, people?* I feel like I was in a car wreck. I *am* a fucking car wreck. Well, sort of. I'm really a grave wreck. That doesn't even make sense.

I hear the answering machine on the kitchen counter pick up. It's one of the few advantages of living in a small condo. But the caller hangs up and calls back. I'm not answering; I still have wine. I hear the machine pick up again, but I can't hear who is leaving me a message. I'll get to it when I get out. I swear.

I sip—okay, guzzle—the rest of my wine. It's the best way I can think of to react to falling into an open grave in front of a bunch of old people, your grandmother, and a smattering of hot men. I'm just glad that my mom and dad are out of the country on a world cruise and did not have the opportunity to see the live-action version of my humiliation. I set my glass down on the floor next to the tub and sink down into the warm bubbles.

I deeply inhale the citrusy scents and let them wrap around me. This is the li—*Thump, thump, thump.* Someone is pounding on my front door. Angrily. Huh. I sigh and pull the plug covering the drain. I stand up slowly because that bruise on my backside is really setting in. My piece-of-shit chair at work tomorrow is really going to burn. I make a mental note to e-mail Uncle Sal, my editor and boss at the paper, to tell him I'll be working from home in the morning.

I grab my pretty amethyst towel and—*thump, thump, thump*—jump at the incessant pounding on the front door as my house phone starts ringing again. Now I'm angry. Who the hell is it? It had better be the police; that's for sure. Without drying my skin, I wrap my towel around my body and storm to the front door, the warm droplets on my skin turning cold in the evening air.

When I get to the entryway, I scream, "Whoever this is, it'd better be good or I'm calling the cops!" But when I open the door, no one is there. I see Pervy Steve across the walkway, and I wave at him.

"Pleasant evening, Shelby." He blushes.

"You too, darlin'." I wink at Steve and close my door.

My house phone rings again, and I race to the kitchen. Standing with my back to the hallway, I answer the phone. "Hello?"

"Hi, ma'am, you don't know me," the strange man on my phone starts.

"Let me stop you right there, pal." I explain, "I have one pervert in my life already, and I don't have the time to take on a second. So while I hope you have a pleasant evening, if you call back here, I'm calling the cops." I hang up.

"The cops are already here, darlin'," Trent breathes lazily from the doorway.

I'd like to say I act smoothly toward a man—whom I have only met twice—showing up in my house and that I take him out at the knees with a judo chop, but I do what any woman raised in the city would do: I scream my face off as loud as I can while throwing my hands up in the air wildly, à la *E.T.*, and running around the kitchen in circles, looking frantically either for an escape or a weapon.

Unfortunately, during my crazed-alien run, I lose my hold on my towel and am now a naked, crazed alien. Granny would be so proud. Finally, I rememberthere is a door to the patio in the kitchen, so I make a break for it. And run straight into the sliding glass door. Just like in the old Wile E. Coyote and Road Runner cartoons, the glass bows out with the momentum of my—*cough, cough*—petite body and snaps back, throwing me to the floor. Where everything goes black.

"Yes, I need an ambulance at one forty-three Sunny-vale Road, Unit B. Yes, I'll stay on the line."

Hey, that's my address. I hope no one's hurt. I open my eyes and realize two things: I'm lying flat on my back on the kitchen floor, and there is a strange man standing over me, staring down with a scowl on his scary yet handsome face. Upon closer inspection, I realize I am naked and there is a strange man standing over me. *What the ever-loving fuck is happening here?!*

"She's come to," the stranger says.

"Ma'am, you had an accident. I'm . . ." But he doesn't get to finish because I jump up screaming.

"A phone pervert! A phone pervert is in my house! *Aaahhhhhhhhhhh!*" I scream and resume my naked alien running. I run to my cooking utensil cup and grab the first thing I can get my hands on, which just so happens to be a pair of metal tongs. I lunge at the phone pervert in my very best impression of a master swordsman. *En garde!* Clapping away like a deranged lobster. "You! Out of my house, Phone Pervert." *Clap, clap.*

Clap, clap, clap. "I told you I already have a pervert." *Clap, clap.* I attack again. *Clap, clap.* "And I told you I would call the police!" Strong arms firmly wrap around me from behind, and I jump, but they only lock tighter around me.

"Lady, I am the police. Now put your claws away and grab a robe before I have to take you in." I let out an *Eep!* when I remember that I am naked. My phone-pervert-turned-police looks over my shoulder and says to the anaconda arms holding me, "Really, Trent, this looney tune is your girl?"

"Hey, I'm not a looney tune." I pout. "I'm just having a really bad day," I mumble. The thought of going to jail naked has brought back all the stress of my shit day.

"What can I say? She's never boring, and Nana loves her." I feel Trent shrug behind me.

"Can you imagine your kids being anything but terrors, with her and Marla's genes combined?" He laughs. "I can't wait to see it."

"Hey," I mumble halfheartedly.

"But they'll be entertaining. And beautiful," Trent adds.

"Beautiful for sure, crazy as fuck for certain." He

laughs again. "Although standing here now, I definitely see her appeal. You ever decide you're done with this asshole, you give me a call, okay, sugar?" the stranger asks me with a chuckle.

A growl rumbles out from behind me, and a warm, calloused palm slides up to cover my breast. Another one moves south, but I slap it away.

"But I don't even know your name," I mumble, looking down distractedly at the large, tan hand on my boob

Another growl, this time more menacing, rumbles up as the stranger laughs again. Apparently, my life is hilarious.

"Detective Kane Green at your service, ma'am." He leans forward and tips his imaginary hat.

"Like the hockey player?" I ask, but I hear a groan from behind.

"One and the same, but now I'm retired." He winks. "The old shoulder couldn't take it anymore, so I decided to follow in my dad's footsteps and joined the local PD."

"I think that's just amazing," I breathe. "I'm a big fan." I blush. And when I say blush, I mean I blush *everywhere*, and *everyone* knows it because I'm *freaking naked*!

"He was just leaving," Trent barks from behind me. Detective Green laughs and heads for the door.

"It was lovely meeting you, Shelby." He winks and

heads off into the night. Kane Green and his shaggy, light brown hair and cold blue eyes are undoubtedly gorgeous, but absolutely nothing compared to the coal-black hair and green Irish eyes of one Detective Trenton Foyle. *I am so screwed.*

chapter TWO

FUNERALS & FIRST DATES

Taylor Swift's "I Knew You Were Trouble" is blaring from the alarm on the docking station on my nightstand where my iPhone is plugged in. I love this shit. This song is my jam. Usually it gets me up and moving, but today I just hurt all over. Almost like I fell into a grave and then humiliated by one of America's finest.

"Shit!" I bark when my feet hit the floor and my bum hits the edge of the bed. I forgot it's the most bruised of all. Besides my ego and my dignity.

Even gingerly standing up is a real bitch, but it's got to happen. Just opening the glass door to the shower stall hurts my body. I'm quietly seething and plotting Trent's death if I ever see him again. How dare he embarrass me like that in front of a bunch of old people and the minister? I'm not counting the Di Francesco sons because as handsome as they are, it'll be a cold day in hell before I jump into anything of any kind with any man. *No, sir, no way!* Been there, done that, and got the mother-humping T-shirt. I am good.

The hot water is loosening my muscles, and my shoulders start to lower from my ears as I relax into the steam and foam. Planning the demise of an asshole appears to be good for me and my mood.

Just reaching down to shut the water off has me cringing already. I gently pat myself dry with one of my pretty purple towels and slip my pink silk robe with the roses on it over my sore body. I step out of the bathroom just as I hear my text ringtone sound Katy Perry's "California Gurls," and head over to where I left it plugged in next to the bed, noticing the text from my boss is not a happy one.

`UNCLE SAL: You are not working from home today!!! I WILL see you in my office in 20.`

"Well, crap," I curse to no one but myself.

I pad my way down the hall to the kitchen for some Advil and wash it down with screaming-hot coffee. If I'm going to leave the house to get my ass chewed, I might as well feel halfway human.

I pound the rest of my coffee and return to my room to dress. To be honest, I'm not even trying. I grab my dark skinny jeans and a Tiffany Blue V-neck T-shirt and toss them on. I throw on my favorite cardigan, which is purple with blue hearts all over it.

I head to the counter in my bathroom, where my makeup is, and start putting my foundation on a makeup brush. I scream when I look up into the mirror, and toss the makeup-filled brush and makeup bottle in opposite directions, splattering light beige gunk all over the place, the glass bottle shattering.

"Holy shit!" I am not prepared for the sight that meets my gaze.

My nose is red and swollen, but thankfully, not broken. Both my eyes are solid black, like a panda bear, and I wish to God that was the worst of it, but it's not.

There appears to be giant goose egg on my forehead. And it is also mottled purple and red as if that goose egg has been sitting out for three solid Easters. *In the fiery pits of hell.*

"Fucking balls!"

I don't have time for this, but I can't leave the shattered glass on the floor. The last thing I'd want is for Miss Havisham to get it in her little kitty paws. So I sweep up the glass and wipe up the makeup. I clap my hands together to get the last of the mess off.

Upon further inspection, I don't have any makeup to cover up this shit show with, and really, if Uncle Sal is going to call me into the office when I look and feel like this, he can suffer, too. So I close the drawer on my makeup.

I grab my purse and slide my feet into my

comfy purple ballet flats and lock up the house. I jump into my car, blast some Sam Hunt because he is kind of dreamy, and head to the office.

My cell phone rings, and Fergie's "Glamorous" plays, so I know it's a phone call. I answer without looking because only my parents would call me this early in the freaking morning.

They must have stopped somewhere on their world cruise if they are calling home. I should check their itinerary online when I get to the office. I miss them terribly, but after my dad retired from the army, they deserved this vacation, so I said I would look after my granny while they were gone. I love them, so much so that I answer with a smile in my voice.

"Hello?"

"Morning, sweetheart," a gravelly voice floats over the airwaves.

I swear I can hear his sexy smile over the phone. I am momentarily speechless. I honestly cannot understand why he is calling me. Last night was epically bad, and I am pretty sure I would never call me again.

I am briefly considering hanging up when I hear him ask softly, "Are you there, baby?" I growl. And he chuckles. *That bastard.* And I remember instantly why I'm mad at him.

"What do you want, Trent?" I ask through gritted

teeth. "I'm about to head into the office, and I don't have time for your shenanigans."

"Shenanigans?" He laughs. "Sometimes I think you talk like an old lady because you hang out with them so much. Tell me, when are you seeing the hell-raisers again?"

I don't answer because the truth is that I'm seeing them after work today for Advanced Senior Yoga at the old folks' home. That is, if I haven't curled up into the fetal position under my desk while I wait to die. It's a real possibility today.

"I'm not answering that," I state firmly. Trent barks out a laugh.

"It's all right, sweetheart. I love them, too. I'm having dinner with the girls and wanted to know if you would like to join us." I hear the smile in his voice. He knows he's got me cornered.

"That's mean using Granny and Marla against me," I huff out.

"Hey, desperate times call for desperate measures, Shelby. Will you go out with me any other way?" he asks softly.

It has me almost worried to give him my answer, so I try to soften the blow, unwilling to let myself hurt this man, which is, by all accounts, batshit crazy. Shit. He's making me like him, and that's dangerous ground.

"It's not you, Trent," I whisper sadly. "If I could, I would date you for sure. But right now? No, I'm just not ready to let my heart get smashed to pieces again,"

I say, surprised to feel a tear track down my cheek. It's painful to remember the damage that James did to my heart. That I let him do to me. But that's not something I am willing to talk about.

"I understand, Shelby, more than you know," he says kindly. "But I am also not a man to give up so easily. I was a Ranger, Shelby. And *Rangers Lead the Way,* babe. I'm in it to win it."

"As cheesy as that was, Trent, I appreciate your understanding." I smile. And suddenly I realize I'm smiling while talking to a guy. I never thought that would be possible. It tells me Trent is already under my skin deeper than I want him.

"Great!" he says cheerfully. "So I'll see you for dinner tonight at Nana's at seven," he says as quickly as humanly possible and then hangs up on me with a resounding *click*. A mother-humping *click*! Argh!

I walk in the front door of the offices of the paper, and before I even get to my cubicle, I hear Uncle Sal bellowing for me.

"In my office now, Shelby!" he screams, and I hear his rolling chair slam against the metal of his cheap office desk.

I drop my purse onto my desk and move toward his office, my head hanging down. Damn, I am fully prepared to get my ass handed to me. I'm probably going to get fired for the goat rope that was Mr. Di Francesco's funeral. I'm probably going to have to move. I wonder if Home Depot will take me back. Probably not after this showing.

"Would you hurry up and get in here," he rails. "And shut the door, too!"

I drag my feet, which feel like cement, through the door and quietly shut it behind me. The resounding *click* has me jumping.

"*Aaaaarrrrrggggghhhhh!*" Uncle Sal shrieks like a little girl when he sees my black-and-blue face.

"Have a seat, Shell," he sighs.

I slink around the armchairs in front of his desk and slide into a seat, still looking at my adorable Target flats in a purple faux suede.

"Look at me, Shelby."

My entire childhood training that is ingrained in my brain recognizes Uncle Sal as both an authoritative figure in my family and my boss, so my eyes immediately snap to his. The same hazel as mine, the same as my dad's—it's a key identifier in Whitmores all over.

Uncle Sal's voice softens when he looks at me and asks, "Care to tell me why a Detective Trenton Foyle has been calling my office all morning, demanding a 'sitrep' on you and how you were doing this morning? Do you know what a sitrep is?" I shake my head. "No? Well, let me tell you. It is a 'situation report,'" he snaps. "And now I can see why! What the ever-loving fuck happened to your face?" he bellows.

I open my mouth to tell him, but before I can speak, he cuts me off. "Wait." He holds up a hand. "I don't want to know." I sigh.

"Just tell me this," he says and then pauses for effect. "Is this related to the assignment I sent you on yesterday?" I cringe.

"Kind of . . . ," I answer hedgingly.

"What does 'kind of' mean?" he presses.

"Well, you know Granny . . . ," I say, evading the question. He pinches the bridge of his nose between his thumb and forefinger.

"Oh no. How did I know she was involved in this," Uncle Sal fumes. I mean, it's his mother. Why is he mad at me? "It was her and those crazy old ladies, wasn't it?"

"Yes, Marla and Bitty Sue were there and were their usual selves."

"So how does the good detective figure in?"

"He is Marla's grandson." Uncle Sal gives me a *Go ahead* look and hand gesture. At least, I hope it's a *Go ahead* and not an *Up yours.* I mentally shrug. I can handle it. "And he might of made me fall into an open grave next to Mr. Di Francesco's burial site and then later may have broken into my house when I was in the bathtub and scared me so much I ran into a closed sliding glass door, which is why my face looks like this," I say in one breath and finish with a big inhale.

"I'll kill him," Uncle Sal rages.

"Well, it's not so bad. He seems nice enough. I'm having dinner with him and Granny and the old gals tonight. So it's probably okay."

"After what that jerkface put you through, I'm not letting just anyone get their hands on my favorite niece. I love you too much, Shell," he finishes on a whisper that has tears welling in my eyes.

"I love you too, Uncle Sal." I smile at him. "I promise it'll be a cold day in hell before I give my heart away to another douche canoe."

"Good girl." He smiles at me. "Now go finish the article on Mr. Di Francesco's funeral and have it on my desk by midnight, sweetheart."

"You got it, Chief." I salute him on my way out his office door.

I barely make it to my desk in my charmingly decorated cubicle when my desk phone starts ringing that annoying trill.

"Funerals and Obituaries, this is Shelby. How can I help you?" I answer, because on my first official day on the job, Uncle Sal made it clear that 'You kill 'em, we write 'em up' was not appropriate.

"Shelby, I'm so glad I could reach you," a sexy male voice floats over the line.

"Well, if it isn't my new phone-pervert-turned-police-detective," I respond dryly. "What can I do for you today? Anyone die?"

"No, not today. Yet, anyway," he says with a chuckle. "I was just calling to apologize. And also, I was hoping to persuade you to go easy on Trent. He's a good guy, and he deserves a chance."

"I have made it clear to Trent, and I will now make it clear to you—not that you deserve it, after seeing me naked—that while I like Trent and think he's a nice guy, I'm not in the market for anything right now. I am still recovering from the last time I got ripped to shreds, and I'm not so sure I'll ever be ready again after that one. So please understand. There're no hard feelings."

"I understand, Shelby," he says softly. "But Trent might surprise you. Also, be warned. He's not the kind of guy to give up so easily."

"That's kind of what I was afraid of." And secretly thrilled about. Shit. What am I going to do now?

SGT Giuseppe H. DiFrancesco (1943–2016)

It was with heavy hearts that Giuseppe Di Francesco was laid to rest beside his bride, Rosemary, who passed in 2010 after a long struggle with ovarian cancer. Mr. Di Francesco's life was celebrated in a beautiful service at the North Park Funeral Home, where stories of his heroics in the service of his country, the love of his high school sweetheart and six sons, and his zest for life were prevalent. You could only feel love in a room full of beautiful flowers, family, and friends of Mr. Di Francesco.

Immediately following the service, family and friends traveled to Veterans Memorial Park by the bay, where he was officially placed with full military honors. Mr. Di Francesco is survived by his six sons: Giuseppe Jr., Thomas, Alfred, Salvatore, John, and Charles.

In lieu of flowers, the family has requested that donations please be made to the Wounded Warrior Project, of which Mr. Di Francesco was an avid supporter.

Boom. Done. I can't believe I was able to turn that mess into a decent piece. Maybe Uncle Sal won't fire me after all. I really have to talk to my mom about monitoring my granny and her friends out in public. One day, they are totally going to get arrested. Probably for public indecency. Hey, it could happen.

I click send, e-mailing it to Uncle Sal so he can review it and format it for the next publication of our paper. I also drop him a quick note to let him know I'm on my way to Advanced Back and Hip Care Yoga for Seniors at the old folks' home.

UNCLE SAL: Better you than me. Love ya.

My uncle is the best. I love him dearly. I close down my work computer. Then I grab the files for the obituaries I'm working on this week. In a city this size, there is a lot of death, and these are my bread and butter. As morbid as that might be. I stuff them into my giant bag, snatching my car keys as I go. I hop into my car and head for some quality time with my grandmother.

When I pull into the parking lot of the senior living center my granny lives in, I walk through the front doors and sign in as a guest, like always. And head up to the tenth floor where her apartment is. I walk down her plush hallway, which has orchids I could never keep alive strategically placed on various tables near swanky chairs I could never afford. I reach Granny's front door and ring the bell.

"Hey, sweet cheeks, what's happening?" she greets cheerily, effectively ignoring the fact that I look like I went extra rounds with Ali. Which is the exact opposite of how my face looked yesterday when she saw me at the funeral.

"I'm good. I just got done at work and came over for some yoga and quality time with you," I say as I wrap my arms around her neck. I love this woman to pieces. "How are you?"

"I'm fabulous. You know how I live for yoga. And it's doing wonders for poor Marla's hip. You remember she broke it a while back, don't you?"

"I do. But you'd never know she broke it by the way she's healed up." I smile at her. I have loved Miss Marla for years. She's a real hoot.

"Well, let's hop to it already!" She claps.

We quickly change into our yoga gear. I should probably be concerned that we match in a cute pair of cropped black yoga leggings with a little keyhole and a tiny black bow on both sides. We each topped them off with a pink yoga tank that has an attached sports bras and cutouts, which make it look like the tank is just barely hanging on, and a band at the bottom so it doesn't hit you in the face when you downward dog. Really, we're just adorable.

I keep an overnight bag complete with shampoo, a touch of spare makeup, and clothes—casual and workout—at Granny's since I spend so much time hanging out with her. This way, I don't have to lug a bag around.

We grab our mat rolls and slide our matching Reef flip-flops on and head for the elevator to take us to the gym. Granny is particularly silent the whole way down to the basement gym, and I'm beginning to worry.

We're not the first to get to class, but we're not the last either. We slide our sandals off and unroll our mats next to each other's, like always. I smile to myself thinking how special this time is with the main gal in my life.

"Did I tell you Trent is joining us for dinner tonight?" she asks casually, not making eye contact with me. Warning bells are going off, and red flags are all over the place in my head.

"No, but he somehow got my cell phone number and called me while I was at work today to tell me he was coming. You wouldn't know anything about that, would you?" I ask, willing her to look me in the eye so I can gauge her truthfulness.

"Well, about that . . ." she says. But she doesn't get the chance to finish because we hear chaos erupt in the room.

"Well, helloooo there, tight end! Where have you been all my life?" is followed by a bunch of old-lady wolf whistles and other catcalls.

"Back off, you she-devil. My grandson is no toy for you!" I hear Marla screech.

I look over my shoulder, and there is Trent, his emerald-green eyes twinkling with mischief as he looks me up and down, long red ponytail to my freshly painted emerald-green toes. I hope he doesn't catch on to my sudden inspirations. But by the look in his eye, I know he does. Damn it all.

And did I mention the reason for the wolf whistles and catcalls? Oh, that would be because the good detective is wearing tight running pants, the kind I usually find disgusting. But on Trent they show the corded muscle and strength in his thighs and calves, among other things. And those are great things. Praiseworthy things.

On top he is wearing one of those compression T-shirts in royal blue, and it only serves to make his eyes greener. Not to mention, Holy Muscles, Batman! Homeboy is ripped. I want to devote my life to mapping his abs and that glorious "V" that points to the Promised Land. Even his bare feet are sexy.

Jesus, I need to get a grip. I am not going there. Maybe ever. My ex left me doubting that there is a decent guy, whom I'm not related to, left out there in tatters on the shit house floor. No, thanks, I'm good.

"Hi, Shelby," he rasps. "You're looking gorgeous this afternoon in your lovely yoga outfit. But I have to say, I think I prefer you naked." I gasp.

"Did you hear that, Verna?" Marla elbows Granny. "They already played 'Hide the Salami.' We're that much closer to great-grandbabies who are so beautiful you could weep." She holds up her index finger and thumb with very little room between them.

"Oooo-wee, I know it!" Granny claps. "If it were anyone else, I'd tan her hide for being so forward on a first date."

"But you listen to me, mister." Granny shakes her finger at Trent. "She didn't go into detail, but it hasn't escaped my notice that my granddaughter looks like she picked a fight with a brick wall and lost. And I will not have that shit. I will not have it!"

"It was more like a sliding glass door than a brick wall, and I swear I had nothing to do with it." He holds up his hands in mock surrender. "It was all Kane's fault."

"Hey now, she was unconscious when I got there," Kane speaks from beside Trent, and I just now notice him. "That sounded way worse than it did in my head. I apologize."

"What the hell were you doing there?" Granny demands.

"I've never tried that ménage business, but I have always wanted to. Is it all that the romance novels say it's cracked up to be?" Marla asks innocently. "I'm just worried that with my hip the way it is now, it would just be a disaster. It was hard enough getting old Harold to give me a second go after I broke my hip, you know, *with Harold.*"

I'm pretty sure there are no words to respond to that. Trent's face is oddly red. Kane is laughing so hard he's crying, and Granny is giving me the side-eye. I'm just standing there, opening and closing my mouth, but no words will come out.

"I'm always here for your needs, Shelby." Kane winks at me. And then Trent lunges, taking him to the mats on the floor. While they're rolling around throwing punches and jabs, I hear their muffled argument.

"I'm just kidding, man."

"Well, I'm not, asshole."

"Jesus, will you calm down? You look like a psycho."

All of a sudden, Trent makes a move and pins Kane. "Candy-ass hockey bastard. Swear to me," he demands, shaking a laughing Kane. "I'm not kidding. Swear to me, motherfucker!"

"I swear, buddy. I'm just teasing you," Kane reassures him.

"I swear I didn't have sex with either of them," I say to no one in particular.

"Well, that's disappointing, but probably for the best." Granny shakes her head as the instructor walks in and heads to the front of the class.

"We're good," Trent and Kane both declare as they brush floor dust off their workout clothes.

"All right, everyone. Toes forward at the front of your mats. We'll begin with blades of grass," the soft-spoken yoga instructor, Harmony, begins. I have no idea if that's her real name, but it's totally fitting.

We each take a deep breath and move our arms from our sides, palms up, toward the sky. Holding our imaginary beach ball between our hands, we sway slightly side to side. I feel all the kinks in my shoulders start to loosen, and then I hear, *bbuuuuurrrrppp*.

"Oh God. Why do they serve chili on Tuesdays to old people? It's like they want us to die," I hear from somewhere in the room. I smile to myself. I love these people.

"Now let's transition to downward dog and the upward-facing dog."

As Harmony has instructed, I reach forward to my toes like everyone else, and I hear Kane and Trent behind me.

"Oh God," Trent whimpers.

"It's okay, dear. It took me a while to get that flexible. Now Harold thinks I'm as limber as a gymnast," Marla exclaims.

"Sweet Jesus, put that away, man!" Kane grumbles. "I'm leaving if I have to look at that monster in your pants the whole class. I swear it's looking at me."

From somewhere in the room, I hear, "You can show me the monster in your pants anytime, baby." I snicker. Kane just growls.

"And again, downward to upward dog," Harmony says, and then we hear a loud *pppffftttt.* "Oh, man, chili again? Bummer," she laments.

We continue the series a couple more times with a couple more farts, but we survive it together. This is a regular Tuesday afternoon for me with my granny.

"And now let's move into sun salutation." Harmony demonstrates the slightly forward bend followed by the stretch backward.

We all do the slow bend forward, *pppffftttt*, and then start to straighten. It's really getting thick in here. My eyes are watering, and I don't know what to do. I'm just glad I'm not wearing makeup, or it would be burning my eyes by now.

"Oh God, nobody light a match," Marla stage-whispers

"Jesus, it's like *Apocalypse Now* in here," Kane gripes.

"I know. It's getting pretty thick in here. I'm choking on all the old-people flatulence," Granny agrees, voicing my sentiments exactly.

"Kane . . . ," Trent admonishes.

"I'm serious!" he complains. "I feel like any minute the captain will tell us it's time to go surfing and play 'Ride of the Valkyries' from the loudspeaker."

We start to lean back. I've been perfecting my backbend for so long that I'm pretty proud of it now. When I lean back, I see both Kane and Trent just standing there, their arms in some sort of bastardized version of mid–sun salutation, jaws open, eyes glazed over. Huh?

"Okay, that's it. Class dismissed. I can't take any more of this shit," Harmony erupts. "I'm sorry, old people. I just need to go smoke a bowl. I'll feel better next class. Let's just try to keep the noxious gases and sexual hormones to a minimum, mmkay?"

And with that, we all roll up our mats, slide our sandals and sneakers on, and with our heads down like little children headed for the principal's office, walk out of class.

"Well, this has been fun, kiddies, but I'm out. Miss Marla, always a pleasure, Miss Verna, lovely meeting you, and, Shelby, just say the word." He winks at me. "I'll see you in the office tomorrow, man," Kane says, clapping Trent on the shoulder. They man-hug, and we all file into the elevator.

Granny's and Marla's apartments are right next door to each other, so we're all headed in the same direction. I'm choosing not to comment on the fact that Trent has had his arm wrapped around me pretty much the whole time. I am also choosing not to admit that he is wearing me down.

"Meet in the hall in thirty for dinner," Granny commands, and we all go to our battle stations.

I go straight to Granny's spare shower to wash off all the yoga sweat and sink into the steam and hot water. I could stay here all night, but knowing my granny, and I definitely do, she'd invite Trent in with me if I took too long. And I am just not ready for that. Although, at the thought of Trent's hard body in this hot shower with me, I feel a trigger burn through my belly. Maybe I am more ready than I thought. Yikes.

I turn the water off and step out of the small glass shower stall. Grabbing my towel off the rack, I dry myself off and wrap it around my body. I grab some leave-in conditioner from the cabinet and scrunch it into my curls, leaving them down to dry in soft waves.

I make my way into Granny's little spare bedroom, where I have my extra clothes stashed. Pulling open the drawer, I take out what I need and then slide light pink lace panties up my legs and grab the matching pink lace strapless bra. I might be young, but I take after my mom and my granny. I've always had a little bit bigger supply up top, and that needs support.

Surprisingly, I feel sexy tonight, and that makes me think of Trent. The damned detective is always on my mind. And that thought spreads a healthy pink blush up my Irish skin, over my chest, neck, and cheeks. In the closet, I choose a jade-green tie-dyed maxi dress. It's strapless but loose at the legs and fitted in the body. I grab my favorite gold sandals and gold hoop earrings.

Next, it's back to the bathroom to throw on some concealer, tinted moisturizer, and powder to cover some of the bruises. Damn. So much for feeling sexy. I look like I went ten rounds with Ali. I then apply light pink blush and matching lip gloss. Mascara is last. With that, I'm as ready as I'll ever be. And done in under thirty minutes to boot.

I walk out to the living room to find Trent, Marla, and Granny sitting together and chatting. Trent immediately stands when I walk in, and Marla preens at his manners. I have to admit to preening to them, too, as a slight blush stains my cheeks.

"You look lovely, as always, Shelby," he says softly as he walks over to me. He towers over me, but with Trent, I never feel afraid. Just the opposite, actually.

"Long time no see," I say back. My in-the-moment wit is off the charts tonight. It's so bad that it's embarrassing. But he just winks at me.

"Well, should we get going, kids?" Marla asks. We all nod as we make our way out of the apartment and down the hall to the elevator. The whole time, Trent's hand is on the small of my back.

We make our way to the top floor where the fine dining restaurant in the building looks out over all of San Diego. I love the view here, especially on a clear night when you can see all of the lights of downtown. The city's skyline on the harbor is so beautiful.

We're seated almost immediately, having a reservation because Granny and Marla have been planning this hostile takeover for a while. It's a lovely spot with an even better view. We sit down and all decide to order a bottle of wine.

The adorably young waitress steps up and tells us the evening's specials, and not once does Trent look at her with the twinkle in his eye that he gives me. And she's pretty! She could totally get a twinkle! Man, I could fall for that twinkle. *Oh, shit. I'm so toast.*

"I went back for you," Trent says, breaking into my thoughts.

"What?" I ask.

"I went back to the store. To look for you," he says with a cheeky smile. "Of course, it was under the pretense of home repair, but really, I was there for you."

"That night was my last night there. I was leaving so I could work for my uncle Sal," I say. "He made me shadow the Community Interest lady before letting me loose in public."

"Ah, that makes sense. I did go back several times looking for you, though. I had to plan my window coverings with Elma, and she's mean and not nearly as beautiful." I giggle. She is mean. And about seventy-five years old if she's a day. "So now you owe me." He smiles triumphantly.

"Excuse me?"

"Well, now you have to let me show you the house, and you can tell me what else I should do and where."

"Seriously?"

"Yes, but I'll even throw in dinner."

"I just bet you will," I mumble.

"Oh! That's a fabulous idea!" the old ladies answer for me.

"I guess it's a date," I say softly.

The rest of dinner passes by in easy company with lively conversation and good food, even if it is healthier fare, being in a senior living center. Poor Trent looked like he might cry when he saw the small piece of trout on his plate next to his three pieces of broccoli and his tablespoon of rice pilaf. But he never said a disparaging word. Not even when he was served an eighth of a cup of lemon ice for dessert.

He was very gentlemanly through the whole showing, and now I can't help but feel like I need to save him. So as we walk the gals to the elevator, I lean in and give Trent some of my secrets.

"Let's walk the girls to their apartments, let me grab my bag and sweater, and I'll take you around the block for a double burger and an extra-large shake," I whisper in his ear.

"God bless you, woman." I can't help but laugh as

the elevator pulls up to their floor.

"All right, ladies. The big guy here finally wore me down, and we're going for coffee. Don't pick out any china patterns or baby blankets while we're gone." I wink.

I grab my boyfriend-style jade cardigan and my huge bag before kissing Granny good night. "I love you," I say to her.

"And I you, my sweet girl." She smooths her hand over my hair. "Don't do anything I wouldn't do!" she shouts as I walk out the door.

"Granny, is there anything you won't do?" I ask.

"Nah, you gotta try everything in life at least once, baby girl." She smiles sweetly at me. "That way, when you're my age, you have no regrets, only happy memories."

On that sweet thought, Trent offers me his hand, and I take it. No regrets. At least, not tonight. And we walk down the hallway to the elevator. All night Trent hasn't pushed me, but he did soften me with gentle touches and sweet words. Almost like gentling a skittish horse. Now there's a thought. But I guess I do seem like a wary animal.

Once on the elevator, the air seems to crackle and snap. My body hums with need for Trent. I'm wondering when this all happened, since I've only known him a few days, really, when I realize he's gotten closer.

"Shelby . . . ," he whispers as he reaches his fingertips out to caress my cheek, and I lean in, almost purring.

We're chest to chest. Thigh to thigh. My hands move up to his abs, as if of their own accord. Trent slides his hand on my face into my hair, and his free hand grabs my waist and pulls me even closer. "I have to," he says to himself before his lips crash down onto mine. And I'm floating. In heaven. I must have died. And I am totally okay with it.

I gasp when his tongue, still cold from the lemon ice, trails over my lower lip, begging for entrance. When he slides it over my teeth, I whimper. I'm calling it a whimper because a moan is so not like me. But I can't stop even if I want to. I'm on fire. Trent is on fire. And it all feels so right. We don't even notice when the elevator stops and the doors open.

"Oh, look, Bitty. I haven't seen a live show like this since the boys from the 73rd regiment took some R&R in *Meh-hee-co* back in '63. Sweet," a man I've never met before says to Bitty Sue. He must be new here.

We jump apart, and I feel my face burn hot. I chance a glance at Trent, and his ridiculous smile goes ear to ear. Figures. Well, it was a pretty damn good kiss. And now I owe the man a burger.

I put my palm over my mouth to hold the laughter in as Trent and I race hand in hand out of the elevator, through the front door of the building our grandmothers live in, and around the corner. Trent doesn't have the same holdups; he throws his gorgeous head back and laughs a throaty, sexy-as-sin man laugh the whole way.

We round another corner into a small alleyway behind apartment buildings, and Trent wraps his large arms around me. The evening air is suddenly warmer, thicker. The sun has gone to bed, and only city lights glow around us.

Just like that, there is no more laughing as I look at Trent's emerald eyes, now dark and murky. Like it's storming in the forest. He instinctually licks his lips, and my hungry eyes track the movement. Lightning flashes in the distance. Trent flips our positions, and now my back is pressed against the wall of whatever building we're standing by. I gasp, and his lips hit mine.

I grab on to Trent's shoulders. Tight. And kiss him with everything I have. I push all my past hurts out of my mind and claw at his chest. His hands, which are at my waist, roughly glide up my sides, chunks of the soft T-shirt material of my dress catching in his fingers. His thumbs graze my nipples. I feel the warm air circle around my legs. Lightning flashes again. I'm on fire.

Trent's tongue glides over my lower teeth as his hands reach for my breasts more firmly. He trails his mouth from the corner of mine to nip at my jawline, and I whimper. My heart is pounding in my chest. He scrunches the top of my dress down below my breasts and into his hands, which are already holding my skirt.

"Oh God," Trent whispers. His forehead against mine, his lips brushing mine. "You're beautiful."

I tip my head back against the building. Trent kisses me again. Harder. I feel his teeth clash with mine.

His hands grip my body more . . . everything. Harder. Fiercer. His right hand weighs my left breast, his thumb circling my nipple through the sweet pink lace. His left palm is rubbing its warmth into my bare thigh.

Trent kisses his way back down my cheek, my chin, my neck. I feel him bite down where my pulse pounds in my neck. His hand on my thigh grazes the edge of my panties and over my center. Lightning flashes again.

"Trent . . . ," I moan. And I know he knows how much I want him.

Trent licks and kisses and nips and soothes his way down to my breast. He uses his talented mouth to pull down the lace cup of my bra and continues his dangerous path around my breast.

Not sure what to do with my hands, but needing to hold on to something when his warm mouth closes over my nipple, sucking, nipping, I grab on to the rough brick of the wall behind me. I need something to keep me attached to the earth. Anything to ground me.

Trent's hand at my other breast tugs the other cup of my bra down under my breast and rolls that nipple firmly between his thumb and index finger. I moan at the sweet little bite of pain as he kisses and soothes my other breast. His hand at my thigh glides up, and his fingers deftly slide under the leg of my panties. He slides his fingers up and down. Up and down. Up and down, before circling that sweet spot with his thumb.

I gasp as he slips a finger in deep. He slowly retreats and reenters Again and again. His thumb circles and circles. Trent kisses his way back up my body, and I wrap my arms around his shoulders, clinging to him.

"Yes," I gasp, but he swallows my cries. Trent slides a second finger in. Then a third, gliding in and out, my hips following the movement. My nails dig into his back, and his cock presses against my waist. I'm close. So close.

"Yes," Trent growls. "Take it. Take what you need from me, baby," he demands against my mouth.

He kisses me hard. His tongue, my tongue. His teeth gnash against mine. His fingers parry. Retreat and reenter. In and out. His calloused fingers circles again and again. My fingers dig impossibly tight into his shoulders.

I grind my hips down and squeeze my eyes shut, and everything burns blinding white. Trent swallows my scream, and everything explodes. Like that summer we camped in Montana. The electrical storm was so strong, and the cabin was struck by lightning. Every window on the house bowed out and snapped back in at once. That's how this is. Every cell in my body bows out and snaps back in.

My back is still against the wall, and Trent's large, muscular frame is surrounding me, stroking me, gently setting my clothes back to rights, kissing me softly, when I return back to my body, my mind. He places his large palms on my shoulders and kisses my mouth softly. He leans his forehead against mine and whispers.

"Come home with me."

"No," I say just as softly.

His eyes go wide, and so do mine. But as much as I'd like to call the word back, I know it is the right one. We've let things get ahead of us here. And as great as the sex would be, it's too soon. The real question is, can we go back to the sweet romance of getting to know each other from before?

SELF-HELP AND HOME IMPROVEMENT STORES

I wake to Taylor Swift's "I Knew You Were Trouble" again, and it's more and more appropriate by the day. Hell, by the freaking minute. The rain is drizzling down the windows, and it is the perfect day for drinking hot cocoa by the window and curling up with a good bodice ripper.

This is my favorite kind of day. I want to play hooky from the office. No one wants to drive in this mess, and all my files are in my bag by the front door. I could easily work from home, snuggled in sweats and blankets with my cat, Missy, and enjoy the rainy day. But I'm restless. Last night with Trent was downright magical. He's kind and sweet. So freaking sexy. And Lord knows his hands and mouth should be labeled lethal weapons with Homeland Security.

But I'm scared. After James, hell, during James,

I swore I would never trust another man. I promised myself and God I would never be vulnerable to another man again. And what happened? A bit of wine and a little thunder and lightning, and there I was with my dress around my waist, his mouth on my breast, and his hand in my panties. I could scream. In fact, I did last night. And not the *I'm being chased by an ax murderer* kind either. But the *Oh God, Oh God, Oh God. Yes, yes, yes, and a little to the left, yes!* kind. Fuck my life. I grab a pillow from my bed, hold it tight to my face, and let loose a scream befitting *Nightmare on Elm Street*.

That scream made me feel a little better. So I put the pillow down and throw the covers back. I head to the bathroom and start the shower running as hot as I can stand it. I strip out of the white, spaghetti-strap cotton nightie I wore to bed last night and toss it into the hamper. It smells like sex, and that is doing nothing for my willpower to avoid men. One big, manly detective to be specific. It is turning me on a little bit, so I might have to take care of that in the shower, too. It's weird that it also makes me feel a little guilty. Like I'm cheating on Pervy Steve by doing it in the privacy of my shower. My life is complicated.

I pull the glass door open and step into the steam. The water is hotter than I expect, but not so hot that it burns. I grab my loofah and body wash and start to lather up. But the sultry steam and the soft soapy suds only remind me of Trent as the loofah rasps over my sensitive nipples. I groan. I drop my loofah to the shower floor. My hands, full of soap suds, follow the trail Trent's hands boldly blazed last night. Over my breasts. Down my soft belly. And over my sex.

My small, delicate fingers circle my clit just as Trent's big, calloused ones had. But where last night my arousal was a wildfire in the dry canyon brush, this morning, it's a small flickering flame over the damp earth. There's not enough there to cause the fire to burn up and out. And I just. Can't. Get. There. Goddammit. That big bastard broke my vagina!

My hands stop their torture and slam against the shower tile. Fuck! Now what do I do? Do I hunt Trent down and apologize and then beg him to fuck me senseless? Because that seems like something I shouldn't do. Or do I let my lady bits dry up—because obviously Trent is the puppet master—and eventually die staring at Georgia O'Keefe paintings, wondering what went wrong, because I'm too stubborn to say he won? Shit. My thoughts are taking dark turns. I quickly shampoo my hair and rinse it clean.

I shut the now lukewarm water off and step out of the shower onto my amethyst bath mat and grab the matching towel to dry off. I bite back the stream of curses when the texture of the towel abrades my nipples. If I ever see Trent again, I'll kill him.

I throw my towel on the floor in a fit and storm to my closet. I slip on plain cotton panties with flowers on them and a white cotton sports bra. I grab a pair of black leggings, the state pant of California, and slide my legs into them. Then I layer purple and hot-pink tank tops over it. I accessorize the whole ensemble with brown Ugg boots that have little bows up the back and an oversized sweatshirt from my college. I comb my long tresses out and twist the whole thing up on top of my head in a messy bun, adding a few pins to hold it in place.

I look in the mirror, and my face is starting to yellow around the edges of my poor bruises. Pretty sweet. I still haven't replaced the bottle of makeup I broke. I have some tinted moisturizer and powder, so that will have to do. I dust a little rosy bronzer on my face, dab a rose-colored lipstick on my lips, and touch it up with a little lip balm. All the while remembering Trent's lips on mine. I sigh to myself more than anything.

I head down the hall to the kitchen and make a cup of coffee and scramble two eggs in a pan. I put two pieces of whole grain toast in the toaster and push the lever down. If there was ever a day to get started with a hearty breakfast, it's today. I sip my coffee while I push my eggs around in the pan. When my toast pops, I grab a plate from the overhead cabinet and set it on the counter. I put my toast and an orange on my plate. Then I turn the burner off and put my eggs on the plate. I set my pan on the back burner to cool down, and head to the fridge to get the butter.

I drop some kitty kibble in Missy's bowl. I scratch behind her ears when she meows at me. Who needs a man when you have a cat? Maybe I should just get, like, eight more and completely devote myself to a life as a crazy cat lady.

I eat standing at the kitchen counter. I know it

seems weird to go through that much effort on a meal just to eat it standing next to the sink, but that's me in a nutshell. The whole time I'm standing here, I see Trent and Kane in this kitchen. Trent really did just want to make sure I made it home all right. Can I trust him? He's definitely on the overprotective side. Do I want to trust him? Yeah, I really do. Man, that sucks. I cram the last bite of toast into my mouth and wash it down with the last of my coffee.

I head to the front door to retrieve my files. I pull them out of my bag and stare at them as if they can answer all of my questions in life. I know there is no way I'm going to get anything done here today, so I set them on the table by the front door and grab my keys out of the bowl. I give them a little toss in the air. I pick up my bag and head out the door.

I lock the door behind me and use the key fob to unlock my car as I run down the walk. I pull the door open and jump in. I put the key in the ignition, and as the engine comes to life, so does Sam Hunt on the speakers. I sit in my spot as he croons about not giving up easily on the girl and that he's going to make her miss him. My mind can't help but wander back to last night when Trent asked me to come home with him. He'd just finished giving me the orgasm of my life when he whispered his request.

"Come home with me."

"No," I said before I could pull the word back in.

"Okay, baby," he whispered with a smile. "But now that I know for sure how you burn up for me, Shelby, I'm going to win your trust. I'm not a quitter, baby. But I can wait for you to be ready. However long it takes."

"Really?" I ask, surprised.

"Yeah, baby." His fingers stroke my cheek. "You're the real deal. You'll be worth every bit of the wait. But we are going to date. I'm going to call you, and we're going to talk on the phone. And I'm going to pick you up and take you to lunch and dinner and the movies and to visit our grandmothers. We're going to laugh and smile and get to know each other. And when you're ready for more, I'll be there. With balls so blue you can hang them on your Christmas tree. And that'll be just fine with me. Okay?"

"Okay, Trent." I laughed. "I'll go steady with you."

"Thank God," he said with a laugh. And then he walked me around the corner to the burger joint, where we filled our bellies with burgers, french fries, and milk shake; miling the entire time.

Day dreaming about my magical non-date with Trent last night is doing nothing for my libido. Nor my resolution to keep my life unencumbered by men. Even just the one. Even if he is really handsome. And really sweet. And understanding. Dammit! That's how these bastards suck you in. Next thing you know, your friends don't return your phone calls, and the man in question is calling all the shots, among other things. And he doesn't seem so great anymore.

Well, I'm getting nowhere sitting in my driveway, stewing. So I put my car in drive and head to points unknown. I like to drive when I'm stressed. Bump my tunes and sing. Badly. And shove everything else out of my brain.

I head down my street and hang a left on Magnifica Ave. Gotta love SoCal and our Spanish names, Saltillo tiles, and amazing Mexican food. Oooohh, speaking of Mexican food, I should stop at Gordo's, a taco stand on the corner, and get some rolled tacos and a Coke. Yes! My day is looking up. I hang a right on Cabrillo Way and then another left at the stop sign. I pull into the first spot available and turn the ignition off. I toss my bag over my shoulder, keys in hand, and head to my favorite neighborhood spot to eat. Gordo's is literally a shack on the corner near a Target, a Toys "R" Us, and a Payless ShoeSource. There's also a nasty bar where my ex's "amazing" dad hangs out and does his best to try it on with cocktail waitresses younger than me. I can hear my own eyes rolling around in my head at the thought of it. Oh, and there's one of those salad buffet restaurants that's actually delicious, but not when the mood for tacos strikes. And I am in the mood. You know, for tacos, not Trent. For a split second, I think about trying to substitute greasy Mexican food for my newly awakened sexual appetite for the good detective, but I am already more than a handful—my booty could not handle that much Mexican takeout.

"Rojo, Rojo!" I hear when I walk up to the little window. "Hey, beautiful," Juan the owner of Gordo's greets me. I'm ninety-nine percent sure he says this to every woman, since I know for sure Gordo is his father-in-law. But it's good for my ego when I need it. "What can I get for you today? The usual?"

"Yes, please!" I smile back at him. "How are you all today?" I ask as I get my wallet out of my purse.

"You know me; I'm always good." Juan winks at me. "One order of rolled tacos and a Coke coming right up," he tells me.

I pass him the five-dollar bill I keep on the side of my wallet for taco emergencies like this.

"Gracias, Rojo." He looks at me quizzically. "Something is different about you. What is it?" He studies me. I see the recognition flash in his eyes when my own go wide for a minute, and then I quickly shake my head no.

"Nothing is new here. You already know I'm working for my uncle Sal at the paper," I say sweetly, trying to diffuse the situation.

"Ah, Ah, Ah. You know my *Abuela* was a *bruja* and I have the sight," he whispers firmly.

"Your grandma was a witch all right. One that starts with the letter *b*." I smirk and laugh. I believe him, but

I would also never admit it to his face.

"There is a man, Rojo. But a good man from far away, not the bad man of the past. You are headed for more evil from your past, but the good man will save you."

"I will never need a man to save me." I laugh. "You know Granny would have my head if I couldn't take care of myself."

"I know. I know your A*buelita* is crazy and all about her world views, but I am telling you evil is coming. Beware, *mi bonita*. Danger is closer than you think," Juan says in a deeper, darker voice. And with that, he hands me my bag of rolled tacos and a to-go Styrofoam cup of cola. "Have a nice day!" he chirps in his usual cheery voice. I try to shrug it off, but I can't help the shivers that race up my spine. Juan might be closer to the truth than I'm comfortable with.

I jump into my car and head west on State Route 56. Only two exits away is the beach. I pull off the highway and park up above the rocky slope that leads to Torrey Pines State Beach, facing the ocean.

I pull out my container of five delicious rolled tacos. Only candy-asses get three. I open the cardboard rectangle and see my beauties lined up in a row like little soldiers and covered with shredded lettuce, sliced avocado, chopped tomatoes, and shredded cheddar cheese. I rip open the paper on my straw with my teeth and poke it into the plastic lid of my cup.

I watch the least terns, the little birds searching for

their next meal, chase the breakwater. There is a small boy crying on a blanket because one of the local squirrels stole his baggie of "fishie" crackers. His mom, a pretty, young blonde, hugs him and offers him a new baggie while a little blonde girl, most likely his sister, dances around them, making silly faces, probably trying to cheer him up.

A handsome blond man in gray dress slacks, a light blue dress shirt, and a striped dark blue tie walks down the stairs and hugs the girl, flipping her upside down over his shoulder. She laughs and squeals with glee. The baby boy stands up and toddles on his chubby baby legs over to the man. The man's smile brightens, and he sets the girl down and picks up the baby. He delicately wipes the boy's fat tears with his strong hands and then kisses the baby sweetly on top of his head. He must have left the office to have lunch with his family. What a sweet moment.

The pretty woman walks over, and the man wraps her in his free arm and kisses her for all he's worth. The kids squeal and cheer. The dad smiles at the mom like he's the luckiest guy on the planet. And he is. They all are. And I never will be. I will never get to have a beautiful family like that one or have the love and adoration of a man like that. Because I am now incapable of that. James took it from me.

With that pleasant thought, I slurp up the last sip of cola, the loud noise of the air bubbles telling me my lunch is gone. I barely tasted it, lost in my interloping thoughts of beautiful families and missed opportunities.

Now sitting in my car again, I turn my key in the ignition, and Sam Hunt comes back on to croon to me about breaking up in a small town and seeing his ex-girlfriend hooking up with his friend around town. Ironic for sure, since my thoughts are still on James and his treachery on my heart, among other things. I wonder if he and Bella are still together. Probably. I bet her magic vagina is still keeping him and his cold heart warm at night.

I get back on the highway and head east to the I-15 interstate. I travel north on I-15 for a few exits, about twenty minutes all in all, when I take the familiar Escondido exit. I need to see some familiar faces right now.

I pull into the parking lot that my car graced for more nights than I can even count and head inside the familiar home improvement store. The glass doors under the big, brightly colored letters slide open and welcome me home. Hilde is at the customer service desk when I walk in, and she practically vibrates with excitement. Hilde is about fifty years old, five feet tall, and one hundred pounds soaking wet. And at least ten of those pounds are her gigantic boobs. She has platinum blonde curls and big blue doe eyes she frames with ice-blue shadow and navy mascara.

"Well, hello, my precious!" she squeals in her raspy smoker's voice and races around the counter to wrap me in a big bear hug. She's so tiny that she is basically motor-boating my boobs, but I don't care. This gal and I have bonded over many hours of shitty customers, and managers with slightly sexually harassing tendencies.

"Hey, gorgeous." I wink at her. "How are you this fine evening?"

"Ugh," she growls. "You would not believe how thick the bullshit is in here tonight!" she yells, throwing her arms up in the air.

"Tell me!" I lean in, resting my elbows on her counter.

"Some yahoo came in here tonight and asked to return a used toilet plunger. Used!" she harrumphs. "Turns out this here plunger did not unclog his *giant* turd to his liking," Hilde shouts as she waves a plunger that has a black trash bag, which is tied in several knots, over the end of it.

"You didn't, Hilde." I gasp, covering my mouth with my hand to hide my laughter. "That's not what I think it is. Is it?"

"Oh! You bet your pretty, perky backside it is!" She leans in, narrowing her eyes on something over my shoulder. "Bill made me take it back. I told that big-turd fucker no, but Bill made me do it!"

"Oh, gross." I shudder. "That has to be some kind of hazmat or OSHA hazard." But really, what's done is done.

"Quit complaining, Hilde!" Bill bellows from behind me. "Please tell me you've come back to me, Shelby."

Bill places his warm palm on the small of my back, just a little too low. His fingertips are just barely brushing the top of my left cheek. The lower one. I'm still leaning over the customer service counter, which is fairly tall, but now I'm stuck here as Bill's big body crowds me from behind and a little to the right. I'm the deer caught in someone's headlights before it gets smoked by a Range Rover. Hilde gives me a sympathetic look. We've all been here before. But there's nothing either of us can do. We just have to wait it out and hope Bill moves on sooner rather than later.

"No, sir," I whisper firmly. "I'm just here to—"

But I never get the opportunity to finish telling my old boss what I was doing in the store because we all hear a low, menacing growl from behind Bill and me. Hilde's eyes have gone so wide I think they might just pop out and roll on the floor. I'm not surprised. I've been there before, too. I know that growl, and I know what orgasmic delicacies of the eyes she's seeing for the first time hold. He is the total package. Speaking of packages . . .

"Get. Your hands. Off. Of her. Now!" Trent rumbles. "Shelby. Get over here. Now," he growls.

Good news is, Bill lets go of me really, really quick. Bad news is, even I am kind of scared right now. I'm not sure whether I climaxed or peed in my pants over Trent's caveman antics.

"Shelby." I jump.

I'm no longer lost in my own inappropriate musings. I look over my shoulder at Trent and see he is practically vibrating with rage, but he's somehow keeping it together. To the average observer, he's just some jealous boyfriend, but when I look at him, I see his steel-straight spine, his fists clenched tight at his sides, and his jaw clenched so hard I can almost hear his teeth cracking and popping.

I nod at him and lower my eyes. Guess today isn't going to get better after all. I look up at Hilde as I stand up from where I was hunched over her counter.

"You okay, babydoll?" she whispers to me.

"Yeah, hon," I answer, squeezing her hand in mine. "I'm okay. It's not what you think," I say as I let go of her hand and slowly make my way over to Trent, whose anaconda of an arm snakes out and pulls me to his side tightly.

"I guess now I should tell you that James was in here not too long ago asking about you," she says softly, thoughtfully. I can see her wheels turning.

"When you say, 'not too long ago,' do you mean a few days ago or . . . ?" I trail off

"About thirty minutes ago. Give or take. In fact, I'm not sure he's left the store. I was distracted by Plungergate. I'm sorry, honey. Real sorry." I nod, unable to say anything else. My brain is going a million miles an hour. I wonder if anyone would notice if I just bolt.

I am weighing the pros and cons of running for my life, in my head, lamenting the lack of Gordo's Tacos in Canada, when Trent puts a toe to the floor and pivots us around with full military precision. His arm is wrapped firmly around me, protecting me. His other hand is resting on the butt of the gun on his right hip. Trent is protecting me. And he doesn't even know what from. I feel some of the ice around my heart crack.

Trent leads me through the store like a US Marshal leading a protected witness into the courthouse. I wonder if this is ingrained or trained into him. We head toward the back of the store. Located near the rear is a hallway that contains the bathrooms, a break room, and management offices.

"What happened back there?" Trent asks me as he turns me to face him just inside the hallway. We are not standing close enough to touch, but close enough for me to see that the anger has bled away from his face, which now only shows concern and confusion.

"It was nothing. Just a surprise," I say, hedging. "Just a blast from my past that I wasn't expecting. What are you doing here, anyway?"

"I needed to order some interior doors. And don't change the subject. Why were that guy's hands on your body, Shelby?" he questions dangerously low. "You have to know I won't share."

"Stop it, Trent." My anger resurfaces. "He's my old boss, and you will leave it be in case I need a job here again sometime soon. If you haven't noticed, my job at the paper is pretty freaking tenuous right now," I snap.

Trent's face softens. "I'm sorry, baby," he soothes.

"I saw his hands on you, and I saw red. But know this: you are never fucking working here again," he declares.

"Excuse me?"

"You heard me. I won't repeat myself."

"Um, I hate to break it to you, but you don't own me," I snap back. Trent steps closer, crowding me into his body. I can feel his chest rumble when he speaks.

"Yeah, baby, I do. You just won't admit it yet. But this body, this brain, this beauty are mine. And I won't stand back and let lesser men mistreat it."

His lips are so close that his breath, spicy from the cinnamon gum he loves, coasts over my lips. I close my eyes, anticipating his kiss. I need Trent's kiss.

"Well, isn't this cozy," a voice I had hoped to never hear again says and sends ice shooting through my veins. "But, Shelby, what the fuck do you think you're doing?" he sneers.

"Excuse me, buddy, but this doesn't concern you." Trent straightens. Now standing tall and strong, he faces the man who destroyed me with no concern whatsoever.

"Actually, *buddy*"—James pokes Trent in the chest—"it does. So I'll ask you kindly to take your hands off my fiancée." Trent just smiles widely.

"I'm not so sure Shelby here is aware of her status in your life," Trent says, but James reaches for me, wrapping his bony fingers around my wrist tightly.

"Is that true, Shelby?" James growls, "You denied our love?"

"Get your hands off of her, buddy," Trent snarls. I can tell he's losing his patience. "I'm pretty sure she became mine when she came like a freight train on my fingers with my tongue in her mouth and her hand wrapped around my cock. PS—It was my name on her lips when she came."

James's fingers tighten even more. I gasp at the pain keeps me from calling Trent out on his lies, but at the same time I don't want anything to do with James. I'm in a pickle. I can see the bruises already forming. My own fingertips are white and purple from the loss of circulation.

"You stupid whore," James sneers. "I told you I would be back for you. I just needed to sow some wild oats before we got married."

"You slept with my best friend," I say through gritted teeth. "You carried on an affair with her for months behind my back."

"I told you I could have anyone I wanted. Look at me—I'm rich, handsome, powerful." He shakes me. "But you, you were supposed to be a good little wife and do as I say. But no, you just had to run off when you found out about Bella. Honestly, I was still trying to decide which one of you I would actually marry when you ran off in that snit. But luckily for you, I enjoy the chase. So I choose you."

"You're crazy." I gasp as his hand tightens. I feel

the tendons in my wrist pop.

"Let her go. Now," Trent demands.

"Stop acting like a willful child, Shelby," James thunders. "You'll have to learn to behave yourself once we're married."

"I won't tell you again. Let her go," Trent warns.

"I told you before; I won't marry you. Not after what you've done," I spit. "Go home to Bella. That is, if she'll have you."

I barely have time to get the worst of my words out because the back of James's hand connects with my face. My head slams back into the wall in the hallway.

"Why, you little cunt . . . ," James snarls.

"Police! Freeze!" Trent shouts. James and I both look over his shoulder. James smiles an evil smile, and my blood runs cold. Trent has a very large, very dangerous gun pointed directly at James. "Put your hands up where I can see them."

James slowly steps away from me and raises his hands up, palms out. Smiling the whole time. I didn't realize I was holding my breath until it escaped from me, my chest burning. My right eye is swelling closed, and I can only see out of my left one. My left wrist is swollen, and I am having difficulty moving my fingers.

"Hands behind your back," Trent quietly demands.

"You have to be kidding." James laughs. "This was just a misunderstanding."

"There is no misunderstanding. You assaulted this

woman in front of a police detective. You are under arrest for assault and battery, assault on a police officer, stalking, and making threatening statements," Trent calmly informs him as he puts away his badge, which had magically appeared when he told James to freeze, and replaces it in his hand with the handcuffs he is locking around James's wrists. My own wrists twinge in sympathy. For his wrists only. "You have the right to remain silent. Anything you say can and will be used against you in a court of law. You have the right to an attorney. If you cannot afford an attorney, one will be provided for you."

"What the ever-loving fuck, Shelby?" James bellows. "Stop this. Right now."

But I'm frozen to the floor in my spot. I don't know what to do. I'm afraid of James; that much is true. But I also can't stop Trent. He is still protecting me. And doing his actual job. And lastly, I don't want to be afraid of James anymore. His reign of terror is over.

"If you choose to answer questions without an attorney present, you may stop proceedings at any time. Do you understand these rights as they have been afforded to you?" Trent finishes.

"Yep. Got it. Loud and clear, dickwad," James spits in Trent's face. "You'll be sorry, Shelby. I promise you that. Your transgressions toward me are huge. And you will receive your penance once we're married. I intend to tear it out of your ass. And it's a true shame since it's a halfway decent ass, even if it is huge." I gasp.

"No, James," I say firmly. Clearly. "We're done.

I am done. And you do not get to beat me or rape me, cheat on me, or lie to me ever again."

I realize I've said too much in mixed company, because Trent's gaze on James has turned murderous. I catch his eye and barely shake my head no, small enough so only he will see. I want Trent to know James isn't worth his career. But I can only see out of one eye, so I can't get a read on him. I let the breath I had been holding go when he opens his phone and makes a call, to which I'm assuming is his dispatch.

"Yes, this is Detective Foyle, badge number 4-4-2-3-9," he says calmly into his phone. "I have a transport to local lockup for processing and need a bus to the Home Improvement on Hidden Valley. Nonurgent. Victim has received a facial blow and likely hit the back of her head on a wall on impact. Victim is conscious and alert. Also needs medical attention for possible broken wrist and damaged cheek and eye socket."

The dispatcher says some other things we can't hear, and I am wondering how my life spiraled out of control. This is ridiculous, but at least now there are no secrets. Trent will know once and for all why I can't be with him, even though I wish I could. I really do. But I'm too broken, too damaged to be a good girlfriend to anyone ever again.

"Yes," Trent says in response. "And if you could get ahold of my partner, Detective Green, and inform him of the incident, I would appreciate it."

I slide down the wall to sit on my backside. My knees are bent upward to my chest, and my arms are draped over my knees. My good arm is cradling my hurt one. I hang my head and cry. I would stop it if I could, but I can't. I feel Trent's eyes on me, but I know he has to watch James until the other police get here. I don't know if I could look him in the eye right now even if I wanted to.

"So, you guys decided to have a party and didn't even think to invite me," Kane says as he strolls down the hall like he doesn't have a care in the world. "I'm hurt, guys, real hurt." He shakes his head in mock disappointment. Bill is stalking down the hall behind him.

"What the hell is going on here?" Bill questions, fuming. "Shelby? The police are here." I can tell when he gets a good look at me, and I must look fan-fucking-tastic, because I hear Bill audibly gulp.

"Are you okay, Shelby?" Bill asks quietly.

"Just peachy, Bill," I say, still looking down.

"Okay," he says calmly. "Don't take this the wrong way, but I'm kind of glad you don't work here anymore. I'd really hate to have to fire you."

"Thank God for that," James grumbles. "You finally have a halfway decent job, Shelby. Something more befitting of what my future wife should be," he says with an air of doucheiness.

"Now is a good time to be quiet, buddy, mmkay?" Kane says helpfully, "Oh, look! Our buddies in the black-and-whites are here. Now we can really get this party started." Kane shoots a knowing look at Trent, who just nods his thanks.

Two uniformed officers walk into the now crowded hallway, shortly followed by two paramedics pushing a gurney with a medical bag on top. Yay, more fun!

"This here is Mr. James Reynolds," Kane addresses the officers, taking control of the situation. "He is being placed under arrest for assault and battery, among other things. Let's go ahead and get him down to Processing. I'm going to take statements from Miss Whitmore and Detective Foyle, and then I will meet you down at the station to wrap up this paperwork. Go team!"

"This is such bullshit," James grumbles.

"Yep, it's definitely bullshit when a man beats up on a woman," one of the uniformed officers says to him.

"You got that right," the other officer replies. "Let's go and get you processed as quickly as possible. You have the right to remain silent . . ." The officer rereads James his rights as they lead him down the hall.

"Ugh," I hear him groan.

"Ma'am, can you look at me, please?" the paramedic asks me. I look up and see a handsome man crouched down in front of me, looking at me with gentle concern on his face. But behind him, Trent and Kane are mirror images of barely concealed rage. "My name is Joe. Can you tell me your name?"

"Shelby," I croak. I clear my throat and close my eyes tight. Then I open them again. "My name is Shelby," I say more firmly.

"Don't you worry about those two meatheads over

there." Joe follows my gaze, which is met with dueling growls, over his shoulder. "We're here to get you taken care of." Joe snaps on some latex gloves, and the sound makes me jump. I hate feeling weak, scared.

"I'm going to touch your cheek and shine my flashlight in your eyes, all right?" Joe questions. I just nod. His gloved fingertips push on my cheek, and I wince. Then they move over and push down again, but I'm ready this time. And again. "I don't think your cheek is broken. Your eye is swollen, and you will need to see an ophthalmologist. Now, follow the light with your eyes only," Joe says as he slowly slides it back and forth, and I feel my eyes cross.

The other paramedic cracks open a chemical ice pack and hands it to Joe, who places it gently over my eye and cheek and asks me to hold it there. It stings and soothes at the same time.

"Now I'm going to clean your lip with an alcohol wipe and tape it until a doctor at the hospital can look at you. Okay?" I nod again.

The cold stinging of the antiseptic wipe fizzes up and makes my eyes water. The other paramedic hands Joe a little bandage packet. He rips it open and peels off a couple of Steri-Strips that he uses to tape the cut on my lip shut.

"Now, can you tell me about the bruising on your forehead?" Joe asks gently.

"I ran into a door," I mumble. I immediately realize how incredibly lame that sounds. The disappointed look on Joe's face tells me he thinks I'm lying.

"Shelby, the man who did this to you is already on his way to jail. You are safe now. So I'm going to ask you again about the bruising on your forehead," he says sternly.

"No, really. The other night, I got startled and ran into the sliding glass door to the patio in my kitchen." I plead, begging Joe to believe me.

"It's true," Kane says. "Trent and I were there and startled her. She jumped up and ran into the door before anyone could stop her. Those bruises are two days old. The eye, lip, and wrist are current injuries, to my knowledge."

"Same here," Trent says. "I witnessed both the incident in her condo and the one here this afternoon."

"And what are you going to do to prevent these things from happening in the future?" Joe demands of Trent. Pop-Pop, my grandfather, would have been so proud of this man's protective tendencies toward me.

"I'm going to ride with her to the hospital, make sure she gets a full workup, take her home, wrap her in Bubble Wrap, and care for her until she's healed. This will distract me from beating the shit out of *Uppity McDouchebag* that was just here," Trent says honestly, and I realize he has a working relationship, if not a friendship, with Joe and his partner.

"That's a true story," Kane agrees. "What an asshole. What did you ever see in him, Shelby? What? Too soon?" Kane questions when we all give him the side-eye.

"You just ignore Detective Green, Shelby. He took one too many pucks to the head in his formative years, and that's my professional opinion." Joe winks at me. I laugh out loud and wince as the sound pings around in my damaged brain like a .22 caliber bullet in a watermelon.

"Yep, pretty sure she's got a concussion. They'll tell you more at the hospital," Joe says to Trent, who just nods, his scowl never leaving his face. "Now let's take a look at that wrist. Can you hold it up for me? Twist it? Wiggle your fingers? Okay. Let's get an inflatable splint on that. Merrily can do that while I have a word with our detectives. Okay?" Joe snaps his gloves off, folding them into each other for disposal.

Merrily comes over and smiles at me weakly. I try to smile back, but my whole body hurts, my right eye is now swollen shut, and I can't move my left hand. My hand! Shit! How am I going to do my job if I can't write? I start crying again.

"It's okay, really," Merrily promises. "You'll get all patched up at the hospital and be as good as new." She smiles at me, and I just cry harder.

"What in the hell is going on over there, Mer?" Joe shouts.

"Nothing! I swear," she pleads. Joe's eyes grow dark as he glares at her.

"No, no, really! She's telling the truth." I try to soothe. "I was just thinking that if I can't move my fingers, if I broke my wrist, I can't do my job as a writer." It doesn't escape my notice that when I said *I* broke my wrist, the faces of all three men turned scary-dark.

"We'll cross that bridge when we get to it, baby," Trent says, trying to reassure me. "Maybe we'll get you a tape recorder and I'll transcribe it at night for you," he offers.

"That's hilarious!" Kane laughs. Trent growls. "You should see the mess this big oaf makes of our reports. He's a disaster!" Kane slaps his knee while laughing. I just cry harder.

"Jesus Christ, you idiot!" Joe grumbles. "What about talk-to-text on your iPhone or iPad? Then your editor can clean it up for you to approve before you submit it for publishing." I instantly brighten. Joe is right. It's not so bad. I can do this!

"Ahhhh!" I squeal. "I love you, Joe! You're the best." I hug him tight. He just saved me. Trent just growls. Kane just laughs.

"Aww, it was nothing, ma'am," Joe preens. "I'm just glad I could help." Merrily just smiles fondly. I'm thinking they have an interesting relationship.

"We do," she answers with a laugh.

"I said that out loud, didn't I?" I ask, blushing as red as my hair.

"Yep." Joe laughs. "That's the concussion talking. You should explain Mer and me to her, though," he says to Trent.

"That's not my story to tell, man," Trent says softly.

Joe and Merrily are guiding me onto the gurney. My legs are out in front of me, and I'm sitting up. The back of the gurney is popped up, supporting me. My good hand is cradling my bad one, and Joe and Merrily are buckling the safety straps around me.

"You know how I love a good strap," Joe says softly.

Merrily blushes beet red and then laughs. Kane and Trent groan audibly, and that seems to just make Joe laugh harder. I must have a confused look on my face, but then Merrily blows my mind.

"Joe is my Dom," she says softly with a smile as she pats my leg. "On three. One . . . Two . . . Three." And they both hit the latches to launch my gurney up off the ground.

"Wait, what?" I say as they all escort me down the hall and through the store. Kane, Trent, Joe, and Merrily all just laugh. Must be the concussion. Yeah, that's it.

Once we reach the front, Hilde is crying. I know she feels bad. She's seen me at my worst with James. I know she's blaming herself, but she has no reason to. She didn't beat me. And I never told her to call the cops.

"It's okay," I tell her. "I'm going to be okay. This isn't your fault, Hilde. Tell me you know," I demand, but she just looks away and nods.

"Let's rock and roll," Joe says as the sliding doors

open and they wheel me out.

Kane fist-bumps Joe and Trent before he jumps into his car to head to the station. Joe and Merrily load me up into the back of the ambulance. Merrily sits in the back with me, while Joe hops into the driver's seat. Trent climbs up and sits on the bench next to me.

"This is Unit Seventeen, ready to transport patient. Please notify San Diego General of our arrival." The doors shut. Joe hits the lights and sirens.

"So, what do you mean when you say, 'Dom'?" I question, and the ambulance fills with chuckles.

"He's my Dominant, and I am Joe's submissive," Merrily says patiently.

"I'm not sure I understand . . ."

"I'll show you sometime if you'd like," Trent says silkily.

My breath catches in my chest. I'm not so sure about that. Merrily just winks at me. Yep, this is definitely the concussion's handiwork. None of this conversation is really happening. Merrily and Joe bust out laughing. Trent, smiling broadly, just looks down at his hands in his lap, but I can see his lips twitching with laughter. Damn it, I must have said that shit out loud again.

"Yep, you did. Still are, really," Merrily confirms.

"Goddamn it!" I grumble. "Stupid fucking concussion. Damn stupid sexy detective!" With that, Trent throws his head back and laughs, too.

Chapter Four

HEALINGS AND HELLCATS

The remainder of the ride to the hospital is uneventful. Well, mostly. Mostly, it is uneventful because I decide to give in to the weight of my head, which is demanding that I lean back and shut the bright surgical lights inside the ambulance out once and for all.

As my breathing slows, I feel the tension bleed out of my body. James is in jail. For now. My face looks even worse, but that would heal. James thinks we are still an item. That's awkward. No, that's motherfucking insane. Pardon my French. But hopefully, the officers in charge at the jail will realize they need to call the people with the big butterfly nets who can inject him with tranquilizer darts large enough to stop an elephant until they can pump him with enough antipsychotics to stop his crazy train in its tracks. Shit, now I am stressed again.

I do my best to channel Harmony, minus the ganja, slowly breathing in the good air and positive vibes, blowing out the bad air and negativity. In with the good, out with the bad. In with the good, out with the bad. This is a bunch of bullshit, and now I'm tired.

I'm just starting to feel the weight leave my body again. My breathing has slowed, but I now realize someone has been watching me. Or, should I say *some-ones?* I know Trent is one of them. I could tell at the store that he was worried. And the other is Merrily. I hope. Because if Joe is staring me down, his eyes are not on the road, and that is not okay. I have had enough accidents, and some not-so accidents, for a lifetime. I think she's just trying to make sure I don't die. I don't have the energy to comfort Trent right now. I just need a few minutes of peace, and then once we are at the hospital, I can tell him that everything will be fine and he doesn't need to worry. None of this is his fault. Mr. Sandman has just about closed the deal when I hear activity stir in the ambulance.

"She's out. You are now free to move about the cabin," Merrily says with a snicker.

"Really, Mer?" Joe drawls.

"What?" I can hear her shrug. "It's paramedic hu-mor."

"Sometimes," Joe sighs, "I think I should have stayed with the engine company.

"Whatever you say, JoJo."

"Did you just roll your eyes at me?" Joe thunders.

"Can you two keep it in your pants for a minute, please?" Trent grumbles. "My girl is hurt, and I need to make sure she's going to be okay."

"She's okay, Trent," Merrily promises softly. "I'm sorry. I won't joke around anymore."

"It's all right. This isn't your fault," Trent sighs.

"Which is more than I can say for that asshole that hit her," Joe bellows. "Do we have a plan for that?"

"No, we don't. And I'm sorry," Trent groans. "I shouldn't have yelled at you."

"So, now that we're all on the same page," Joe says smoothly, "who is this girl? And don't say, 'Shelby Whitmore.' I know that much from her driver's license. Who is she to you?"

Well, if that isn't the six-million-dollar question. Jesus, I'm getting as bad as Granny. So damn nosy. And yet I'm dying to know. Am I the girl he caused to fall into a grave? The girl he made out with in an alley? I'm not about to mention the other stuff that happened. Am I just the girl that sold him his new kitchen cabinets? The granddaughter of a friend of his grandmother's? The list goes on and on. And I am pathetic. I stifle a groan of my own self-pity, hoping that no one notices.

"She's everything," Trent states firmly. Quietly. I'm holding my breath. I think Joe and Merrily are, too. "She's the granddaughter of Nana's friend, and Nana has been trying to set me up with her since before I moved here. She's the girl that sold me my kitchen cabinets and knocked me on my ass that night with her beauty and smarts."

"I was wondering if she was your 'angel of the home improvement store,'" Joe says with a laugh.

"She's more," Trent sighs. "She's it, and I can barely get her to give me a chance. Although, after this eye-opening encounter with her ex, I'm pretty sure I know why. How do I show her that I'm not him? That I will protect her from him or anyone else that would hurt her?"

I can hear the frustration in his voice, and it hurts my heart to hear it and know that I am the one who put it there. But I don't know how to change. Suddenly I'm not feeling so good. Joe appears to be taking every bump and sharp turn he can, and my stomach is flopping around. I can feel the sweat from the fear of impending doom roll down from my hairline. My body starts to shake, and saliva is pooling in my mouth. Oh God. I can't stop it. I squeeze my eyes tight, feeling unforeseen regret for having my favorite tacos and soda for lunch. Joe takes another sharp turn, and I can't help it. I lean over the edge of the gurney and empty the contents of my stomach. All over Trent's lap.

"Boom, bitch!" Joe shouts like he's at a football game. "That is for that shit in basic training. Booyah!" He laughs.

"Did you know that Joe and I were in the army together?" Trent asks Merrily and me. I shake my head, but Merrily just smiles a sly smile.

"I did know that. And I've heard *all* about basic training. You probably had something coming, Trent." Merrily laughs. "Although, I'd say this is more Shelby's concussion than anything Joe cooked up. Here are some paper towels and a trash bag. We'll see if we can get you some scrubs at the hospital."

"Thanks, Mer."

Joe pulls into the breezeway in front of the emergency room with all the pomp and circumstance to be expected. He swings the rear double doors of the ambulance open, and Merrily hops out. They pull the stretcher I'm strapped to out through the doors, and the legs and wheels pop down like an airplane getting ready to make a landing at Lindbergh Field downtown. As soon as I clear the doors, Trent jumps out and moves beside me, taking my uninjured hand.

As if we are some special ops team, we move as one. Or synchronized swimmers. I'd like to say I don't know how that one jumped into my head, but there is a lot rattling around in there tonight. That and the fact that Marla and Granny once tried it at the old folks' home. It was before Marla broke her hip in an unfortunate elderly sex accident but after they failed at pole dancing. It's been a wild ride since Granny moved into Marla's building after Pop-Pop died and before Trent got here to help me keep some order amongst our elders. As I said, we're like a special ops team . . . or synchronized swimmers, Joe at my feet, pulling me through the sliding doors at the emergency room bay, Mer at my back, pushing us along with a purpose, and Trent at my side, his warrior face on. I can officially say I have never seen his warrior face before, and I hope to never have it aimed at me. He obviously means business. I just want out of here, and I have only been in the building for about forty-five seconds.

"Victim: twenty-five-year-old female," Joe barks at the nurses and doctors who meet us at the door. "Possible concussion, possible broken wrist and hand, lacerations on right cheek and lip. Detective Trenton Foyle, San Diego PD, off-duty witness and reporting."

"Patient is conscious. Let's move her to bay three," someone in blue bunny scrubs shouts. Shit. I must have hit my head harder than I thought.

"Lost consciousness in the bus. Also, patient shows signs of confusion and disorientation," Joe says.

"No, I don't," I declare. Joe gives me a hard glare.

"She's also having trouble holding thoughts on the inside," Trent says and chokes back a laugh. The bastard. "Everything seems to just be coming out. Like diarrhea."

"Or the . . ." Joe leans in and sniffs. "Tacos? She puked all over you in my bus." Trent growls.

"Oh, Trent," Blue Bunny Nurse practically purrs. "You poor thing. Let me see if I can get you some scrubs after we get our patient checked out." She zeros in her gaze on me.

"And now, was that any way to treat an American hero?" BBN barks at me. I feel my eyes go wide. What the fuck did I do?

"Well, for starters, you put your nasty vomit all over poor Trent here." Are you shitting me right now? I must have said that out loud again. Damn.

"Yeah, baby, you did," Trent says with a chuckle. BBN glares at him.

"I wasn't aware you two were acquainted," she huffs. But then she rallies. "Maybe if you called me once in a while . . ."

She runs her stripper-red fingernail down Trent's pec and over his abs toward his belt buckle. She trails the pads of her fingers back and forth over the plain silver buckle on his worn, brown leather belt. Thankfully, she doesn't go any further. I'm not quite sure if it's because she needs to maintain some semblance of workplace decorum or because my vomit mostly hit his impressive package. Either way, I'm pretty sure BBN is ovulating loud enough to be heard in fucking China.

"Don't you have any manners?!" BBN shouts at me. Mer and Joe bust a gut laughing. "And, you two"—she turns to them—"don't you have a run to close out?"

"I said that out loud again, didn't I?" I ask Trent.

"Yeah, baby, you did." He runs his hand down his face in an attempt to wipe his smile off. Bastard. "So, just out of curiosity, on a scale of one to ten, how impressive would you say my package is?" I just sigh as

I lean my head back and close my eyes. There is no point in asking if I said that out loud; it's obvious that everything I'm going to say in the foreseeable future will be out loud.

"Shelby and I are seeing each other," Trent says softly, and I know without opening my eyes, he directed those words to BBN. She growls and glares at me. I'm assuming this, since I feel the lasers burning my eyelids, but I can't be bothered to open my eyes.

"You stole my boyfriend, and you're not even going to look at me!" BBN demands. What the hell is going on here today? Is there a full moon or something?

"One, he pursued me, not the other way around. I have told him no repeatedly. And two, he did not tell me he had a girlfriend."

"Because he doesn't," Joe grumbles from the corner.

"Why are you even still here?" she shouts.

"Shelby is one of us now; we're here for her," he responds calmly. "Another crew has been pulled in. 03 is out of service for the time being."

"So you just don't care that we had a thing before you horned in on it?" she demands.

"Brandi . . . ," Trent warns.

"No, it's okay." I hold a hand up. It's hard for mere mortals to be confident when they look like Quasimodo, but this chick is working my last nerve and it's been a rough couple of days. I need to go home with a big bottle of super-strength Xanax and sleep this off. Or morphine. "I didn't horn in on anything, and as you can see, my ex-boyfriend beat the hell out of me in the hall outside of the break room of my former place of employment. This was two days after Don Juan over here made me fall into an open grave . . ."

"Smooth move, asshole," Joe says and chuckles. Trent just shrugs it off.

"And I ran into a sliding glass door. That hurts by the way," I say as I tick each statement off on my hand. "And one day after we did hot yoga with Kane and a bunch of horny senior citizens and had a dinner that left me starving, Romeo here gave me the best orgasm of my life in a back alley behind an old folks' home. A lot has happened in the last few days, so excuse me if my 'give a damn' is busted right along with my face. Now, how can I get some happy juice and get the fuck out of here?" I finish strongly.

I here Joe and Mer laughing in the corner, but Brandi, the artist formerly known as BBN, just squeals and storms out of my little area. Great news! Things are looking up. But she didn't send me a new nurse, or a doctor either. I am a sadface.

"I know, sweets. We'll get you seen soon." Joe smiles sweetly. If this is what having a Dom is all about, I could totally get behind that. Trent growls and Joe laughs. I must have said that outside of my head again. I should go back to sleep.

"You can't go to sleep until we get some labs and scans done of that big head of yours." A doctor and a very irritated BBN walk back into my little cubby. I sigh. Being awake is getting me into trouble.

"Well then, let's get you upstairs for those scans and see if we can't keep you out of trouble, Miss Whitmore." The doctor smiles indulgently. He's like a sweet grandpa of the ER. He chuckles.

"Finally," I say, exasperated. "Somebody gets me."

Trent lifts me like a fairy princess, something soft and special, delicate even, and gently puts me in a wheelchair BBN has provided. I sit back, and she rolls me to the elevator for my labs and scans.

I'd like to say the ride in the elevator is relaxing, leaning my head back and taking a deep breath after the last few days, but sadly, that's just not going to happen. I can feel BBN's eyes shooting daggers at the back of my head and her hot dragon breath breathing down my neck.

"So . . . how is it that you seem to know Trent, again?" BBN demands. It isn't until I hear Trent groan that I realize he followed us into the elevator. I'm embarrassed to admit that I'm actually a little relieved.

"Our grandmothers are neighbors," I say politely.

"Well, isn't that convenient," she huffs.

"Not really," I share. "Miss Marla tells me all about his penis all the time, and my Granny is constantly asking if I've seen it or if I have slept with him. As you can see, since I am in your hospital for being roughed up by the last man I trusted with my heart, I'm not necessarily in the market for another."

"Are you trying to say that Trent is comparable to that monster?" she asks with faux rage, trying to ingratiate herself back with Trent. But it's Trent who visibly bristles.

"Of course not," I sigh, both exhausted and exasperated. "I merely meant that I have steamer trunks full of baggage. Who would want to take that on? It's not really fair of me to ask that of anyone."

"She's right, Trent," BBN says softly. "That's too much baggage for anyone to take on." And she gently places her palm on his forearm.

"Maybe for most men. But, baby, I'm not most men," Trent says, his eyes locked on mine. "And there's a big difference between your asking for it and my offering it up."

"You can't be serious?" BBN demands, her nails biting into his arm as her grip tightens. "Baby, you need someone to support you and your career, not to mention your libido. I can give you that. You know she can't." But Trent's eyes never leave mine.

"You're mine, baby," he says softly. "You have been since that night I walked into the home improvement store."

I nod softly, tears burning behind my eyes. BBN huffs out a growl, and I roll my eyes. Trent, his gaze never leaving my face, barks out a laugh at my response. I just hope BBN isn't going to be a problem. My vision might still be a little on the blurry side, but I'm thinking she looks like the kind to carry a grudge.

The elevator dings to let us know we have reached the floor that Radiology is on. When the door opens, BBN roughly shoves my wheelchair into the opening, just catching my right shin on the corner of the door as she slams me into the elevator wall.

"Whoopsies," she says, and I can almost hear the evil smile she's unsuccessfully trying to hold back. "Right this way, folks."

After BBN's awkward soul-bearing in the elevator, she's quick to abandon us at the radiology department and make tracks back to the emergency room. Honestly, I'm glad. I wasn't sure how much more I could take. And truth be told, I wasn't sure if she would lunge to scratch my eyes out or if she and Trent would start making out and dry humping in the elevator like a couple of teenagers. For a minute there, I was sure it could go either way. Now that we've obviously moved past the eye-scratching for revenge, it's a little scary.

"Well, folks," she says with her saccharin-sweet, fake-ass smile. I smile right back, which has to be at least a little bit frightening because only half of my face works right now. This, of course, makes hers waver a bit, but she manages to regroup. I'll give her that. "Jorge here will take your x-rays and get you right back down to us in the ER. Then we can figure out what to do with you." I swear I hear her say, *I know what I'd like to do with you.* Yeah, I bet it involves this wheelchair going right out a fourth-floor window.

Jorge, Trent, and I all watch BBN porn-star-strut to the elevator and poke the button with one of her feral-cat claws. She throws a smirk and a wink over her shoulder as the elevator dings and the doors open. When the elevator takes off with her in it, we all breathe a collective sigh of relief. I'm half fantasizing that the doors opened but the elevator wasn't there and that she then fell into a black hole leading to a parallel universe when Jorge breaks up my psychotic ramblings.

"That chick gives me the willies." He emphasizes that with a shiver. Trent just nods solemnly, eyes wide.

"Well, Big Chief over here"—I throw a thumb over my shoulder to indicate Trent—"obviously played 'Hide the Salami' with her, and now it appears I may have a contract on my head."

"You noticed that, huh?" Trent asks casually.

"Oh yeah." I laugh. "China noticed the signals she was throwing your way." I give him the side-eye.

"On a scale of one to ten, how much trouble am I in?" he asks, looking at me with big puppy dog eyes.

"Weirdo, I didn't even know you. But if you have more crazy-town train wrecks lying in wait, I am definitely putting that in the cons list of whether or not I should date you." Trent just winks at me. I'm in so much trouble.

Jorge is amazing and funny. I feel bad, though, because all of his efforts aren't really helping my melancholy. My bitchy side says BBN still has her sights set straight on Trent, and that really burns my biscuits. I didn't want him before, but I do now that I have pushed him away and the ugly truth of James and my history—and apparent present—appears to have left the door wide fucking open for Brandi and her stupid blue bunny scrubs to hop right onto Trent's impressive man parts. I sigh loudly.

"We'll have you out of here as soon as we can, Ms. Whitmore." Shit, now this poor guy thinks I'm pissed at him.

"No, it's not you. It's my life." I sigh again. "You're just doing your job, and I'm being rude. How is your day going?" I smile with only the working side of my face.

"Pretty great now that I have a good-looking woman smiling at me." He winks, and I feel my smile turn more genuine. He is adorable. "Now, come lie down on my table and let me get some pretty pictures of your head," he tells me. I do what he asks and let him get all the x-rays he needs so Doctor Grandpa can decide if my Humpty Dumpty is cracked for good. It kind of feels like it is.

"All right, you're done. Hop up." He smiles sweetly as he helps me up and back into the wheelchair.

"Thanks." I smile back as he pushes me down the hall.

"Here is your next stop, Shelby." He smiles again as he stops me in front of the lab doors and says, "I hope they go easy on you."

"Me too, me too."

"Hello, my name is Hannah, and I'm going to be drawing your blood today," the woman, who, ironically, is wearing red scrubs, says crisply. Trent just groans. I'm going to take a stab in the dark here and say the appearance of Hannah the Phlebotomist is not a good sign.

"Hello," I say politely.

"Let's get you into a chair around back," she says coolly to me. "You, you may not come back. You wait here." She points to a chair out front for Trent.

Poor Trent opens his mouth to say something, but I quickly shake my head in the negative. If this woman is already trouble, his fighting to come with me will only cause more problems in the long run. He sighs loudly and nods his head, accepting my decision.

Really, how much trouble can I be in? I know he didn't sleep with her, too, because BBN would never have allowed it. I don't realize until she has me locked into her blood drawing chair, with the arm down and holding me in, that it is worse than I thought—I look up and see a snapshot of BBN and Hannah the Phlebotomist scantily clad in what could only be described as hooker wear, with their inflatable boobs barely covered by the strings holding up their dresses. Their arms are around each other, cosmos in hand, in some uber-trendy nightclub down in the Gaslamp District. Shit! They're BFFs, besties, ride-or-die chicks. Fuck, I'm going to die because this "bee" is surely going to kill me.

When I turn my gaze back to Hannah, she smiles evilly, and I realize that BBN is not a feral cat but a she-wolf in nurses' clothing and that these wolves travel in mother-effing packs. She snaps her rubber gloves on kind of aggressively and preps her needle pack. I'm starting to sweat. I can feel it beading at my temples, and I am starting to feel a little sick again.

Hannah roughly grabs my arm, pulling it straight out in front of me and just shy of slamming it down on the armrest in front of me. She squeezes my hand into a fist so tight you can hear my knuckles pop, and I let a whimper escape my lips. She just winks at me. Winks! Next, she snaps the rubber band around my upper arm, and I know that I am in trouble. I have to swallow several times to get all of the saliva that's pooling in my mouth down.

"You know that Brandi and I are friends," she says calmly. I just nod slowly.

"I am coming to realize that," I say softly as she absentmindedly pokes my inner elbow with her finger.

"And that we are close." I just nod again. "Close enough that sometimes we share . . . everything," she says, making eye contact.

I'm not sure what that means. Shoes? Lip gloss? Tampons? I have no idea.

"Okay . . ." I mean, what else am I supposed to say? Then she takes the needle and jabs. "Ouch."

"I mean *everything*." She jabs again. "So imagine how disappointed I was when Brandi had an amazing moment with Trent but never got a call from him again. Because on the second night, I was going to get to join in. And from what I hear, there is more than enough to go around."

She jabs me again. *And again.* Now this is not a my-arm-is-hard-to-draw-blood-from jab. This is *a-you-stole-my-toy-so-I'm-going-to-hurt-you-as-much-as-I-can-get-away-with* jab.

"I haven't slept with him," I say softly. *Jab.*

"But you will. You have what I want and what Brandi really wants. And that is a problem." *Jab.* I'm trying hard not to flinch, but this shit hurts.

"Hannah, there's a man in the waiting room, demanding to be brought back to see Ms. Whitmore," says another woman wearing red scrubs as she pops her head in.

And I am saved by the freaking bell! Hannah sighs but immediately sobers and slides the needle effortlessly into my awaiting vein. Blood starts flowing into the little vials, one after another, when Trent rounds the corner.

"You okay, baby?" he asks, stroking my hair away from my face.

"Yeah," I say softly, but in my head, I'm thinking, *Fuck no, I'm not. I am going to die at the hands of some sex-crazed, slutty nurses, and it's all Trent's fault!*

"Okay." He gives me a sweet smile.

"It was the funniest thing," Hannah butts in. "She had the trickiest veins I've ever seen. I had to stick her multiple times before she would cooperate." *Bullshit!* I want to shout, but I don't since she still has a direct line to my life force. I bite my lip in an effort to censor my thoughts. Trent just narrows his eyes on her.

Hannah the Phlebotomist takes more blood than I thought could actually be in my body. I think BBN is seeking vengeance for Trent's interest in me. By the twelfth vial of my life force, I'm beginning to think she might be a sadist. Still feeling queasy, whether from my head injury, Hannah's interrogation, or BBN's sluttiness, I do not know if she is and I don't care. As Hannah places a cotton ball over the needle in my arm and releases the needle with a snap, taping down the little ball of cotton that's supposed to stop my bleeding, I don't even fight the newest wave of nausea as it swims up. I feel the sweat on my face. My body feels both hot and cold.

"Are you okay, baby? You don't look so good," Trent asks.

"No, I don't think so," I say weakly.

He gives me the side-eye. After his ride in the ambulance with me and his new acquisition of blue scrubs and a plastic bag with all of his soiled clothes in them, he has to know what's coming. I watch him take a small step back, gauging my reaction, and then another and another until he's out of the splash zone. I feel a shiver rack my body. Hannah looks at me with only a small amount of concern; she'd probably be happy if I died from blood loss. I shake my head from side to side. Then she tilts her head down to take a closer look at me, and I throw up all over her face.

"You bitch!" she screams.

"I didn't do it on purpose," I defend. "I have a concussion." I nod solemnly.

"Well, we best be going," Trent says as he loads me up into my wheelchair as quickly as possible. We're hauling booty toward the elevator at some serious speeds. Trent must be in really good shape.

When the elevator door dings open, Trent hustles us inside. He is back to giving me the hairy eyeball. I'm sure he is seconds from bolting for the door, but I'm feeling too tired and sore to care right now.

"I'm not sure whether to be horrified or impressed," he says to the empty elevator.

"Well, let me know when you decide," I sigh, not sure what to do with all of the different emotions swirling around in my brain, and worse, my heart.

"Whoa. You're mad at me?" he questions. "I should be mad at you. Do you realize what kind of trouble you bought us tonight with the boob twins?" he growls.

"Mad at me?" I huff. "Should I remind you how my last few days have gone? Mostly because of you! I am tired and hurt and embarrassed. I just want to go home, Trent." His gaze immediately softens.

"I know, baby," he says softly. "As soon as I know you're okay, I'm going to take you home." I just nod because there is a big lump in my throat that I can't seem to talk around. Trent just might make me fall for him after all. And I have a sinking feeling that wherever Trent is concerned, I don't stand a chance.

The elevator dings to let us know we're back at the emergency room. By the look on Trent's face, I can tell he's dreading it, too, because Hannah the Phlebotomist has no doubt informed BBN of how awful I was. Trent pushes me around the corner and back into the cubicle with the curtain and parks my wheelchair. He lifts me up into his arms and gently deposits me onto the hospital bed. He sits down next to me and wraps me in his arms. Trent has this way about him of making me feel small and fragile and precious. A girl could get used to that.

Trent has me scooped up into his arms, like a doll, with my head on his shoulder. He is softly raking his fingers through my hair, and I love it. I sigh happily. I'm just starting to relax into him when the curtain gets pulled back and Dr. Grandpa and BBN appear. Judging by the grin on her face, I'm sure this is going to be good. Trent sees it, too, because I feel his whole body stiffen and go on red alert.

"Well, it looks like you'll live, Ms. Whitmore, Your wrist is just badly sprained and your lip should heal soon enough," The doctor sighs. "But you should have told us you were pregnant so we could have done tests other than the x-rays."

My jaw drops open, and I can't think of a reply. I know I'm not pregnant. I haven't slept with anyone since the last time I was with James, and that was a year and a half ago. Well played, BBN, well played.

Trent still hasn't said anything, but I feel his gaze on my face. I'm trying to make words come out of my mouth, but I can't. BBN is looking like she won this round when we hear a mix between a whoop and a battle cry from behind the doctor and BBN.

"Woo-hoo!" Marla cheers. "Did you hear that, Verna? My grandson slipped one past the goalie already! Yeesssss!"

"Hoo boy!" Granny hollers. "I knew those two would make us a gorgeous grandbaby! And did I not tell you he looked virile, Shell?"

"Yes, Granny, you did," I sigh. Deciding to just rip the Band-Aid off, I go for it. "But I still haven't slept with Trenton."

"Still?" she asks. I just shake my head. "Damn. False alarm, people. No baby. Yet."

"I told you she was trouble, Trent," BBN says hotly. "She's having someone else's baby."

"No, she's not, you dumb hooker!" Marla shouts, and I swear I hear Trent chuckle. "I have watched this girl for years. *Years*. And if she hasn't slept with Trent yet, she hasn't slept with anyone since *Douche McDoucherson.* So if she's pregnant, it's the Second Coming, honey, and you'd better brace yourself. Do you hear me? *Brace.*"

"Thank you, Miss Marla." I touch my fingertips to her hand. "And also, you're accurate. Well, not the part about baby Jesus. I'm not pregnant. At all. By anyone," I clarify.

"I would have raised that baby as my own if it meant I could have been doing it with you, Shell,"

Trent says softly, his fingertips to my cheek.

"Well, we aren't going to find out anytime soon," I say to him.

"That's our boy!" Granny cheers. BBN just huffs. Again.

"I do think that Brandi and Hannah might have some explaining to do as to how tests showed that Shelby is expecting," Trent says firmly. This must be his cop voice. I wouldn't mess with him.

"Yes, I agree," the doctor says. "I will definitely be looking into it. Nurse Brandi, a word." They step outside my little ER cubicle and close the curtain.

"How did you two get here?" Trent narrows his gaze on our grandmothers.

I feel my own eyes go wide. I hadn't even thought of that. Both women shuffle their feet side to side and are staring down at their sparkly sneakers. All of a sudden, they both snap their heads up in defiance, shoulders rolled back. Oh boy.

"We borrowed Harold's Caddy," Marla states firmly. She's challenging Trent to call her on it. And he does.

"Nana!" he shouts.

"What?" she barks back.

"Neither of you two has a driver's license. That's what!" he yells. Well, that clears that up for me. "And you don't even have two working legs. How are you even driving?"

"Well . . . ," she says, stalling. "I clutch, shift, and steer, and Verna hits the gas and the brake for me."

"Are you fucking kidding me?" he bellows.

"No! And don't you take that tone with me, mister," she shouts back. People from New Jersey don't even play. Oh boy. "I could still whoop your butt if I had to!"

"Okay. I'm sorry," he acquiesces. "But no more driving."

"It was an emergency!" Granny shouts. "I can't let that bastard hurt my Shelby after what he did to her and my Herb," she chokes out. And I stiffen.

Now that I can admit I have real feelings growing for Trent, I don't want him to know that Pop-Pop's death was my own fault. That he would still be here today if it wasn't for my careless choices. I know Trent feels the change in me. I try to slide off of his lap, but his arms tighten around me.

"What?" he asks.

"Can we go? I'm not feeling so good," I say.

"Okay, baby. But we're going to talk about this later," he says firmly.

I glare at him, but he just smiles. Stupid hyper-observant bastard. I am rethinking my feelings for him when a different nurse, along with Kane, arrives at my cubicle.

"Hi, all, my name is Sarah, and I have your discharge and care paperwork," Nurse Sarah says as she breezes in like an angel of freedom. *My freedom.* "If you could just sign here, here, and here, then you'll be free to go. Now, what you're signing says that you will have someone wake you up and ask you questions every hour for twenty-four hours to make sure you don't slip into a coma. It also states that if you have brain or spinal fluid discharging from your nose or ears, you'll come back to the ER. Your stomach will be upset for a while, so don't be surprised if there is any nausea or vomiting." Trent, Kane, and I all snicker.

"I see we've already had some of that, which is fairly normal. Mild foods until it passes. Lots of rest. And contact your regular practitioner to follow up with this hospital visit. All right, kiddos, you're free to go. Detective, don't forget your nasty clothes. I don't want those." She winks and breezes back out.

"You ready to go, my little hellcat?" he asks as he smiles sweetly at me.

"I was born ready," I answer honestly.

"You take good care of my baby, you hear, mister?" Granny shakes her finger lovingly at Trent. "And knock her up while you're at it. She's not getting any younger."

"Granny!"

"We mean it, Trent." Marla reaches up to pat his whiskered cheek"

"I'll do my best, Nana," he says with a laugh. I can admit that I like seeing that twinkle in his emerald eyes.

"We love you both. Take care of each other."

"We will, Nana." And with that, we are ready to get out of here. But before we leave, Kane questions how Granny and Marla got here.

"They did what?" Kane balks and visibly blanches when he hears how the grandmothers got here. "Who there in *God's Waiting Room* even has a license, let alone a car?" he grumbles.

"Ha!" Granny chuckles. "That's a good one! I prefer *The Road to El Diablo.*"

"How about I take these two lovely ladies out for an ice cream cone and then on home?" he kindly offers. "I'll have Jenkins return the getaway vehicle. Jenkins! Get in here!" Kane shouts around the curtain.

"Here are the keys," Marla says in her soft voice. "Treat it with kindness. It's Harold's baby."

"What kind of car is it, ma'am?" Jenkins inquires.

"It's a light blue 1959 Cadillac Eldorado Biarritz convertible, dear," Marla says with a sweet smile.

Poor Jenkins just stands there frozen, his hand still outstretched, reaching for Harold's keys. I think he might have had a ministroke. Either that or he just came in his pants like a fifteen-year-old.

"Jesus, did the poor kid just have a stroke?" Granny voices my thoughts.

"Or jizz in his pants?" Marla adds my other thoughts. Trent groans, but Kane chuckles.

"I did," Jenkins answers. "I think I just jizzed in

my pants. This is the coolest day ever. I love my job!" he shouts and then runs out the door to the parking lot.

"This is the weirdest day ever," I say.

"Yeah, it kind of is, baby," Trent says softly. "Let's go home."

Home sounds nice. Home sounds fantastic. So I let Trent load me up into his Tahoe and head for home. It's when we are traveling east and not south to my condo in the city, that I realize we are heading to his ranch home on the hill.

chapter FIVE

RIVERDANCING KILLER BUNNIES

I wake up to the sun shining in my face through sheer, dove-gray curtains on windows that overlook the canyon rock and scrubbrush plants. The birds are singing their joyful songs and there is a team of *Riverdancers* clogging away all over my body and inside my head.

I groan and open my eyes to the light, immediately closing them again. I kick my feet softly against the silky sheet, as I do every morning. It's almost like a gentle running while on my side, like a puppy who is dreaming. I like the way the sheets feel on my feet, but these are not my sheets. I pop my head up from the covers and see a huge pine bed with dove-gray bedding. This is also not my bed.

The pillow next to mine has an indent from someone sleeping there, but the bed is empty. The realization of just whose bed I have been sleeping in causes me to let out a startled "Eep!" and dive back under the covers. To the tune of male chuckles from what I am assuming is the doorway.

"Come out, come out, Goldilocks," Trent's gravelly voice says with a laugh. "I know you've been sleeping in my bed because I put you there myself."

"Nope," I whisper. "No one's here."

He just laughs again and peels back the covers. I feel a breeze and look down. And instantly dive back under the covers.

"Why am I naked?" I squeal, which sounds a bit muffled because I'm hiding under a big, fluffy down comforter and other blankets and sheets.

"You can't sleep in clothes," he answers honestly. "I wanted you to be comfortable."

"I was in leggings and a sweatshirt. That's the very definition of comfort!" I snap.

"But you were in a hospital, and those are just chock-full of germs. I did us both a favor. Who knows what we could have caught if you'd have stayed in those clothes."

"I feel like that depends."

"Depends on what?"

"Depends on how many times you boned Nurse Brandi and her henchman." I watch Trent flinch, and I immediately regret my words, feeling guilty for such a nasty comment. "I'm sorry."

"It's okay." He shrugs one manly shoulder. "I deserved it. But hear me now. I deserved it. Deserved. Past tense. Present tense, all I want is you." I gulp. Trent is nothing if not direct. "Plus, you have to be nice to me because your gremlin of a cat has been watching me all morning."

"Missy is here?"

"Her name is Missy? I would have thought it'd be more along the lines of *The Lorax*," he muses.

"She speaks for the trees," I deadpan. Trent throws his head back and laughs a deep, sexy rumble that I would thoroughly enjoy if my head wasn't pounding.

"Don't be mean. She's beautiful to me," I say as Missy jumps up onto the bed and starts purring loudly as I run my fingers through her fluffy black-and-white coat.

"Huh, I never would have seen that coming . . ."

"I can't believe you went and got my cat. That's so sweet."

"Actually, Kane did. He owed me a favor."

"Of course he did. Where is the good detective, anyway?" I ask.

"Not. Here," he growls. I just roll my eyes but then squeeze them tight. It hurts to eye-roll. "Anyway, you and Missy here aren't his favorite people right now, so I guess you're stuck with me," he says.

"Why? Kane likes me," I answer, genuinely confused.

"But Missy doesn't like him. She hissed and snarled

and clawed all over poor Kane."

"Miss Havisham, were you naughty?"

"Meow," she coos.

"I didn't think so." I smile as I continue to softly run my fingers through her long coat.

"You named your cat after a scary spinster?" he asks after a moment.

"Of course. We're going to grow old together," I answer in all seriousness.

"Baby, you're not going to be an old spinster if I have anything to say about it."

I'm almost more shocked by the fact that he's read classic literature than the fact that he's giving my naked body some serious looks. He seems to notice my nervousness and offers me a reprieve. Sort of. I can tell Trent is just waiting for me to get comfortable before he pounces again.

"Why don't you go on into the shower and I'll get you some sweats to wear," he offers.

"Thanks, Trent." I smile weakly. "I really appreciate that." He smiles his cat-that-ate-the-canary grin, and I know I am still in trouble.

"No problem, baby," he says as he leers. "Bathroom is right through there." He nods his head toward the door on the other side of the room.

I just sit here for a long while with the sheet pulled up over my naked breasts and tucked tightly under my arms. The longer I sit here, the longer Trent leans against the doorjamb with his arms crossed over his chest and his legs crossed casually at the ankles. His lean hips are subtly canted forward, allowing me to see the not-so-subtle bulge in his jeans. The longer he stands there, the bigger his stupid grin on his stupid handsome face with its stupid sexy, dark stubble grows, and it's starting to freaking grate on my freaking nerves.

"Can I have a little privacy?" I ask.

"Nope." He grins even bigger, his eyes crinkling in the outer corners with laughter, and damn if that isn't sexy as all get-out.

I growl and try to tug the sheet free to wrap around myself, but to no avail. It appears a fitness regimen isn't the only holdover from Trent's army days. Apparently, hospital corners and sheets so tight you could bounce a freaking quarter on them are, too. I wrestle with the sheet for what feels like an eternity. All the while, Trent just lazes in the stupid doorway. Just when I think I've finally made headway, when I fall off the bed and onto the floor, with no sheet to show for it. Yes, I am now totally naked. Yay, me!

I chance a glance over the bed at Trent, and that bastard is biting his lower lip so hard I am surprised it's not bleeding. I can tell he wants to laugh, but he knows I will kill him if he does. *Kill him.* Head injury or no. I stand as gracefully as I can. Yes, still naked. But my pride is a funny thing. I can't let Trent's laughing at me get to me. I will never let another man laugh at me. I am not here for his personal entertainment regardless of how sexy he is. So I do what any self-respecting woman would do. I roll my shoulders back, stand up straight, and throw up my middle finger over my head. I turn and proceed to the bathroom with my head held high, but I am once again stopped in my tracks.

"I can't decide which is sexier, baby," Trent interrupts my dramatic exit. "That ass or that attitude. That ass could bring a man to his knees, but that attitude, baby? That attitude makes me forget you just spent the night in the hospital. That attitude makes me want to throw you onto the nearest available surface and fuck you until you can't remember your own name and mine is what you scream."

I would like to say I have a witty retort I sling right back at him and then continue my power strut to the tune of "I'm Every Woman." But that is not what happens.

I am mostly sure, even if I will never—and I mean *never*—admit it out loud, that I let out a pathetic "Eep!" and then scurry off to the bathroom like the scared little mouse I am. All the while, Trent laughs his deep, sexy, booming laugh. And it is sexy.

I slam the bathroom door and collapse against it, hoping against hope that my racing heart will slow itself the heck down. Or that when it explodes, I die a quick and painless death. I also hope that my sad, spinster body cools itself down so I can avoid the temptation that is in fact Trent. But most of all, because I am bored, I hope I can juke left and dodge him right so I can escape this den of sexual temptation and hide out in a movie theater. I'd really love to see that new *Wonder Woman* movie.

I reach into the gorgeous, walk-in stone shower and turn the water on. Too cold. Like, arctic cold. If it works for guys, it should work for me, right?

"Holy shit. Fuck balls!" I scream when the cold water hits my overheated skin. A knock sounds on the bathroom door. Jesus, I hope I locked it. The last thing I need is to be naked in a closed room with a naked Trent and soapy bubbles.

"Everything all right in there, Shell?" Trent asks, his voice full of concern.

"Just peachy," I reply in a clipped tone.

"Okey dokey," he says, and I can hear the smile in his voice. "Just let me know if you need me to scrub your back. You know, because of your wrist and all."

"I'll be fine."

I look at the bar of soap and wonder, why in the hell do all men have a bar of soap in their showers? Do they revoke your man card—or, God forbid, your wiener—if you own just one loofah and some shower gel? But I digress. I take the bar of soap and immediately reach over my shoulder to scrub my back as I always do, wrenching my wrist in the process. I instantly drop the soap and yelp.

I grab my wrist and fold my body over and around it, when the bathroom door bangs open and splinters apart. No joke—this fool just kicked his own bathroom door in. But my wrist hurts too much for me to enjoy it.

Trent quickly strips off his clothes and moves toward the opening of the doorless shower.

"Holy mother fuck!" he roars when the cold water hits his tanned skin. Quickly adjusting the shower to his preset temperature, he sighs in relief when the water heats up. Then he turns around to shoot me a knowing smirk. "Whatcha doing taking a freezing shower? PS—You're probably safe for at least an hour, or forever. We may never see my balls again," he deadpans.

Since I'm still bent over clutching my throbbing wrist, I am eye level with certain parts of him that beg to differ. Some such parts that could be used as a flagpole. Just saying. He sees me hunched over and quickly scoops me up so I'm standing again and my injured wrist is cradled in his big hands.

"You hurt it bad, didn't you, baby?" his deep voice rumbles. When all I can do is just nod, Trent runs his fingers over the injury until all my muscles uncoil and I start to purr. Then he rubs some soap in his hands and continues his delicate treatment of my injured arm.

My head tips back against the cool stone, and my eyes drift closed. Trent's hands leave my arm again to gather more soap, and slowly he rubs my other arm with smooth circles and gentle fingers. He leans forward and places the sweetest kiss on my forehead. Moving his hands to my shoulders, Trent turns me slowly so my back is to him.

Trent gathers more soap in his hands and gently kneads my shoulders and the back of my neck over and over again, and I'm putty in his hands. I am surprised that I'm not a big pile of goo being washed down the drain. His hands roam down my back and up again, slowly working all of the kinks out of my muscles. His hands trail down even farther, over my ass and back up the outer sides of my thighs. He keeps moving hands up and up until he is kneading my soft belly. And then they travel north again until he cups my breasts in his hands. I lean my head back on his shoulder, the back of my body pressed up against his front. As his hands continue to skate over my body, I arch into his touch and wiggle my bottom against him with a whimper.

"Please," I moan.

And as if a bucket of cold water had been dumped over Trent's head, his hands immediately fall away from my body and he takes a step back. Trent grabs the bottle of shampoo from the shelf and pours some into his hands. Lathering up the suds, he gently rubs them into my long, dark red hair. When he's done, he taps me on the shoulder and lifts my chin to lean my head back under the cascade of water to rinse the shampoo out.

Once my hair is rinsed out, I think, *Now things are going to heat up again.* Trent has a habit of keeping me on the edge for all of eternity. That might be a bit dramatic, but that's what it feels like. All of a sudden, he grasps the shower knob and shuts the water off. Trent reaches out of the shower for a big, fluffy towel and thoroughly, but not at all sensually, dries me off before grabbing his own fluffy towel and wrapping it around his waist. He quietly leaves the bathroom with me standing there in a towel, my jaw on the floor. Talk about hot and cold.

Apparently, Trent went to the closet for another pair of well-worn, butt-hugging jeans and a light gray T-shirt because when he walks back into the bathroom a few minutes later, he is dressed but barefoot, which is sexy as hell. Trent strolls over to me and carefully places a faded green shirt with the word *ARMY* stamped in bold letters across the front over my head and waits patiently while I slip my arms through the sleeves. Next, he squats down and helps me into the matching sweatpants with elastic ankles. The pants are huge, and I have to roll the waist several times, but I am warm and covered. Lastly, Trent rolls his big, thick socks over my feet, and I could probably die of comfort right now. When I am fully dressed and toasty, I sigh a happy sigh.

Trent, still in a catcher's squat, drops to his knees and wraps his arms around my body, touching his forehead to my belly. He closes his eyes and holds me there for a while. I don't know what possesses me, but I gently put my arms around his head, hugging him to me. I think seeing his warring emotions play out across his face brings out the caring side of me. And I guess I do care for Trent. Much more than I should. So I drop my injured hand to his shoulder, and the other I use to run my fingers through his dark hair, which is slightly longer than the military regulation length.

We stand like that for some time, just soaking in each other's comfort, when all of a sudden, his eyes open and he looks at me and smiles the sweetest smile. Trent has come to some resolution. I can see it in his eyes, and it won't be long before he shares his plans for me. My biggest fear is that if he gives me more of these happy, boyish smiles, I'll be dead in the water—there is no way I wouldn't give him anything he asked for with one of those smiles.

"So, how do you feel about some scrambled eggs and *killer bunnies*?" he inquires happily. It's definitely not what I thought he was going to say.

"Um, what?" I laugh.

"Breakfast and a board game." He winks at me. "Those are your two choices for entertainment today."

"Breakfast. I'm starving. Then, this 'killer bunnies' business."

"Well, okay then."

And it really is. It's actually more than okay. I like being around Trent, and if I sleep another day away, my brain is going to rot and fall out of my ears. I can feel it happening; I swear. "Off to the kitchen with you," Trent says as he playfully swats my bottom. Yeah, I didn't figure that Trent was too far off from losing his marbles either.

As I make my way down the hall to the kitchen, I feel Trent's eyes on my ass. I can practically see his resolve crumbling. Time to make a serious decision about Trent. And that decision is . . . I don't want to spend my life being lonely, when I can be with Trent. I look over my shoulder and toss a wink at Trent as I smile at him for being caught blatantly checking out my ass. He growls, and I run faster to the kitchen.

I land in a barstool at the counter after rounding the corner to kitchen freedom. Trent smiles at me like he knows I know that I just dodged a bullet. Just because I say I am going to take the leap doesn't mean I am ready right this second. Sheesh. He casually slides a large mug of coffee in front of me, just the way I take it—mostly sugared-up creamer with a splash of coffee. He smiles at me from behind his own mug as I sigh in delight at my delicious coffee.

Without speaking a word, Trent starts scrambling eggs and popping slices of bread into the toaster in the corner. The silence is comfortable. I can see us spending many mornings like this for years to come. I shake my head to dislodge the thought. Just because I said I would take a leap—a baby step, really—doesn't mean I'm ready for forever, or years even. I'm ready to take it day by day. I'm thankful that Trent is standing with his back to me so he doesn't see my willpower crumbling. Plus, it's not like he proposed or anything. And, I mean, the last guy who did that is still kind of in jail.

Trent slides two heaping plates of cheesy eggs and buttered toast across the counter. One in front of me, the other in front of the seat next to me. Like he doesn't have a care in the world, Trent saunters around the counter and takes his seat next to me. And when I say "next to me," I mean our thighs are touching. He picks up his fork and takes a bite. My stomach growls. Loudly. And my face flames with embarrassment. I pick up my fork and follow suit. The eggs are delicious, and I can't help the moan that falls from my mouth. We both make quick work of our breakfasts. I had no idea how hungry I was, but really, I shouldn't be surprised. I'm not one to skip a meal. *Ever.*

We make quick work of loading the dishes into the dishwasher and then finish our coffee. It would be a shame to let good coffee go to waste. I sigh as I rinse my cup out in the sink. This has been a good morning. It feels good to be up and moving. Even if I can feel all the aches and pains from my run-in with James.

"Come on. Let's go," Trent says as he takes a square-shaped box out of the hall cabinet and tucks it under his arm. He holds his other hand out to me, and I take it, letting him lead me back down the hall to his bedroom.

We both climb onto the bed, and he immediately opens the box and starts shuffling cards. I pick one up to look at it. I arch an eyebrow in question as I look at the goofy yellow bunny on the card. Trent quickly snatches it back and shuffles it in the deck with the rest.

"No peeking," he chastises, but I just laugh. "Although, you could probably use all the help you can get. I'm pretty good at this game." He smirks.

"How good do you need to be to play a kids' game of silly bunnies?" I laugh. He clutches his heart and gasps in mock outrage.

"You wound me!" he laments and then narrows his eyes on me. "This is a very serious game. But if you'd like to move along on today's agenda, we can skip it," he leans in.

"No, no," I say with a laugh. "Let's play the silly, scary bunny game." I laugh again nervously.

It turns out Trent was right. Killer Bunnies is a serious game. A game that I really got into. For hours. And also, a game that he killed at. Literally. Trent literally killed all my bunnies. All. My. Fucking. Bunnies! Argh.

"Nooooooo!" I wail as he sweeps my last bunny off the board. His bunny-money pile looks like it belongs to Richie Rich, and that fucker just took out my very last bunny with a nuclear warhead. "A nuclear warhead! Was that really necessary?" I question.

"Yes. Yes, it was." He laughs. "That's what you get for making fun of my bunny game. Total annihilation."

"But I had the bubonic plague! I was going to wipe out all of your bunnies," I whine.

"But, you didn't." He chuckles.

"And you deserved it for that lawn mower accident! That poor bunny," I sigh.

"You know he's a cartoon, right?" Trent smiles at me softly.

"Yes, I know he's a cartoon, but did you have to be so cruel?" I ask.

"Yeah, I kinda did," he tells me as he pulls me into his arms. I sigh, because really, who wouldn't when wrapped in Trent's strong arms, staring into those green eyes.

He smiles at me, and then, careful not to reinjur my healing lip, he kisses me. Soft and sweet at first, but when Trent feels my body melt into his, he moves to deepen the kiss, gently sliding his tongue across my bottom lip. I gasp and open to him. He digs his hands into my hair as he takes my mouth.

Slowly Trent leans me backward, laying me down in the middle of all the bunny cards on the bed, and follows me down with his body. Not content to just make out, I wiggle my body under his, and he snakes his warm hands up my body and under my T-shirt, brushing the sides of my breasts. Trent pushes my loaner shirt up and up until he has to break our kiss to pull it over my head, which he does.

Tossing it onto the bedroom floor, he resumes the slow glide of his hands over my body. My arms, my belly, my breasts. He pinches my nipple between his thumb and index finger, pulling a gasp from my lungs. He kisses me again. I slide my hands underneath his T-shirt and rake my nails down his abs. Trent groans in my mouth, and I pull at his shirt until he reaches behind his neck and pulls it off one-handed. Damn, that's hot.

Trent slides his palm down my breast and over my belly with purpose. He gently bites my bottom lip and pulls as he tugs on the drawstring of my borrowed pants. He scrunches my pants down to my knees, effectively restraining my legs and opening me up to him in equal measure.

"Shelby," he gasps in mock shock. "Are you not

wearing any panties under my sweatpants? I like it," he growls as he trails his fingers between my legs.

"No," I say, breathless. "I'm not."

Trent groans as he kisses my mouth again before sliding his lips over my jaw, my throat. He nips at my shoulder blade but then soothes the hurt with another soft kiss. My fingers tangle in the sheets on the bed we never made this morning.

Trent trails his mouth down over the tops of my breasts and then in between them. Down my belly, over my belly button, and farther south until his head is between my thighs.

"Trent . . . ," I whisper.

"Shh," he says as he pins my hips farther open. Almost to the point of pain. My lower legs are still tangled in the sweatpants.

And then he's there. He licks me once. Twice. And I gasp and grip the sheets tighter in my hands. I feel him smile against my overheated skin, and I fist my hand in his hair, pulling. He licks me again and again before adding a finger and then another, stretching me. I burn. My body is on fire.

"Trent . . . ," I whisper as he stands and slowly undoes the row of buttons on his fabulously worn jeans and slides them down his muscular legs. His eyes are searing into mine. I bite down on my bottom lip, watching him.

Trent slowly pulls my borrowed pants down my legs, freeing them, but I still can't move. Watching

Trent is like watching a tiger prowl. He tosses the sweatpants to the floor and then crawls up the bed toward me. I release the breath I had been holding when he places his large palm on my shin and pushes it forward until my knee is under my arm, along the side of my body. I am totally open to him. His eyes never leave mine as he slides in deep.

He rests his forehead on mine, squeezing his eyes closed tight and letting out a deep breath before snapping his eyes open again. But now, he sees me differently. He gently brushes my hair out of my face and kisses me again. I wrap my other leg around his back and wiggle, trying to get him to move.

Trent smiles against my mouth before pulling his hips back and then thrusting back in, in long, sharp strokes. Again and again. I wrap my arms around his neck and arch into him. He groans into my mouth.

"Trent." I arch into him again. "Please," I beg.

"What do you need, Shelby?" he asks against my mouth.

"More. I need more."

Trent kisses me again, his hand gripped tight on my leg, the other tangled in the sheets by the side of my head, as he picks up his pace. Pumping harder, faster. I'm so close I burn. I arch into him and rake the nails of my cast-free hand down his shoulders.

"I'm close," he groans against my mouth. "Got to get you there, baby."

"I'm there," I tell him. "I'm there."

I cry out as his pace becomes desperate. He thrusts into my body again and again. Trent bites down where my neck meets my shoulder, and I come. He calls out my name as he follows me over the edge.

Trent rolls to his back, taking me with him, his body still connected to mine in every way. We cling to each other. The only sounds in the bedroom are our labored breaths. Until he chuckles. I give him a questioning look, and he runs his hand over my ass, removing a lazy bunny card that had gotten stuck to one of my cheeks during our postgame interlude. I snatch it out of his hands and toss it over my shoulder.

"I guess I won after all." I wink saucily at him, and he growls before pulling me down to kiss me again.

"Wicked witch," he calls me between kisses. I feel him harden again. "What spells you cast on me."

I sit up intending to give him a quick but wild moment, but Trent has other plans. He sits up, too, and wraps my legs around his waist, his own legs stretched out in front of him, underneath my bottom, his cock still deep inside me. He glides his hands up my sides to cup my breasts as his hips pump up into me. I gasp and rock against him.

"Slow," he says against my mouth. "This time we go slow." And we do. As we touch and taste, we rock leisurely against each other.

It's a slow build this time. Lazily rolling over me like a wave at the beach. I lean back as far as his arms will let me, which is not far, dropping my head back onto my shoulders. I come on a sigh, his name on my lips.

"Trent," I say softly.

Something about his name and the way I have spoken it lights a fire in Trent. He rolls us so I am again on my back, his hips cradled in between my thighs, my whole body holding him as he continues to rock into me. Trent braces himself on his forearms on either side of my head as he picks up the pace, albeit still sweetly and softly, and makes love to me. I come again, but this time it rolls over me swiftly, I wasn't expecting it. But Trent was. As if he was waiting for me, I feel his body shudder with the force of his climax as he whispers my name.

"Shelby," he says. Softly. Reverently. Like a benediction. And he follows it with no other words, knowing I'm not ready to hear them. Judging just by the way he says my name, we both know those words could mean everything.

Chapter SIX

LIONS AND TIGERS AND MARBLES THE MORAY EEL, OH MY!

I wake up to the sun shining in my face through sheer, dove-gray curtains on windows that overlook the canyon rock and scrubbrush plants. The birds are singing their joyful songs, and there is a team of *Riverdancers* clogging away all over my body and inside my head. I groan and open my eyes to the light, immediately closing them again.

I kick my feet softly again the silky sheet, as I do every morning. It's almost like I'm running on my side. I like the way the sheets feel on my feet, but these are not my sheets.

I pop my head up from the covers and see a huge pine bed with dove-gray bedding. This is also not my bed.

The pillow next to mine has an indent from someone sleeping there, but the bed is empty. The realization of just whose bed I have been sleeping in causes me to let out a startled "Eep!" and dive back under the covers.

It's happening again. It's like I am trapped in *Groundhog Day.* You know, that Bill Murray movie? The one where the guy played by Bill Murray wakes up to the same day every day. The. Same. Freaking. Day. I am living that day.

Since the day after I was attacked by James at the old home improvement store, I have been waking up in Trent's bed. This lifestyle entails waking up, showering with Trent, eating breakfast with Trent, sleeping with Trent—and I don't mean the restful kind—and lather, rinse, repeat. I'm not complaining.

Trent has the body of a god, a great sense of humor, and for all intents and purposes, appears to be a stand-up guy with a great job who is hell-bent on taking care of me. Also, let's not forget he's dynamite in the sack. But didn't I just say I'm never going near the opposite sex again? Now here I am, and every time he gets within three feet of me, I turn into a completely different person. I need time to evaluate these life decisions. And I need space. Lots and lots of space. Without Trent. Or condoms. Or a bed. Holy shit, did we even use condoms? I can't remember! But I digress.

And I'm bored. A woman can only live on scrambled eggs and wild monkey sex alone for so long! I am at that threshold of survival where I need cocktails and fancy shoes. And a burrito. Or a grilled cheese from In-N-Out Burger. Man, I need a grilled cheese. Again, I digress. It might be the head injury. Or the cabin fever. I do not know.

I am pondering these thoughts when, from behind me, I feel a large, warm body climb into the bed. The mattress dips down and an anaconda-sized arm slides around my belly. I freeze. Stiff as a board and unsure what I am supposed to do.

Ship's Log: It has been three days that I have been here receiving the Detective Trenton Foyle treatment. And let me tell you, it's good treatment. But, and it's a big "but," I really do think I need some space. We've never even been on a date, yet he has felt me up in an alley and I have been sleeping in his bed, naked as the day I was born, for three nights and counting.

When Trent feels my less-than-receptive body language, his hand reaches up to my chin and tilts my head back against the pillow so he can look into my face. He rolls me over so that I am on my back with my knees together and Trent is straddling my belly. He studies my face, and I know he sees everything.

"What's going on in there today?" he asks me softly.

"Nothing." I shrug, not quite meeting his eyes. "I'm just bored," I say.

"Well, let's get you unbored." Trent smiles wickedly, and he coasts his hands all over my body.

I feel myself softening toward his touch, and I know I am going to lose the battle against what I should do and what I want to do. I hear a sexy purr. Shit, was that me?! Oh, damn, it was.

Trent trails his lips down my cheek and across my jaw. He gently lifts the loaner T-shirt that I was sleeping in over my head. His mouth finds my neck again as he gently nips and sucks at the magic spot between my ear and shoulder that he stumbled upon the other night. Well, *stumbled upon* aren't the right words—there is nothing *stumbly* about Trenton Foyle in bed. Everything he does is with determination and purpose. And let me tell you, he knows his way around a woman's body, *my body.*

I whimper and feel him smile against my skin. Trent skates his rough palms up and down over my sides a few times, and then he changes their change course and heads for my breasts. Just barely gliding over my nipples.

I arch into Trent, and he reaches for the borrowed boxers I have been sleeping in just as the front door busts open, tripping the alarm system on Trent's house, its sirens blaring over and over, ringing in my ears. I put my fingers in them to stop the noise from ricocheting around my battered brain like a pinball. And then the two most likely to surprise me in the middle of a sexual moment bust in.

"Trenton!" Marla screams. "*Treeeeennnnntooonnn!* Are you home, baby?" she inquires as she starts to search the house for the occupants, who happen to be naked and not in a position to be seen by their grandmothers.

"Shit!" I whisper-shout.

Trent, the traitor, just chuckles against my neck. So I do what any rational, sane young woman would do in my situation. I summon up all of my anxiety and fears, shape them into superhuman strength, and shove his ass off of me and onto the floor. I jump up and run into the closet and grab a pair of Trent's sweatpants and one of his white T-shirts.

"Hey, Granny, Miss Marla, what are you two up to today?" I ask the grandmothers, noting that Trent has somehow found himself in a pair of well-worn jeans. Meow. Shit! These thoughts are what keep getting me into trouble!

"We've come to spring you from the pokey, baby." Granny smiles at me lovingly.

"Huh?" I inquire eloquently.

"We've come to rescue you from Trenton's *Den of Iniquity,* dear," Marla says sweetly while shooting Trent the side-eye.

"I'm thinking we need to ban your use of the phrase 'Den of Iniquity,' Nana," Trent says in a mock-stern tone.

"Are you going to try to tell me that that woman has not been thoroughly assaulted with your friendly weapon?" She aggressively points to me. "Do not lie to me!" she shrieks.

"I think we need to add that one to the banned list as well, Nana," Trent says with a smile on his face. The bastard thinks this is funny!

"Regardless, we're taking Shell out this afternoon,"

Granny says.

"Thank God." I grasp at any hope of getting out of here and getting my head on straight and figuring out what needs to be done about my life, my head, and my vagina. We're not all in agreement over here. Trent shoots me an angry glare but wisely stays silent with the grandmothers present.

"Excellent!" Granny claps and tosses me a small duffel bag. "Here, we brought you clothes. Don't worry. It's your boring wear from your closet," she assures me when she sees me eyeing the bag like it's full of rattlesnakes.

I grab the bag and run into the bathroom that connects to Trent's bedroom. I cautiously open the duffel bag. Amazingly, they packed me medium wash skinny jeans with rips in the knee and a black crew neck, cap-sleeved top that has a scalloped trim on both the sleeves and the waistline. They also packed silver ballet flats and a hot-pink, crossbody Kate Spade envelope bag. The grannies did good. Damn good.

I toss my wavy red hair up into a loose bun on top of my head with a few wisps framing my face and grab the jewelry I was wearing when I left my house several days ago—a pair of diamond earrings Pop-Pop bought me when I graduated college and a funky silver necklace with a little piece of turquoise in the middle. I think my mom said it's Aztecan or something. She got it on one of her travels, but I stole it from her closet years ago. I throw it all on and head out the door. I bet they're taking me out for coffee or lunch. I could totally use a good cup of coffee to jog my brain.

I walk out the door and see Trent has acquired a T-shirt in the time I was dressing in the bathroom. He is leaning against the wall in the way that he does. It says he owns the world and doesn't give a crap what anyone else thinks. His arms are folded over his strong chest, and his hips are canted forward toward me. There is a smirk playing on his lips that I find I don't much care for, but I don't have time to ponder it because the grandmothers interrupt my thoughts.

"Don't you look lovely, dear," Marla says sweetly.

"Thank you." I smile at her. I really love her.

"Is that the drug spoons necklace I gave your mother?" my granny asks, interrupting my sweet moment with Trent's nana.

"What?" I laugh. "No, Mom told me it was Aztecan. She got it somewhere around the pyramids in Mexico," I tell her.

"No, your mother is full of shit." Granny cackles. "That necklace is made from drug spoons Bitty Sue, Marla, and I bought in Thailand," she says so calmly I know she is telling the truth.

"Um . . . what?" I ask.

"Drug spoons, dear," Marla responds to me as if I'm slow. "I'm not sure what they do with them, but we met this guy who melts them down into these necklaces. Pretty neat, huh?"

"Yeah, neat . . ." I'm starting to freak out. Fucking

drug spoons? And when the hell did they go to Thailand? "Here's the thing—I've worn this necklace to class, to work, to funerals. Hell, Granny, I have even worn it while traveling. For all we know, I could've been put in a TSA holding cell because you got a drug spoons necklace from some dude in Thailand!"

"Well, I think it's important to remember that you got it from your mother, who knowingly lied to you about its origin." When I shoot her a murderous glare, she shrugs. "What? It's true."

"I feel like I shouldn't be present to a conversation that involves my girlfriend getting drug paraphernalia from her grandmother. Paraphernalia that was acquired in a foreign country while my grandmother was a participant," Trent says.

"I mean, they could have been vintage absinthe spoons . . . But I guess we'll never know now." Marla shrugs.

"I'm not your girlfriend!" I shout at him.

"Really?" Trent challenges. "Were you not my girlfriend when I cared for you the last few days? Or were you not my girlfriend when my cock was so deep inside you we both forgot our own names?"

"I'm just saying that we never discussed titles," I mutter petulantly.

"And I'm saying that we shouldn't have to. This isn't high school, where I'll ask if you want to go steady. I won't because I already know the answer," he bellows. And then I shout a loud "No!" at the same time he shouts, "Yes!"

"I'm not him, Shelby, and I'm never going to be," he says softly.

"Well, that's just great, guys, but we've got to go. We just caught a homicide," Kane says from the front door, which I just now notice is open and contains both Kane and a beautiful blonde that looks kind of like Tinker Bell. "This is Sophia. She's hanging with you today, Shelby, until Trent and I can get a feel for this one."

"Great!" Granny shouts, jumping up as fast as her eighty-two-year-old body can. "We're going to Hunk-O-Rama. The more the merrier!"

"Um . . . what?" I ask, totally not okay with this afternoon's grandmotherly revelations.

"It's okay." Sophia shrugs. "You should see some of the freaky stuff that happens backstage at the skating shows. Once you've seen an orgy, you've kind of seen it all," she finishes honestly.

"Huh?" I say, because it's all I can say.

We're all staring at Tinker Bell here, with new eyes. Kane definitely looks like he's seeing her for the first time. Now, isn't that interesting. I chance a glance at Trent and see by the twinkle in his eye, he sees the same thing I do.

"Well, I guess we all better be going, right, Kane?" Trent asks.

"Yeah, we better hurry," he says distractedly.

"I'll just run and grab my shoes and my gun." Trent smirks at me, and I shake my head at him.

"Well, this is going to be a fun day. I sure have some orgy-related questions for you, dear," Marla declares.

"Oh, I couldn't tell you," Sophia says softly. "I'm still a virgin." And with that, poor Kane looks like he swallowed his tongue.

"What did I miss?" Trent asks when he returns from his trip down the hall with both his shoes on his feet and his gun on his hip. He has also grabbed a brown leather jacket and his badge, so he seems to be doing well.

"You wouldn't believe me if I told you." And with that, I pat his cheek, and Sophia and I follow the old gals out to Harold's baby-blue Cadillac, leaving Trent and Kane in the dust.

I'd like to say the ride to Hunk-O-Rama was uneventful, but that would be a lie. Who knew a couple of old ladies would have so many question about double penetration. I am feeling a little queasy by the time we pull up to the pink building with purple neon lights declaring the establishment "the best male review this side of Vegas." I'm still not sure about that. Not that I have ever seen a male review before, but I'm guessing they dance and flop around. There is no line out front, which I feel is telling. We are ushered inside by a man both Granny and Marla seem to know quite well.

"Welcome, welcome!" A man that appears to be about the same age as the grannies shakes my hand vigorously after giving each grandmother a bear hug and a pat on the bottom. "My name is George Amos."

"Shelby," I say, shaking his hand.

"Shelby is my granddaughter," Granny says proudly.

"And Trenton's girlfriend," Marla volunteers, which earns me an eyebrow wiggle.

"Sophia," she says, shaking George's hand when it's her turn. "No relation."

We all laugh. She's lucky, that one. This is a hell of a family to be a part of.

Once you're in with our family, there is no going back. She might not be blood, but based on Kane's reaction to the little figure skater, she's going to be around for a while.

"Now tell me what you're doing here and not at that horrible place across town," Granny demands with a wink, softening her words.

"And where is Sylvie?" Marla chimes in.

"One of Sylvie's bouncers called in sick, so I'm watching the door so Bruno can do his job. Sylvie is inside and will shit kittens when she sees you. As for The Pink Pussycat, it's fantastic and basically runs itself. Speaking of which, do either of you two dance?"

he asks Sophia and me.

“No, sir,” I answer firmly with a hand on Sophia’s arm when she opens her mouth to speak.

“What a shame,” he says more to himself. “Well, go on in, ladies,” he says with a bow.

Bruno shows us to the best table in the house, and a scantily clad man wearing nothing but muscles, a bow tie, and a Speedo tells us our drinks are on the house.

“Why did you do that?” Sophia asks in her soft, tinkling-bells voice. “I actually dance quite well.”

“I am sure you do, but sister to sister, he was asking if you and I strip,” I say softly.

“Oh, yeah, no.” She shakes her head. “I have one more shot to make it to the Olympics before I will allow myself the dissatisfaction of being a Dalmatian in a Disney on Ice show. Those spots really chafe.” And there you have it, folks.

We order a round of drinks, and I take a minute to look my compatriots over. Everything happened so fast at Trent’s house that I never realized what the two grannies had on. Good Lord! Granny and Marla are both wearing LuLaRoe leggings, which I am fairly sure they both stole from my closet, and black oversized T-shirts with the neck cut out so that they hang off one shoulder. In hot-pink letters on the front is the message “Bitch, don’t kill my vibe.” And they have both completed the look with their sensible Keds shoes. I swear you can’t make this shit up. You just can’t.

“Jesus, Joseph, and Mary!” Granny exclaims.

"Would you look at the ding-a-ling on that one?"

And oh, *Lord, who art in heaven,* you can't help but look. It's kind of like a car wreck. There is a man, or maybe a yeti, on stage dancing to some Beastie Boys song, which is horrible enough. Ugh. I like what I like and the Beastie Boys don't fall inot that category.

"Jesus, take the wheel! Are they supposed to be so hairy?" Marla queries.

"Holy cats, it's hairy all the way down," Sophia gasps. And it appears there is more to life that she could learn.

"I don't think so," I say.

"Land sakes! That's like a woolly mammoth's trunk." Oh God, where is my drink? Or a horse tranquilizer?

"Look at the way he flips it around. It's kind of like the elephants at the zoo," Sophia says, but I'm not so sure she meant to say it aloud.

I think the ladies are more stunned than anything. Hell, I am, too. Oh, thank God—elephant trunk is done dancing for now. I slip him a dollar from my purse, because really, it was impressive, if not horrifying. Our drinks have since arrived. I shoot back my glass of whiskey and immediately ask for another. I think it's going to be a long night.

"Woo-hoo! Look at this chunk of hunk!" Marla screams as the music changes to B.o.B's "Magic." Apparently, she cannot hold her alcohol. Good to know.

In all fairness, the chunk of hunk is pretty good-looking. He has black hair closely cropped to his scalp and light mocha skin so flawless it could be a painting. He also has the brightest hazel eyes I have ever seen, and I have to admit, I am halfway in love with him. Then he starts to dance. He has muscles upon muscles and is wearing a tiny white Speedo, which leaves absolutely nothing to the imagination. I think the Speedo is approximately three sizes smaller than the anaconda in it. Now I am more than halfway in love with him. And Trent has pretty impressive parts, too.

Our next round of drinks arrives, and thank the heavens for that. I'm not sure what is going on between the hell-on-wheels grannies, Sophia, the ice-skating virgin, and the six plus feet of beautiful man and muscles that seem to be dancing on the stage. He puts his fingertips into the waistband of his Speedo and swirls his hips in a way that suggests he knows what he is doing as he slowly spins in a circle, stopping with his back to the audience. He shoots a jaunty wink at me over his shoulder as he hula-hoops his hips one more time, and my jaw drops to my chest. Then Magic Man bends forward, dropping his drawers to the floor and showing us and God an ass you could bounce a quarter off of. My granny echoes my thoughts.

"Jesus, you could bounce a quarter off that," she exclaims as she, in fact, starts looking for said quarter in her pruse that is so large I think Jimmy Hoffa might be found in it, and alive!

"I could serve tea on that," Marla cries.

Magic Man starts to swivel his hips again as he begins to dance around. And then I see it. We all see it. And I am stunned. He is some kind of genetic improbability. Magic Man's erection, if you can call it that, is enormous and as thick as a Coke can. It frightens me. Jesus, he could hurt somebody with that! I can't even describe it.

"Now I know what they mean when they say that it's like a baby's arm," Sophia shudders.

"That's no baby's arm," I declare, for lack of anything else to say.

"Good Lord, what is that?" Marla exclaims. "It's like a moray eel climbing out of his body," she wails in shock with her palms on either side of her face. But it's Granny who voices what we all are thinking.

"But look at his balls!" she gasps. "I've never seen any so tiny. They're like tiny little baby balls. They're like marbles. He's Marbles the Moray Eel." And it was true. I have never, in all my life, seen balls so tiny.

"It really does look kind of like an eel," Sophia whispered. "Why does this one look different?" she asks softly.

"Oh, because he's uncut, baby," Marla answers honestly. But with one look, I could tell poor Sophia was still confused.

"He's uncircumcised," I whisper to her. "You know, he still has his foreskin." I can see the clarity dawn on her face.

"Jesus," I exclaim. "Check, please!"

Really, it devolved from there. But the worse the situation got, the more shots of whiskey I drank, and that wasn't great. I was in no shape to lady-sit. And the more I drank, the more the old ladies drank.

When Mr. Incredible takes the stage—, and let me tell you, he's called Mr. Incredible for a reason, the old biddies come undone. Sophia will probably have a form of PTSD after this episode. I know I will never be the same.

"All right, ladies!" Granny screams from on top of our table. "Unfurl the flags!" And with that, Granny and Marla reach under their tops and unhook their bras, sliding one strap off and out the sleeve and then doing the same with the other strap. Sophia and I stare on in horror as they pull their bras through the last sleeve and toss them toward the stage.

"Another round?" the waiter asks me with a gentle pat on my shoulder.

"God bless you." I nod solemnly.

The nice waiter, who is my new best friend, places a glass in front of me. Being the kind soul that he is, he had the foresight to bring me another drink before I even said yes. I think I might be in love with him.

"Ladies and Gentlemen!" the announcer calls over the sound system. "I think we have a criminal in our midst. Someone had better call the police!"

I should have been paying better attention. I must be going soft in my old age. Otherwise, I would have noticed the weird winking side-eyes Marla and Granny were shooting Sophia and me. Or even seen the two steroid twins dressed as police officers flank us.

"I think we found our perpetrators. What do you think, ladies?" And the crowd goes nuts. So much so that no one could hear me scream for help. I try to hop off of my barstool, but my movements and fine motor skills are hampered by the truckload of alcohol I had consumed.

"No, no. Nope. No perpetrators here." I shake my head vehemently.

But it is no use. Steroid Twin A pulls my chair as far away from the table as it can go and circles me in my seat, running a fingertip over my shoulder and collarbone as he passes. Steroid Twin B does the same thing to Sophia on the other side of the table.

All of a sudden, they bend over us and stuff their heads into our cleavage. Mine is ample enough that I am briefly worried he will never find his way back out. Then they run their noses up along the side of our necks. When he gets to my ear, he whispers, "Please don't kick me in the nuts." And then he hauls me up over his shoulder like a fireman.

They walk up the steps to the stage to the sounds of raucous women screaming and stomping their feet. When we get to the top, they drop us into chairs that sit facing the wings of the stage. And then "5-1-5-0" by Dierks Bentley started blasting from the speakers.

"Oh no," I say.

"What's happening?" Sophia asks me, panicked, her baby-blue eyes darting wildly around.

"This should be over soon. I hope," I reply with a nonanswer. "Then we can murder a couple of old ladies who have clearly lost their damn minds!" The last part I say while making eye contact with Granny and dragging my index finger across my neck in a throat-slitting fashion. Granny and Marla just throw their heads back and cackle.

The fake policeman in front of me smiles and places his hat on my head as he straddles my lap and grinds against me. I want to close my eyes, but I'm afraid of what will happen if I do. I realize I haven't checked on Sophia when I hear her shriek. And by the sound of it, there is a penis touching our poor, sweet, ice-skating virgin. I'm not sure when it happened, maybe somewhere between all of the double-penetration talk and the fifth of hooch, but I adopted this sweet figure-skating fairy on ice. I feel responsible for her. I look over my shoulder, and sure enough, there's a dick on her shoulder. Shit. She's totally going to need therapy. I hope that thing's had its shots.

I turn back around, and my policeman winks at me and then rips his clothes off in one swoop and chucks them to the side of the stage. I let out a little shriek when I realize he is almost completely naked and circling my chair again rather closely. Trent is going to be so pissed!

My policeman dips his fingertips into the waistband of his poison-green Speedo as he thrusts his hips around my face. I cringe. Please, God, don't let him hit me in the face with that monster. I can handle a lot of things in life, but a mushroom stamp isn't one of them.

He doesn't, but he does flop it around near my face a bit before his song ends and he takes a bow and exits the stage, leaving me his cap as a souvenir. He's really cute and was a good sport about the whole stripping-on-me-under-duress thing. But if I'm honest with myself, and whiskey always makes me honest, the only policeman for me, real or fake, is Trent.

I make my way over to the bar, where I am happy to nurse a Jack and Coke while Granny, Marla, and Sophia, who seems to have come out of her shell a bit, party it up. A couple more guys dance on the stage, but I'm over it. I have officially seen more dudes' junk today than in my entire life. Some good, some bad, so really effing ugly.

I am cozied into my barstool, drunkenly swiveling side to side with my straw in my mouth, when firm arms wrap around me from behind and a strong chin rests on my shoulder. I let out a shriek until I hear Trent's manly chuckle.

"I'm not sure how I feel about you in another policeman's patrol cap, but if you want to wear mine and nothing else, I'm happy to help out," he growls and then runs his nose up the side of my neck. "Oh God. You smell like him. Let's go. I only want to smell me on you." And with that, Trent pulls his wallet out of his back pocket and drops more than enough money to cover my bar drinks and a very generous tip onto the bar.

He deposits his wallet back into his pocket and spins my stool around so I'm facing him. I offer up a jaunty smile. Trent then picks me up and throws me over his shoulder, à la *Top Gun*, and I barely manage to catch my new hat as it flies from my head. As we exit the bar, I wave to the grannies and Sophia, who appears to be in quite the carnal clinch with Detective Kane in the corner. Huh, who knew?

BOMBSHELLS AND BITTY SUE

The next morning, my alarm goes off to the tune of Sam Hunt's "Make You Miss Me," and it rings true with me. I miss Trent. But before you get your panties in a wad, let me tell you that Trent spent the night here last night.

After whisking my drunk self away from the scary strip club and our grandmothers in a very romantic fashion, Trent loaded me up into his SUV, and I giggled at the way he carried me around like a caveman.

"We're at my house," I said when I looked up and realized that Trent had pulled into my condo complex.

"The drive was significantly shorter," he said before stepping from the truck.

Trent walked around the vehicle, unbuckled my seat belt, and pulled me from the car. He stalked up the short walk to my front door like a man on a mission, and he stopped and looked me in the eyes.

"Keys," was all he said.

I deposited my key ring into his waiting palm and watched as he balanced my body in his arms, against his chest, while unlocking the door and letting us in. He promptly locked the door behind us and dropped my keys unceremoniously onto my little table by the door.

My condo is tiny, and it takes only one quick look to realize there is only one way to the bedroom. Plus, he was here the night of Mr. Di Francesco's funeral, so Trent stalked his way down the hall to my bedroom, where he set me down on my feet and promptly stripped me of all of my clothes.

Trent grabbed me by the hand and led me into the attached bathroom and over to the glass shower enclosure. He let go of my hand to reach in and turn the knobs. Soon we were blanketed in thick steam.

I leaned back against the counter and watched as he slowly stripped off his clothes for my own enjoyment, his deep eyes meeting mine the whole time, and a seriously sexy smirk played around his mouth.

"Get in," was all he said as he held open the shower door for me.

Trent followed me into the small shower stall, but that was where the distance between us ended. The hot water pelted my oversensitive skin, and I turned around just in time for his mouth to meet mine.

Trent squirted some of my favorite shower gel into

his palms and rubbed them together. I watched as the foam built between his strong hands. I closed my eyes as he massaged my body with his soapy palms, paying extra special attention to my breasts, pinching the hard tips as he went, causing me to whimper.

I wiggled my bottom against the glass wall of the shower and pulled at his shoulders, hoping for and prodding him to move further. I wanted him to kiss me, but he didn't. No, Trent just stood there and watched me come undone against the clear glass.

My efforts were finally rewarded when he pushed one palm down my back and held the cheek of my ass in a firm grip while the other skated down my belly. Trent used his foot to kick my feet out wide, and I happily complied.

His finger teased my soft folds before swirling around my clit. My breath caught in my throat, and I tossed my head back. The reverberations of its smack against the glass rang out in the room, but all I could focus on was Trent, his green eyes on me.

He carefully dipped one and then two fingers into me, pumping harder and harder, as his thumb played wicked tricks on my clit. My head was swimming, but not from the alcohol. From need. I needed him. I needed Trent like I have never needed a man before.

"Please," I begged. "I need you."

"I know what you want, and I know what you need," he growled. "You want my cock, and you won't get it a moment before you come on my fingers. I need

you to come now."

I tossed my head side to side against the glass, my eyes squeezed so tight that a bright light pulsated behind them to the beat of his thumb on my clit and the fingers he continued to thrust deep.

"Trent," I whimpered.

"Now, Shelby." And I did. I screamed as I came. His mouth crashed down on mine, and he swallowed my cries.

Before I knew it, Trent was lifting me up, my back pressed firmly against the glass shower wall. He used his hands to hold my thighs wide, opened to him. His hard cock stood tall and poised at my entrance. I was given no warning before Trent slammed deep inside.

We both cried out at the sensation, the feeling of his cock seated deep in my pussy, stretching me to my fullest. He bit down on his bottom lip and squeezed his eyes closed as I clenched around him. When he opened them again, he was renewed with purpose, and he pulled out from my heat and pumped back in again and again.

It was building again, and I had no hope to stop it even if I wanted to. Trent increased his pace as he continued to slam home, and the climax he was pushing me toward took off like a runaway train.

I threw my head back and screamed again as the orgasm barreled through me. Trent thrust powerfully once, twice, and then a third time before he held deep inside me, his head buried in the crook of my neck, and he came, groaning, calling out my name.

After he pulled free from my body, Trent leaned back and shut off the taps. The water had long since run cool. Trent toweled off my body and then his own before scooping me up into his arms like a bride, like something precious to him, and carried me to bed.

He pulled the covers back and laid me down, but he did not have sleep on his mind. Trent gently covered me with his own body before softly kissing my lips, then my jaw, my shoulder. He kissed his way down my body until he settled his shoulders between my thighs and kissed me in the most intimate way.

Trent licked and kissed and nipped until I was gasping and writhing under his ministrations. I clenched the bed sheets tight in my hands, my body burning for him, for his touch. I was getting closer and closer to the edge, but then Trent slowly climbed up my body. He carefully unhooked each hand from the sheet and held it softly in each of his on either side of my head. He lined his cock up with my opening, and as I softly whispered his name, he gently slid inside.

This was not rushed or hurried, but soft and slow. His cock slipped in and out of my body as he tenderly rocked me to another climax. In fact, Trent made love to me—there was no other way to describe it—as I tipped my hips up to meet his gentle thrusts every time. His eyes opened and locked on mine, his mouth barely touching mine, as together, we both fell over the edge.

Trent repeated the process of worshipping my body, ringing climax after climax from me even when

I felt there were none left, until the wee hours of the morning. And yes, I wore the hat. But sadly, murder waits for no one, so my sex god turned back into a pumpkin—I mean, homicide detective—and went to go investigate a crime scene.

So here I am, in the middle of my big bed that smells like Trent and sex. I am warm and relaxed and happy. All thoughts of James and the loss of my grandfather are there, but in the background. Trent, as always, seems to do his best to make everything okay. I give one last stretch of my arms overhead and pull the covers back so I can pad my way into the shower.

When I stand up, I smile to myself. I did not go to sleep naked. I remember putting on a slip at some point in time, but here I am, naked as a jaybird. It seems Trent has a sneaky side. I grab my robe from the back of the closet door and make my way into the bathroom to turn on the shower.

While the water heats up, I wander into the kitchen and make my cup of coffee, adding more cream than coffee—but that's just how it goes.

With my cup in hand and a few fortifying sips burning my throat, I make my way back to my bathroom. I set my cup on the counter and drop my robe, stepping under the hot spray. The scorching water softens my stiff muscles, and I feel myself relax. I make quick work of washing my hair and body. Shutting off the taps, I grab my soft purple towel and wrap it around my body.

I head over to the counter, where I yank a comb

through my long tangles and use my dryer and a big round brush to tame my mane into soft waves.

The bruises on my face are healing nicely, and a little powder goes a long way in covering them up. Just because I feel fantastic, I decide to throw caution to the wind and swipe a shimmery gold shadow across my lids and gunk up my lashes with some extra dark mascara. I pop my lips together, smoothing out my favorite soft-pink lipstick, smile at myself in the mirror, and then head to my closet to dress for my first day back at the office since the incident.

Surveying my massive closet that holds no room for a man's belongings, *ever,* I settle on a champagne-pink pleated silk skirt that hits just above my knees and a black V-neck silk blouse with short sleeves and big flowers all over it. I top the look off with black pointed-toe heels that have a sexy little strap that wraps around my ankles. This morning, I am feeling on top of the world!

I grab my purse and my keys and head out the door. Pervy Steve is leaving for work at the same time, so I offer up a small wave and a wink to him.

"You look nice today, Shelby," he says softly.

"Thank you, Steve. So do you."

I lock my front door and walk to my car. I beep the locks open and climb behind the wheel of my Jeep. I love this car. When I turn the key in the ignition, Beyoncé blares from the speakers. *Hell yeah! We do run the world!* I am crushing it today.

The drive to the paper is not too long. Traffic is never fun during rush hour in San Diego, but it's the price we pay for sunshine, palm trees, and salt air. I drive through a Starbucks on the way and grab my go-to caramel macchiato.

I pull into the entrance of the staff's parking lot of the paper and flash my photo ID badge. The arm lifts up and lets me in. *Yes!* I mentally cheer, pumping my fist over my head. I luck out a get a great parking spot. Today is my day!

I swipe my badge on the card reader at the door and let myself in. I set my coffee on my desk in my cubicle and lock my purse in the bottom drawer of my filing cabinet. I can hear my phone ringing Maroon 5's "Payphone" from my desk, but there is a yellow sticky note from Uncle Sal on my computer, telling me he wants to see me ASAP, and that has all my attention.

I snap the sticky note off of my ancient monitor and make my way down the hall to the editor in chief's office. I knock on the doorjamb and wait for him to acknowledge me. Uncle Sal is big on that one.

"Come in!" he bellows. I can hear him slam his phone down onto his desk.

I push his door open and smile wide at my favorite uncle when his eyes meet mine. Uncle Sal has always been another dad to me. With no kids of their own, he and his wife, Anita, spoiled me rotten.

"Hey, Shell," he says softly. "Glad to see you're looking better. And that that moron is behind bars where he belongs."

"I'm okay, Uncle Sal." I wink at him.

"Well, Auntie Anita and I will be the judge of that," he says in a mock-stern tone. "And what the hell is Ma clamoring about that you're hooking up with a detective? Do I need to break his legs?" he asks honestly.

"We're not really Italian, Uncle Sal." I laugh.

"It doesn't matter. I can still break his legs even if we're Irish. I sure wish you'd become a nun, though. It would save me a lot of grief." He nods sagely.

"Moving on," I say. "You wanted to speak with me about something." I wave the sticky note, which is stuck on my finger, in the air. My fingers on my other hand are crossed behind my back, praying he didn't send me an office note about Trent.

"A couple of things. First, I really like what you did with Mr. Di Francesco's write-up and obituary. Good job on your first write-up." He smiles warmly at me. "And the family is really happy. They said something along the lines of being surprised you could turn that circus into such a positive article. You have anything you want to tell me about that?"

"I have no idea what you're talking about, Uncle Sal." I hold my eyes wide and give him my best *I'm innocent* act. He knows I'm full of shit, but he loves me regardless. It's kind of awesome.

"And second, here are the death notices for the week." Uncle Sal hands me the list that has been reported to the paper by friends and families.

It contains both the local deaths and the list of families that want obituaries written about their loved ones. I take a quick glance at the sheet of paper in my hand and feel all the breath robbed of my lungs.

"Oh, shit!" I bark out when my lungs refill harshly. Bitty Sue bought the farm. Sure, it's a given. Eventually. They are elderly people living in a senior living facility, but I kind of thought those three old ladies defied death. Kind of like Rasputin. "Granny is gonna be pissed."

"Really?" Uncle Sal asks, seeing what has caught my attention. "I thought Bitty Sue was one of the crazy old ladies from hell. I figured Mom would be upset, but not mad."

"Oh, I bet she's pissed. Bitty Sue still owed her ninety-seven dollars from last month's poker game at Peaceful Sunset."

The game is not sanctioned by Peaceful Sunset Retirement Village. And the villagers refer to their home as anything but. Usually they call it *Not Quite the End of the Road* and *Ready to Meet El Diablo.* Or my personal favorite, *The Hotel California,* where "you can check out anytime you like, but you can never leave." Honestly, all of the monikers fit that crowd better than the name Peaceful Sunset.

"I gotta go," I shout as I jump up and head down the hall to my desk.

"Better you than me, baby girl. Better you than me," he shouts at my back. "Call me or Auntie if you need anything. Kiss Mama for me!"

I toss a wave over my shoulder and break out into a full run for my desk. When I hit my cubicle, I barely slow down to open the bottom drawer and get my purse. I open my big Coach tote and grab my car keys. My phone is ringing "Highway to Hell," and I know it's my granny, but I just have to keep going to get to her. Our bond is so strong that I know in my heart she needs me, no matter how tough she is.

I unlock the doors of my Jeep Cherokee and jump in. I turn the ignition, and the radio comes to life, playing T.I.'s "Dead and Gone." I pull the gearshift into drive and peel out of the parking lot. I hit the highway and drive like a maniac. I briefly wonder, *If I get pulled over, can I claim I'm sleeping with a detective for a free pass, or is that in poor form?* I don't know, so I'll cross that bridge when I get to it.

I take the next exit and come screeching to a halt as the train-crossing lights start flashing and the safety arm comes down before the cars in front of me so a Coaster can safely pass. Goddammit!

I hate lunch hour traffic. You would think it would take all of five minutes to get from my office at the paper, which sits in one of the high-rise buildings of the main city skyline of downtown, to my granny's place, but alas, downtown traffic was sent straight from hell. Peaceful Sunset Retirement Village is in the Gaslamp District, along with all of the restaurants, the Convention Center, and the new ballpark, and angled perfectly so the sunsets over the city's skyline and the sailboats and big boats in the harbor can all be viewed from the residents' balconies.

Finally, after what feels like a lifetime and a half, the Coaster passes, and I burn rubber. Fortunately, my dad's old office used to be down here, so I can navigate the grid of east-to-west and north-to-south roads and one-way streets. I know this area like the back of my hand.

The song on the radio rolls over, and Sam Hunt starts singing "Goodbye" as I make a right turn on a one-way street and head up a few blocks only to make a left on another. My heart is in my throat. My phone is ringing Granny's ringtone again, but I can't answer. My hands are white-knuckled on the steering wheel. In my head I'm praying to God to the tune of "No cops, no cops, no cops." So far he seems to be answering. "In Jesus's name, Amen!"

I make another left and head up a block to make the right I need to bring this zigzag trip to a close at my granny's building. As I near the intersection, the light changes to yellow, and I know I won't make it, but I forge ahead anyway. I make the right turn just after the light turns red, and my "no cops" karma wears out as an unmarked SUV flashes the lights in his grill at me. Doubly unfortunate, this isn't just any police officer; it's the one who left my bed sometime after four o'clock this morning.

"Fuck."

The driveway for the old folks' home is about a block after that right turn, and I figure I'm damned if I do and damned if I don't, so I slow down, put my signal on, and turn into the circular drive that ends under the portico, where I will hopefully, fingers crossed, hand the valet my keys and head in the front door instead of being arrested by a certain sexy detective.

I throw my car in park and grab my oversized Coach tote with my life in it off the seat next to mine and head for the door. I wink at the young valet, who smiles his usually flirty smile at me. It's a thing we do.

I am almost to my goal—maybe I won't get my ass chewed after all—when a strong, masculine hand reaches out and grabs my upper arm, spinning me around to stare at eyes the color of the Irish hillside his ancestors came from, eyes that usually steal my breath and all rational thought. Right now, those eyes are spitting mad, and all I can say is, "Oh, fuck."

"You think?" he barks, and I cringe. "Oh no you don't! You don't get to cringe away from me, Shell."

"Trent . . . ," I whisper.

"No," he bellows, pulling me closer. His arms wrap around me, and we're chest to chest. "Shelby, you know I would never hurt you. But you do need to get how fucking mad I am right now."

"I know," I say softly.

"No, you fucking don't. Do you know what I thought when I saw you hell-bent for leather?" I shake my head, biting my bottom lip. "I thought, 'How am I so wrapped up in this girl, and one day, probably sooner than not, I'm going to get a call from dispatch saying that she died in a single MVA when her car drove off of the Coronado Bridge or that her car is upside down in a tree?' How am I supposed to feel about that, Shelby?"

"I don't know," I answer softly.

"Do you care about me? At all?" he whispers. I probably would have been okay if he yelled—that I could handle—but it's the hurt in his voice that guts me.

"Yes, of course, but that's not what this is about." Instantly I regret my words. I don't want Trent to think I don't care about him, because I do, I really do, but my granny and I have been tight my whole life. She needs me. And that's before you take into account the fact that she is all alone and it's completely my fault.

"Well then, enlighten me," he snarls. "What is this about?"

"Granny," I say softly. That one name says it all for me. "She needs me."

Trent just hangs his head back on his shoulders. He appears to be counting. I don't know. On a labored sigh, he drops his head forward in resignation.

Trent drops a soft kiss to my less bruised forehead and unwinds his arms from around my body. He grabs my hand and walks me inside. Trent flashes his badge so we don't have to waste time checking in with security for visitors' badges.

They know us here anyway, so it's okay. Without a word to me or anyone else, he leads me to the bank of elevators, and we pass a single rose in a bud vase and the sign marker notifying residents of Bitty Sue's passing.

The whole ride up in the steel box as we make our way to the floor where our grandmothers' apartments are located is tense. Trent is still angry, and I don't know what to do to fix it. He seems to be making some decisions up there in his head all alone. And I can't help but think that after all the time he spent pursuing me, making it known to me and everyone else that he was all in, that I was worth it, he is now deciding that I'm really not.

I'm not gonna lie; that stings. I can't believe this asshole would make me start to fall for him and then decide he really doesn't like who I am after all. *Just like James.* I wonder which of my friends Trent will sleep with when he realizes he's bored with me. This is why I said "no more men." Next time, I won't be swayed by my vagina!

The elevator dings our arrival, and we both appear to snap out of our inner musings. I chance a side-eyed look at Trent in time to catch his grimace. Well, I guess it's been a fun week. Before we even make it down the hall, Granny is running to us. But she's not her usual put-together self. Her hair is still in rollers, and she is in a hot-pink velour track suit.

"Thank Christ!" she hollers. "Where the hell have you two been?"

We both open our mouths but can't seem to get the words out. Between Bitty Sue and the apparent end of Trent and me, we didn't stop to figure out how we would approach our grandmothers with this news.

"Oh, who the fuck cares," she growls, grabbing our hands. "Just get your asses in here."

Granny drags us down the hall toward her apartment and slows only to throw her front door open and shove us in. Marla is sitting in a recliner that used to be Pop-Pop's favorite chair.

She is in a matching velour track suit, only hers is punk-rock purple. Marla's hair is also in rollers, and she has fuzzy slippers on her feet.

The most noticeable difference is the massive ice pack on her hip and the pain etched into the corners of her mouth and her eyes. All thoughts of my fight with Trent are quickly forgotten.

Trent kneels down next to Marla's chair and bows his head to her. She raises a shaky palm to his cheek and whispers softly to him, love flowing between them. Granny wraps me in her thin but strong arms as we watch Marla and Trent share their private moment.

"How are you, Nana?" His strong voice is soft, and it's humbling to see this powerful man literally brought to his knees over the well-being of his grandmother.

"I'd be better if my sweet boy wasn't hurting." She smiles sweetly at him. "Real love is hard, isn't it, my boy?"

"How did you know?" he asks.

"Oh, my boys always wore their hearts on their sleeves," she answers. "But it's obvious you've never loved like this before—not even Amy," she says wisely. And I think, *Who the fuck is Amy?* And on the heels of that thought is how much I don't like her.

"Oh, for fuck's sake!" Granny shouts, shoving me away. She claps her hands together. "There are more pressing matters right now than these two morons." I gasp. Trent laughs. Leave it to Granny to break the ice.

"I'm so sorry about your friend, Granny," I say softly. "She was a really nice lady."

"Nice!" Marla shouts from her seat, and we all jump. "Bitty Sue was a nut. And kind of a tramp. And she owed me money. She was a hell of a gal, but she'd be pissed as all get-out to hear you call her nice."

"True dat!" Granny shouts with a fist bump. "Ride free, bitch. Ride free!" Trent smiles at his shoes and shakes his head in an effort to hold in his laughter.

"Well, if we're not a crying, screaming mess, what are we doing here, ladies?" I ask.

"Finding a killer, dear," Marla says firmly.

"What?" Trent and I say at the same time.

"Jinx," we both say.

"Double jinx," I shout and then stick my tongue out at him.

"Damn it," he growls.

"Really, children?" Marla raises a stern eyebrow.

"What?" Trent shrugs his shoulder.

"You're here because Bitty Sue was murdered,"

Marla says calmly.

"Now, Nana," Trent starts.

"Don't you 'Nana' me."

"All I mean is that she was getting on in years. People die," he says softly. By the looks he's getting from the grandmothers, I feel a need to wade in.

"You've said it yourselves tons of times. This place is the "Hotel California"—you can check out, but you may never leave. You know it's true. And who in the hell would want to kill Bitty Sue?"

"Well, now that's what we're going to find out," Granny says smartly.

Trent seems to weigh the situation for a while, gazing back and forth between Granny and Marla. Oh, shit, he's getting ready to cave in to these two old bats.

"Watch, he's getting ready to cave," Granny whispers as she elbows me in the ribs.

"Okay, ladies, tell me why you think your friend was murdered. Convince me," he sighs dramatically.

"Oh, shit," I say when I can't think of anything else.

Granny ushers Trent and me over to the sofa and sits us down. It's awkward and uncomfortable to be so close to him when I know he is still unhappy with me. Hell, I'm not even sure there is a Trent and me at all anymore.

"Well, it all started when we went downstairs for our daily ration of diesel," Marla says.

"What?" Trent asks.

"We have to go downstairs to the café to get our daily one-cup allotment of high-test, high-octane regular coffee for the day," Granny laments.

"Ah."

"As I was saying," Marla clears her throat to get our attention before continuing. "Verna and I went downstairs to get our morning coffee. When we were passing the elevator bank, we noticed the announcement for Bitty Sue. We were both surprised."

"Understandably." I smile sweetly at her.

"So after we grabbed our coffee to go, we decided to go into her apartment to see if we could reclaim the money she owed us from last month's poker night."

"Granny!"

"Nana! That's breaking and entering with the intent to commit burglary!"

"No, it's not! She owed me that money," Marla yelled back.

"That doesn't matter!" Trent bellowed louder.

"Of course it does!"

Both are standing with their hands stretched out to emphasize the legitimacy of their claims. I can see a subtle tremor to all of Trent's muscles as he tries to rein in his emotions. I can see the struggle running over his face, his shoulders, his back, down to his clenched fists. I force my gaze to leave Trent and take in the pulse of the room. It is not lost on the others present that this is taking a toll on Trent.

"Trent . . . ," I whisper, too afraid to go to him.

I'm still not sure where I stand with him. Is Trent done with me? Is he falling for me like I am for him despite all my best efforts. Will he forgive me and understand this little bit of crazy is just how I am? I don't know.

"Not now, Shelby," he growls. "Not now. I can't."

"What?" I whisper, but I know I don't want to know.

"I can't do this." Trent firms his back and shoulders. "I can't watch you do something crazy and kill yourself. I need order. I need to do my job, and I need to look after my grandma, but I don't need you." I suck in a breath.

That one hurt. I figured he was going to break up with me, but I didn't think he was going to go for blood on the way out the door. Then again, I keep being surprised by the cruelty of men whom I have more feelings for than they do for me. One day, I swear, I'll learn from these lessons.

"Oh." It feels like someone sucked the air out of my lungs. But I stand tall, just the way Granny taught me to. "Okay."

"I'll see to it that your stuff is returned to you." And with that, he runs a hand over his face, turns, and strolls out the door. It doesn't slam but quietly snicks closed.

Wow. I did not know it was going to hurt this much. I knew he was going to leave—they all do—but I didn't think it would be this soon. Or hurt this bad. It feels like an iron fist is clenched tight around my heart. Well, what do you know; maybe I wasn't falling after all. It would appear I already fell. I feel a sob bubble up from my throat but tamp it down before it can get all the way out.

"Shelby . . . ," Marla says softly. But Granny firmly shakes her head once. She knows I need to rally myself. No one can protect me like me. That has become abundantly clear.

"It's okay." I hold up a hand. "I'm okay."

"You're not," Granny says. "But you will be. Now, let's get down to work and figure out what happened to Bitty Sue. We owe it to the old bag."

I slowly take a deep breath and make my way back over to the living room and sit on the sofa, Marla next to me, holding my hand.

"It'll be okay, baby," she says softly, her wrinkled hand brushing my hair out of my face.

"It won't be, but I will." I take another shuddering breath before looking Granny, who is pacing the floor in front of us, in the eyes. "Now, tell me about Bitty Sue."

"Bitty Sue has been on the make for a man since we all moved in here," Granny says when she stops pacing. "Her husband died back in Vietnam. She had no kids and never remarried."

"That's right," Marla says. "Her husband was the captain on the tour that your pop and my Hal were lucky to make it home from."

"What? I didn't know about that," I tell them.

"They didn't want you to know," my granny says softly, her eyes sad. "You know Pop-Pop wanted to protect you from the world."

I feel the tears sliding down my cheeks. There is nothing to keep them in check. I will never not miss my grandfather. He was the greatest man I have ever known. And I will bear the burden of knowing I caused his death for the rest of my life.

"They were surrounded," Marla says. "No hope of getting out. So the captain called fire on their position. Do you know what that means?" she asks when she sees the confusion on my face.

"No, I don't."

"Well, it's when there is no hope for them, so they radio to have their current position fired upon by their own artillery to take out the enemy." I gasp. "They hope to get into foxholes and be protected, but that's not what happened that night."

"That's right," Granny says. "Just about everyone died. Except for your grandfather, Trent's, Mr. Di Francesco, and George, whom you met the other day. They were the only ones to make it out."

"Okay," I say, trying to gather my thoughts before they come tumbling out of my mouth. "But what does this have to do with Bitty Sue now?"

"Oh, it does. You see, she went clear off the rails when her husband sacrificed himself. She loved him so much she knew she'd never replace him."

"So she turned into a tramp," Marla finishes honestly.

INVESTIGATION SHMESTIGATION

"So what does Bitty Sue being a tramp have to do with her death? I still feel like I'm missing something here, guys," I address the room.

"Maybe it was a jealous lover?" Granny asks.

"You're not sure?" I shoot back.

"Well . . . ," she hedges.

"What do you mean 'well . . .'?" I rally. "Do you even think something is really going on here, or are we just going on a wild-goose chase? Because I have to tell you, ladies, I don't have it in me right now."

"What your grandmother is trying to say, child, is that we saw the evidence ourselves," Marla says in her soft voice.

"That's what I'm talking about!" Granny cheers.

"No, what are you talking about?" Both women

groan and share a frustrated look. "Okay. Here's what we'll do. You both had better start at the beginning."

"So, it's like Marla was saying before Trent got up on that big, ugly high horse."

"Granny, don't be mean," I scold.

"Ugh. Okay. Fine. All I'm saying is that it's going to be a doozy of a fall off that one," she gripes.

"Granny. I don't have time for this," I warn.

"Yeah, Verna. Shit or get off the pot," Marla chimes in.

"So, as I was saying, Marla and I decided to go into Bitty Sue's apartment before her family got here to clean it out."

"Which, as Trent informed you, is illegal, but go on," I sigh.

"Hey, she owes me money!" Granny defends.

"Me too," Marla adds.

"Okay, let's move past the illegal debt collection. What happened after you went to the apartment?" I ask, trying to placate them. I need to get this show on the road before we're all as dead as Bitty Sue of natural causes.

"No, it's what happened in the apartment," Marla answers.

"Right, so we let ourselves into Bitty Sue's place," Granny begins. We went to that ugly little doggie cookie jar she keeps in the kitchen. No money . . ."

"Granny."

"Then we looked in her flour jar. Again, no money."

"I'm not sure I should be hearing this . . ." I give them the side-eye.

"Then we went into her bathroom and lifted the lid off of the toilet tank. Again, no money."

"You two are kind of frightening."

"Then we realized we had to go into her bedroom, which we did not want to do for a variety of reasons—the main two being that one, rumor on the street is she died there . . ."

"What street?"

"And two, we could catch the clap or any number of those icky things from her sheets," Marla finishes for Granny. "I didn't live to be eighty-two just to catch a wayward case of venereal disease." She shudders.

"So we opened the door and looked at her bed. Bitty Sue was crazy enough that she just might have put all her money in her mattress. But when Marla and I started moving the pillows off the bed to get a good look at the mattress, we noticed something strange."

"What's that?" I ask.

"Her makeup was on the pillowcase," Marla tells me.

"I was going to tell her that, you old witch!" Granny shouts.

"Well, you took long enough already," Marla snaps back.

"She's my granddaughter!"

"Well, she will be mine, too, when Trent pulls his head free from his asshole!" Marla rallies.

"Do not even get me started on that boy and his misconduct," Granny growls.

This situation is clearly deteriorating. I need to get this train back on the tracks. And quickly. So I clap my hands sharply, like a kindergarten teacher whose class is in serious need of some Adderall.

"Ladies!" I shout. "I am going to need you both to not bring up Trent for at least five days. Now, tell me. What does a stained pillow have to do with the money?"

"We didn't find the money." What? Now I'm confused. I thought the whole point of this conversation was the freaking money.

"What?" I ask. "Then why are we talking about you looking for the money?"

"Because the money is why we went into Bitty Sue's apartment in the first place," Granny tells me. "The pillowcase is what's important."

"Okay. So then tell me about the pillowcase," I sigh.

"The pillowcase was stained with Bitty Sue's signature makeup," Granny says.

"Yep, black mascara, red lipstick, and more rouge than you'd see in a whorehouse," Marla chimes in.

"But, so what?" I ask, still confused. "My pillowcase is constantly stained with my makeup when I'm too tired to take it off. Hell, even one of Trent's has been marked with my signature makeup."

"Bitty Sue slept like the dead, honey. You sleep like Evander Holyfield in the ring," Granny says with a sweet smile.

"Dead on her back with her arms crossed over her chest like she's in a coffin," Marla adds as she leans back in her chair with her eyes closed and her arms folded over her chest. I do have to admit that she does look like a corpse. I'm not even sure if she's breathing. It's creepy.

"And with a full face of makeup in case that night is the night she passes on to be with the captain."

"So then, why is the pillowcase stained?" I ask.

"Good girl," Marla says proudly, tossing me a wink.

"The pillowcase would only be stained if it touched her face, baby girl. And since everyone knew Bitty Sue slept like the dead, the only way it could have done that was if someone had placed it over her face," Granny says.

"So it really is reasonable to believe that our friend was murdered, don't you think?" Marla says softly. And yeah, it did. So I nodded my head to tell them as much.

"Do you know what her cause of death was?" I ask.

"No. They wouldn't tell us anything more than that

she had died," Granny answers.

"Okay, well, there is our first step." The grandmothers look at me, confused, but I have a plan.

I stand up and walk over to the table in the dining room, which is where I left my purse. It takes me a minute to unload all of my crap. Makeup bag, book, earbuds, the heels I took off in exchange for my sneakers when I was hell-bent for leather to get to my granny's, condoms—*where the hell did these come from?*—phone! Here is my phone. I pull up my contacts and dial the number I have saved for the medical examiner's office.

"Hello, yes, this is Shelby Whitmore with the *San Diego Metro News,* Funerals and Obituaries," I say when the call is answered. "I'm looking for information on the death of Bitty Sue Reynolds. Cause of death, surviving family members to contact, that kind of thing."

The lady on the other end of the line informs me that there is no next of kin, which we kind of figured. Personally, I think that's sad as hell. She also tells me that there is no autopsy pending because the cause of death appears to be respiratory failure/cardiac arrest. I bite my lip to hold in a gasp. Respiratory failure could definitely be as a result of being smothered with a pillow. Oh, shit. *Shit!*

I take a deep breath and squeeze my eyes tight. Shit, I could really use some tacos. Damn it! Okay, deep breath. There is no use getting the old biddies worked up over this news because we don't know what it means yet.

"Yes, ma'am. Thank you," I say into the phone. "I will follow up Wednesday. Thank you again. Have a nice day," I tell her.

Okay, today is Monday, so I have plenty of time to get my shit together and show these old ladies that Bitty Sue, while hell on wheels, was human. And also elderly. So she probably did die of natural causes.

"Well, don't keep us hanging here, chickadee," Granny interrupts my musings. "What did the medical examiner say?"

"Well," I start. "That was the secretary in the ME's office, and she told me that Bitty Sue just passed, presumably in her sleep, because she was an elderly widow living alone and that there is no cause to do an autopsy to provide a death certificate for burial."

"Well, what does that mean?" Marla erupts.

"It means that Bitty Sue's cause of death has been unofficially ruled as natural causes." I pause to let them collect their thoughts. "There will be no autopsy."

"But did they tell you *specifically* what they thought it was?" Granny asks, eyes narrowed on me. Smart old lady. Damn it.

I really need to take away her ability to google. I take another deep breath and muster up my confidence, narrowing my eyes slightly on the woman who taught me how to run the world more than Beyoncé did.

"She said the ME is pretty sure it's respiratory failure, cardiac arrest," I tell her as calmly as I can muster.

"I knew it!" She slaps her thigh.

"Now, we don't know anything," I say blandly, holding up my palms in an effort to stop what's coming.

"Yes, we do!" Granny shouts belligerently.

"She could have just passed in her sleep, Granny. It happens all the time here," I say in an even tone.

"But what about the makeup on her pillow?" Granny snaps.

"I have no earthly idea how it could have happened," Marla says softly.

"You got me. I don't know either. But I do know you guys can't go off half-cocked," I tell them with a raised eyebrow.

"We would never do such a thing." Granny gasps with a hand pressed over her heart. Marla is clutching her pearls. These two old ladies are so full of shit. And I tell them so.

"You two are so full of shit."

"Watch your mouth, young lady!" Granny barks as she smacks the back of my head. But she softens the blow with a wicked wink to me.

"We're going to have to investigate," Marla says sweetly.

"That's right! We're gonna be like those PIs on TV," Granny cheers. "We're the Granny Grabbers. No . . ."

“Okay, Cagney and Lacey, let’s not get ahead of ourselves here.”

“No,” Granny says softly before gaining speed. “We’re the Dangerous Dames.”

“Hear! Hear!”

Oh, shit.

“Now, you two know you’re going to have to tell Trent about these discoveries you’ve made, or he’ll be royally pissed,” I tell them.

Damn, just saying his name sears a pain so sharp through my chest. Absentmindedly, I rub the burn over my heart, grimacing. This pain is far worse than any betrayal James dished up. In my heart of hearts, I know this pain will never go away. At least I have a few decent, or not-so-decent, memories to keep me warm on cold nights. And if I hadn’t been so lost in my own thoughts, I would have seen two sets of age-wizened eyes narrow on me and my actions, all too aware of my thoughts and feelings as if I had voiced them allowed.

“Well, I will do no such thing,” Marla declares with a haughty tilt to her chin and shoulders. “If you want to tell him, you can do it yourself.”

“What?” I gasp. “Don’t you think that’s just a little harsh given what happened in this very room earlier today?”

“Nope,” she says letting the *p* pop off her lips. And that’s it. That’s all she gave me. What the fuck?

“Granny?” I ask, reaching out for support that I

now know will never come.

"What?" She looks right into my eyes. "You're both grown-ups. You should be able to figure this out on your own. And you know I have never once, in all my eighty-two years, been a narc!" she finishes triumphantly. Jesus, help me.

"Well, fine," I say defiantly. "I hope you're both very proud of yourselves and your childish behavior, but I'll be damned if I let you two get yourselves killed. You're all I have here while Mom and Dad are overseas. And he'd have my head if I let something happen to you."

I stand up and walk over to kiss my granny on the forehead and then over to Marla to do the same. Before I straighten back up, she wraps her arthritic hand, which has poison-green polish on her nails, around the back of my neck, leaning her forehead to mine.

"He'll come around, sweetheart," she says, her green Irish eyes, so much like Trent's, locked on mine. I just nod because what can I do? I can do nothing but agree with her. But I know it's over for sure. Unfortunately, now I need to call him to inform him of the plan our grandmothers are hatching to catch a supposed killer. How is this even my life?

Maybe I should move to Dubai. No, that's too hot. Alaska. That's it. I'll move to Alaska and live in leggings, Ugg boots, and parkas, and no man will ever find me attractive again. Then I can live out my days with a slew of cats. Or a polar bear. Maybe I'll get eaten by a bear, and it'll put me out of my misery. I sigh to myself.

"I need to get going," I say quietly to the room. "I'm going to catch up on some work from home. Call me if you gals need anything."

They both give me a hard stare. I know they want me to call him. It couldn't be more obvious that they want Trent and me to patch things up, but it's just not in the cards for the good detective and me. Hell, they told anyone and everyone that would listen about how we were all going to be a family and their pact to join our two families would be complete. How beautiful the babies we were going to make would be. And I was starting to warm up to the idea. I will be okay with that. Eventually.

I throw my big Coach purse over my shoulder and head out the door, letting it close softly behind me. The long hallway is eerily quiet. Almost menacing for the middle of the day. The back of my neck tingles like someone is watching me, but when I glance over my shoulder, no one is there. Damn, I have to stop letting Granny's and Marla's wild ideas get to me. One thing is for certain, though; I have to call Trent. He has a right to know what those two are up to. Marla is his grandmother, after all.

I ride the elevator down to the main floor and walk out the front sliding doors into the warm California sunshine. The valet guy knows me well, and he can see it's as plain as the nose on his face that I'm not in the mood for chitchat. Also, he witnessed my big blowup with Trent before we went upstairs so he could break my heart and Granny could set us on the trail of a would-be killer.

"Um, I'll just run and grab your car," the poor kid mumbles to me.

I see my car pull around the corner from the garage. I smile to the kid in hopes that he doesn't hate me or think I'm a crazy person. The last thing I need is to be visiting my granny and having the big men bust out their butterfly nets and elephant tranquilizers. That would be awkward, to say the least.

I jump into the driver's seat and quickly adjust the seat and mirrors. Why is it that every kid who works valet is, like, seven feet tall? I put my Jeep in gear and head for the highway. I'm going home to get some work done, and then I'll come back and brainstorm with the grannies later. I turn the radio off and pull my phone out of the cup holder where I had set it.

I dial the number I know so well, and it rings and rings and rings, and then nothing. What? I told him I would check in with him about his grandmother. He dismissed my call. Harsh. I shore up my courage and dial again. It rings and rings and rings, and then . . . *nothing.* Now I'm getting really pissed. So I take the freeway exit for my condo and dial again. It rings and ring and rings, and then I hear his voice. And he's pissed.

"What could you possibly want right this minute, Shelby?" he answers. Ouch.

"I was trying to let you know that our grandmothers

are extremely convinced that Bitty Sue was murdered for being promiscuous and have decided to embark on an investigation of their own. But since you're not interested in the goings-on of the elderly and I'm not a fan of being a narc to a bunch of octogenarians, I'll let you go. Good-bye, Trent." I go to hang up.

"Wait, Shelby . . ."

"What?" I ask. I'm over it and over this conversation.

"Why didn't you try to talk them down?"

"What makes you think that I didn't?" I snap back.

"You have to admit, you're a little bit of a nut," Trent answers.

"I have to go," I growl.

"I'm sorry," he says. "I'm having a bad day."

"You're having a bad day?" I screech. "I just got dumped for worrying about my grandmother, and when I try to do a nice thing by keeping you in the loop, I get my ass chewed . . . *again.* No, thanks. I didn't sign on for this." And then I hang up.

I pull into my parking space in front of my condo and park my car. I grab my big tote and start to head inside but realize my mailbox has to be overflowing with bills and Victoria's Secret catalogs. So I head on over and open the little metal door. It explodes with paper envelopes and catalogs. I stuff as much of it as I can into my tote bag and fill my arms with the rest. And then I head to my door. All to the tune of Trent's ringtone on my phone.

If I was a smart woman, I would have pulled my house keys out of my purse before I stuffed a week's worth of mail in my bag, but I'm not, so I didn't. I shuffle through as many of the papers as I can, moving some this way and that. I find my keys, but I also find a little mailbox key. It's the key they leave you when you have a large package and it's placed in one of the big boxes.

I open the door and drop my keys and the mailbox key onto the table by the front door and then take my purse into the kitchen to dump all the mail out onto the kitchen counter. I upend my bag and just let it all flop out as my phone rings again.

"Hello," I answer, placing the phone between my ear and my shoulder as I'm sifting through envelopes.

"Don't do that again." I immediately get my back up.

"Do what?" I ask as I go back to sorting my mail.

"Hang up on me," he says, and I can hear his jaw clench.

"You don't get to make the rules anymore," I say softly. I hear him sigh.

"Look. I'm sorry," he says to me. "I'd like to be civil if that works for you."

And damn if that doesn't burn. *Civil*. It's so cold when before there was so much more. But this is the way it always is, isn't it? Better now than when married with a baby. I abandon my purse and head for the entryway and the keys.

"Okay," I tell him as I walk out my front door.

"Okay. Now tell me why you couldn't talk them down," he says as I walk back to the mailboxes.

"Hi, Steve!" I wave as I pass him. He makes a startled face and then jumps into the bushes.

"Shelby," Trent tries to redirect my attention back to himself.

"Well, when they broke in to Bitty Sue's place to look for cash," I start to explain to Trent.

"Don't say 'broke in'! Don't say incriminating things about my grandmother to me," he growl-whispers into the phone as I grab a box with no labels but my own on it. I laugh.

"Okay, when they entered the premises with a key, they were looking for a missing item that may or may not have been cash. And while they were looking, they noticed makeup stains on the pillow," I tell him as I reenter my condo, closing and locking the door behind me.

"And the makeup means something?" he asks as I make my way into the kitchen and set my funny little box on the counter.

"I guess she slept like a corpse. She never moved in her sleep. And she slept with makeup on every night, always had," I say, cutting into the tape on the box and pulling it open. It's filled with tissue paper, so I start pulling it back.

"And they make a jump from makeup smudges to murder, just like that?" he asks. "You're going to have to tell them that old people die, and as much as they don't want to believe it, Bitty Sue was old."

But I don't hear him because I drop the phone and scream a scream worthy of Tippi Hedren. Shit. I need to call the police. I look around for my phone and realize I dropped it and Trent is shouting for me.

"Trent! I have to go," I tell him.

"Shelby! Shelby! What happened?" he shouts.

"No time! I have to call the police," I gasp into the phone, still shaking.

"I am the fucking police!" he growls.

"No. The real police!" I shout, trying to explain.

"I am the real police!"

"No, the police in this area. Shit. I've got to go." And I hang up. I immediately dial 9-1-1. The operator picks up right away.

"Nine-one-one. What is the nature of your emergency?" she asks me.

"Someone sent a threatening package to my house."

"How do you know it's threatening?" she asks. I'm a little surprised by her question.

"Um, because of the note that says I'm going to die?" I ask.

"Is there anything else? Or is it just a threatening note?" Does she not believe me? Or does she hear about threatening packages all the time?

"Well, the dead bird kind of clinched it," I tell her, growing more frustrated by the minute.

"Ma'am, what is your address?" she asks. I tell her my address and my name. "A police officer will be arriving shortly. Please stay on the line."

"Okay, thank you," I tell her. I make my way out of the kitchen, leaving everything exactly where I last touched it.

I walk into the living room and sit down on the sofa. I don't turn on the stereo or the television. Not even a lamp. I just sit there in the dark, waiting for the police to show up. I see headlights pull up out front, and I'm sure this is them.

"I think they're here," I tell her just as there is a knock on my door.

"Okay. Stay on the line until I have confirmation of the responding officer." I answer the door, and a frazzled Trent and a serious-faced Kane are standing on my doorstep.

"This is not the officer I want. Take him back!" I wail.

"Ma'am, the responding officer is Officer Beaumont. He is still three minutes out. Is there a fraudulent officer at the premises?"

"No. He's a real one," I grumble.

Trent holds his hand out for my phone, and I hand

it over willingly as I move out of the doorway so they can come in. Kane puts his hand on my shoulder, but I just shrug it off.

"This is Detective Foyle. My partner and I are responding. Thank you," I hear him say before he hangs up.

"You okay, kid?" Kane asks. But I just shake my head no. "Want to show me what's going on?" he asks.

"Yeah, I guess. I mean, you came all this way," I say as I lead him to the kitchen. Ironically, it's where we first met after Trent scared the hell out of me. "It's over there on the counter."

Kane pulls on gloves and uses a pen from his pocket to move things around a bit. "It appears to be a bird with its neck snapped," he says to Trent.

"And there's a note," I whimper.

"What's the note say?" Trent asks, snapping on his own gloves.

"It says, 'This little birdie can't sing anymore, and you won't either if you don't stop asking questions.' That's kind of sick," Kane comments. No kidding.

"Still think old people just die, Trent?" I ask. I can't help but get a little dig in.

"We don't know that it's related. You have a winner of an ex that posted bond this very morning," he tells me. I didn't realize James was out. This is not good. But still, that zinger cut deep.

"And another winner standing in my kitchen, acting

like an asshole," I mumble, but from the way Trent's spine goes rigid, I know he heard me.

"Kids!" Kane claps his hands. "This is serious. Time to put your lover's spat behind you," he chastises.

"It's more than a spat," I tell him. "The good detective ended things this afternoon in front of our grandmothers." Kane turns to glare at Trent.

"Dude, that's harsh." Kane shoots Trent an *Are you kidding me?* look.

"Do we really need to air out our dirty laundry, Shell?" Trent glares at me. Um . . . okay.

"Did you really need to dump me in front of both of our grandmothers and then run?" I snap back.

"Dude, you ran like a girl?" Kane laughs from behind me. Trent just growls.

"I had my reasons," he mumbles.

"Reasons that left me trying to soothe two upset old women when you did the upsetting!" I yell. "Why are you here, anyway?"

"I get a call when your name comes over the police band," he says softly, and I just shake my head.

"Well, you should cancel that order," I tell him, feeling the tears burn behind my eyes.

"No way!" Kane shouts. "We're thinking about giving you your own code," he tells me gleefully. Bastard.

"Yeah, I'm good," I tell him.

"Somehow, I don't think so," Kane says to me. I look up into his blue eyes and feel like he sees everything. I shrug. Whatever. But I feel Trent's gaze burning holes through my skull. I don't need the help. I'll figure it out on my own. I will.

"So?" I tap my foot and cross my arms in front of my chest. "Why are you here, anyway?" I question again.

"When I heard you scream and then tell me you had to call the police, I couldn't just sit there. I care, Shell," he says softly, almost too quiet to hear. "I probably always will," he finishes.

"No!" I shout. "You don't get to care, Trent."

"It's not that easy."

"It is," I snap back. "You don't get to come and go as you please. You need to go," I say firmly. He just looks at me sadly.

"I'll just take this and log it as evidence," Kane says as he wraps the sinister package in a big plastic bag for evidence.

"Shell . . . ," Trent says, pained.

"No," I cry.

The tears are starting to burn down my face. He follows Kane back to the front door but stops just before passing through it, his strong hands gripping the frame.

"Shelby," he says, looking back at me. "I don't know what you want from me?"

"I want you to go," I say as calmly as I do not feel.

"Why are you being this way?" he demands.

"What way is that, Trent?" I snap. "Because I'm just trying to follow the rules that you yourself keep changing on me. Go back to your stupid big-boobied nurse," I say, seething, as I slam the door in his face.

I lock the door and then slide down it, hugging my knees as I slump down. A sob erupts from my chest, and I bury my face in my knees now that the tears are freely flowing. A loud sound thumps on the other side of the door, above my head, rattling the wooden door.

"Shelby . . ." I hear Trent's muffled moan from the other side of the door, but I don't make a peep. I just sit there and cry by myself, letting him go just like he asked me to.

"Come on, buddy. Let her go for now." I hear Kane try to softly coax Trent away from my home. Those are the last words I hear as I curl up on my side on the cool tile of my entryway and cry myself to sleep.

GRANNIES AND GHILLIE SUITS

Elizabeth Susan Mackelroy (19412017)

Elizabeth, known to her friends as Bitty Sue, passed on earlier this week. She leaves her friends. She is survived by no children or immediate family. She resided at the Peaceful Sunset Retirement Village in the Gaslamp District. She was predeceased by her husband, Captain Franklin Mackelroy, United States Army, who was killed in action in Vietnam.

The sun is blistering my eyeballs through my eyelids, and there is a John Philip Sousa tribute band marching around in my head. Damn those fucking symbols! My mouth feels like there's a whole bag of cotton balls in it. I lick my lips and crack one eye open.

Well, at least now I know why my body hurts. I'm

not in my big, comfy bed. No, I am on the rug in front of the front door. On my side, in the fetal position. Like a baby. I must have slept here after my epic cryfest.

"Meow." Missy head-butts my face.

"You're the only one I can count on, huh, baby?" I coo as I pet her while lying on my side.

I sigh and carefully push myself up with my one good arm onto my knees and stand up. All the while noticing every creaking muscle. I have never been more aware of the fact that I'm getting older. Unfortunately, this train of thought is taking a direct path to *I just got dumped*-ville and on to *I'm going to die alone*-land. These are not great times.

I walk to the bathroom and lean over the sink to splash some cool water on my face. When I look up into the mirror, I scream a scream worthy of Elm Street or Carrie's Prom. Holy shit! I look like Rocky Balboa! My whole face is red and swollen, and there's snot and eye crust stuck to my face. I'm not even sure Missy would like me right now.

I head to the kitchen, in desperate need of coffee, and stop when I hit the entrance. Looking at the island, with all of my mail piled up on it, I can't help but remember the dead bird and the nasty note in that box of doom. I know I'll never look at another brown box with a stupid smile on it or an online-clothing-purchase package the same again. And that really makes me sad. Silver lining? I might die before I have a chance to purchase the shoes I've had my eye on and can't really afford right now. I make a mental note to ask Granny if she'll take Miss Havisham in if something happens to me. This little furball is . . . unique. And I'm not sure many would appreciate her for her true character.

I take a deep breath and roll my shoulders back before heading to the coffeemaker. I put a mug under the spout and a pod of the strongest stuff I have in the cabinet into the holder. As soon as it's done brewing, I chug the whole mug—black, without any cream or sugar to cut it. The second cup, I doctor the way I like it but take it with me to the bathroom, ready to leave behind the macabre feel of my once happy kitchen with Pioneer Woman dish towels and Tiffany Blue mixer.

I make the shower as hot as I can possibly stand it and drink the rest of my coffee, standing under the hot water. This is my tried-and-true way to rally on tough mornings. I set my empty mug in the cutout for soaps and shampoo bottles and wash my hair and body as economically as possible. There is nothing to be enjoyed today.

I towel-dry my body and then comb and blow-dry my hair so my crazy red curls are soft waves. I tap some concealer under my eyes and then gunk up my face with as much product as possible. As hard as it is to believe, I looked better after Trent caused me to fall into an open grave. Trent . . . Now my heart feels like an open grave.

I put on a tight but stretchy medium-blue pencil skirt and a dove-gray boyfriend cardigan and matching shell. Bue pointed-toe heels and my diamond studs and I'm ready to go. I pick up my brightly flowered bag and look at it. It feels wrong to hold something so happy. I almost go back into my closet and get a plain black bag but decide that Granny would tan my hide if she heard me now. So I shake it off and grab my keys before reminding Missy to hold down the fort. I'm pretty sure we both know that she's just going to take a nap and then puke on something that I love.

I walk outside and muster a half smile and wave to Pervy Steve as I get into my car and head toward the office. Even the highway traffic toward downtown doesn't rile me up, so I stroll around the corner and grab a coffee and a chocolate croissant after I park my car in the lot.

I take my coffee from the barista and wave my thanks with a mouth full of chocolatey goodness. My purse over my shoulder and my hands full, I head back toward my office building. Someone tries to talk to me in the elevator, but I just growl and rip a big bite off of my croissant with my mouth.

He decides not to talk to the crazy lady and gets off on the second floor and heads for the stairs. I could probably eat all my meals at that coffee shop, and then I would never have to go back into my kitchen again.

I ball up my paper bag and toss it into the trash can next to the elevator door and head toward my cubicle as I sip my icy mocha blend with extra whip. I'm not going to lie—it's the extra whip that gives me the will to live.

I sit down and fire up my computer. I have a long list of dead people to announce to the greater San Diego area. I'm making great progress. The list of death notices for the week is e-mailed off to the editor, and I'm cleaning up a few obituaries and funeral notices when my phone chimes with a text. I would ignore it, but it's playing "Hells Bells," and that's Granny, so I pull my phone out of my purse in the drawer and take a look.

```
GRANNY: Come to the home PDQ!!!
I need you. It's URGENT!!!!
ME: On my way!!! Hang tight!!!!
```

Oh my God, I think, *Granny was right about everything, and now she is in the clutches of a deranged killer!* I mentally clutch my pearls at my throat like a good Southern woman who was born and bred in San Diego—not the South—and haul my ass out of my desk chair.

"I gotta run, Sal," I shout through my boss's office door as I make tracks past it. "Something's wrong with Granny. She said it's an emergency."

"Go! I'll call the police and have them meet you there," he shouts.

I hit my car and make the land speed record getting

through town. But I have to get there on time. My granny needs me! I pull into the first spot I find and throw my car in park. I jump out, not even bothering to shut my door, and take off for the building.

I'm running through the parking lot of the Peaceful Sunset Retirement Village in my pencil skirt and heels from work, and this is how I died. Not really. I can't bother to notice how my feet are pinched in these damn shoes, but holy hell was I on point at work today.

I'm halfway through the tree-lined parking lot when a monster jumps from between the trees. It's tall and dark and covered with leaves. Oh God. I'm going to die at the hands of a tree monster. I think, *Do tree monsters have hands or paws? Does it even freaking matter—I'm going to die!*

A bloodcurdling scream rents the air. And I am flying through the air. Into a puddle in the parking lot, full of rainwater, mud, and oil from all of the cars. I land hard on my backside, and the splash of this disgusting tidal wave comes up and over my head, soaking my carefully curled red hair and running my makeup down my face.

I look up in time to see the monster take a step toward me. This is it. I think, *This is the end. I'll always love you, Granny. I'm sorry I never took your advice and made a beautiful baby with Detective McHottie! Tell Mom and Dad that I love them.*

"Jesus, Joseph, and Mary, what in the hell are you talking about, child?" the monster asks as he pulls his head off. Wait, that's not a monster. That is my grandmother pulling the hat and mask off of a ghillie suit.

"Jesus Christ, Granny!" I shout. "You scared the hell out of me." She smacks the back of my head with the flat of her hand.

"Do not take the Lord's name in vain! I raised you better than that," Granny shouts. "And I'm not too old to take my wooden spoon to your backside either." She smirks. "But if you're aiming for a good spanking, I bet the sweet and charming detective could help you with that. How are you today, Trenton?" She winks over my shoulder. *Winks!*

"Fine. Thanks, ma'am," that deep, deep voice that puts Josh Turner to shame replies. "Now, am I Detective McHottie, or should I be jealous? Because if it's me you want to make a baby with, I think we could come to an agreement," he says as he offers me a hand up.

"I said that out loud, didn't I?" I ask as I take his warm hand and stand. "In all fairness, I thought I was going to die. And I most certainly wouldn't be talking about you even if I was about to die." I turn to walk away.

"You wouldn't be about to walk away and break my poor, miserable heart by watching your fine yet bruised ass walk away, would you?" Trent asks.

"Stop the games, Detective Foyle. I can't play them anymore," I tell him as I start to walk away.

"Shelby," he starts, but I interrupt him when an unfortunate thought crosses my mind.

"How would you know if my ass is bruised?" I ask and think about it, taking note of the breeze that I feel blowing past my cheeks. "I ripped my skirt open when I fell, didn't I?"

This wouldn't normally be a problem, but seeing as I was running late this morning and my skirt was fairly tight, I made the executive decision to forgo underpants. My mom would be shocked, but Granny—she just looks on, smiling proudly. I sigh.

"Yep," he confirms my nightmares. I hang my head and turn away. Again. I try to leave with as much of my dignity as I can when Trent adds, "I'm going to need you to stick around. I have to question you and then write you a few citations."

"Citations?" I all but shout. "You've got to be kidding me, Trent!"

"No, ma'am," he replies calmly. "There are reports all over town of you speeding and driving like a maniac. Then there is the little matter of making a false report to the police, which is a fairly serious matter. And lastly"—he leans as he ticks my last transgression off on his fingers—"by the looks of you and your grandmother, you are gearing up, if you haven't already, to interfere in my investigation. I warned you before, Shelby. I will not do it again. But I am very tempted to take you over my knee and warm that beautiful ass with my own hand. Or paddle. Your choice."

"You wouldn't dare," I reply with all my strength and pride, thrusting my chin up.

"Go ahead, darlin'." Trent leans into my bubble of personal space—these things are important!—his nose just inches from mine, and states firmly, "Just. Try. Me."

"And what investigation?" I put my hands on my hips and lean toward him. "Last I checked, 'old people just die. Let it go, Shelby.' Wasn't that what you were saying when you ended things in front of my grandmother. Or last night when you told me the dead bird and nasty note someone mailed me was not related."

"What dead bird, Shell?" Granny asks, but I'm too busy staring down Trent, that no-good bastard. "Damn it, Shelby! Answer me," she yells, snapping me out of my standoff with Detective McHottie.

"Last night, when I got home, I had a package in with my mail. It had a dead bird and a threatening note. Trent and Kane came out and said it's not a big deal." I shrug it off. Somehow, I don't think she believes me.

"I never said it wasn't a big deal, Shelby," Trent says softly. "What I said was that I cared, and then you lost your fucking mind," he adds. I draw in a gasp.

"I did not!" I shout. "What I said is that you don't get to drop me like a bad habit and then pretend to care."

"I'm not pretending!" he shouts back.

"Well, you have a funny fucking way of showing it!" I scream at him. I guess now we're letting it all hang out.

"Do you know how long I stood there and listened

to you cry last night, Shelby? Do you? Knowing I couldn't hold you in my arms and comfort you. Do you know that it killed me? It fucking killed me, Shelby," he says brokenly.

"I'm trying to let you go like you asked, Trent," I say softly. "You can't keep coming back and pulling me in, only to hurt me all over again. Either stay or go, but I want off this merry-go-round," I tell him.

"What if I told you I wanted to stay?" he asks me, but I can't bring myself to trust him, to hope. He chased me. I didn't want this. I didn't want to be hurt again. But Trent started this.

"I would say it's probably too little, too late," I tell him. I look up into his eyes, expecting to see resolve, hurt even, but I don't. I see the glitter of a challenge in them. Shit. "Can you write me the tickets that I'm not going to pay now? Please?" I try to diffuse the situation, but Trent only rises to the challenge.

"Did you just admit to breaking the law, ma'am?" he questions me.

"No. Nope, not me," I stammer. I see what he's doing here.

"I believe you did. I'm going to need you to put your hands against the vehicle," he tells me. That bastard.

"What are you doing?" I question.

"I'm following police protocol," he tells me. "Now, put your hands on the vehicle before I have to force you."

So I put my hands on the vehicle. Trent pats me down but takes some leeway over my ass and in between my legs. I'm not going to admit to him that I'm a little turned on now. Nope, no way. That shit is coming with me to my grave.

Trent glides his hands up my arms, and for a moment, I forget that we're in the middle of a parking lot, surrounded by people. That is, until I feel the metal cuffs bite around my wrist as he pulls my hand down and behind me. Then the next one is clicked into place.

"What the hell?" I demand.

"You're under arrest," he tells me before launching into my Miranda rights.

"You can't do this," I implore him.

"I believe I just did." He smirks at me as he shoves me into the backseat of the black-and-white, telling the officer to drive me straight to the precinct because *Detective Asshole* will be booking me himself. I growl, but he just laughs. "Don't make me add resisting arrest to your list of crimes, love."

I'd like to say the drive to the police station is the most humiliating moment of my life, and it is, up until we pull into the actual police station and I am walked into the back to be processed with my hands cuffed behind my back.

"Shut it!" I shout as I'm marched past a laughing Kane. "I don't want to fucking hear it," I growl at him, but he just howls louder.

"I think it's safe to say he cares, doll." Kane chuckles.

"No, he doesn't," I snap. "I'm not listening."

Trent stomps in, clearly pleased with himself, and follows the officer and me toward the back. Kane is trailing him with a maniacal look of glee on his face. He takes a key from his pocket and unlocks the cuffs before shoving them back onto his belt. Before I can move away, Trent is there, snatching up my hands and rubbing my wrists where the cuffs scraped them.

"This isn't how I imagined you in my cuffs, Shelby," Trent grumbles in my ear.

"Then don't do this," I implore him.

"I'm just doing what I have to," he says.

I'm shoved in front of a scale with height increments marked up it. I measure in at five feet six inches. I am told to face forward and hold a board with my name and booking number on it while my picture is taken for all to see. Then I'm turned to the side so they can get a profile shot. I'm sure the mug shots are just magical, seeing as how I am soaked in mud and rainwater from my fall in the parking lot.

Trent grabs my hand in his and leads me over to a big machine with a blue screen, almost like a giant photocopier. He enters some information into the computer and then, one by one, rolls each of my fingers across the blue screen.

As soon as all of my fingerprints have been scanned, my driver's license photo and information pop up on the screen, and I cringe. It was taken in July, and my hair was so curly and wild. I had on a black Rusty tank top with white letters and a pink hibiscus flower across my breasts and very little makeup. I was on my way to the beach, if I remember correctly. And now, now I look like shit.

Trent quickly re-cuffs my hands behind my back. I roll my eyes at him. This isn't really necessary. I'll play his game, and then when I finally get out of here, I will avoid Trenton Foyle like a bad case of the clap.

So here I stand, like a drowned rat, soaked from head to toe in mud, my bruised behind and my even more bruised pride hanging out for all to see, with my head tipped down as I am booked by the incredibly sexy, Detective McHottie for a variety of things I am not actually sure I did. Clearly, I have died and gone to hell. I'm hoping the ground will open up and swallow me whole because there is no way I can survive this humiliation if I'm not really dead.

"Now, if you'll step this way for your cavity search," Trent tells me as he grabs me by the elbow and leads me down the hallway.

"You're kidding, right?" I ask. "You can't be serious."

"Serious as a heart attack. This is police procedure," he says with a straight face. Barely. I see his lips twitch in the corner.

"Trent . . . ," I say.

"Buddy, I wouldn't do that," I hear Kane tell him from behind me.

"It's standard procedure," he shoots over his shoulder to his partner.

"But I didn't do anything wrong!" I shout as I dig in my heels and fight. I am not getting a cavity search.

"It's your life. Or your balls, really. She looks like she's about to chew them up and spit them out," Kane tells Trent, who winces but brushes it off quickly. "Dead man walking," Kane shouts from the hallway.

I bend my knees and lean toward the ground. I am actively doing anything I can to not end up in the body-cavity-search area. I'm on my side, with my hands cuffed behind my back, and kicking my legs wildly to get away from Trent as he tries to get a purchase on me so he can drag me off to impending doom. I land a good kick to his nuts and hear an *oompf* come from him as he bends over to catch his breath. I am busy doing my best impression of an inch worm as I wiggle away.

"Kane! Dammit, Kane! Help me. Please!" I scream at him as I make my way back down the hall.

"I can't help you, doll. I'm so sorry. I was hoping he'd come to his senses, but it's not looking so good. Just relax and it'll be over before you know it." I'm shocked. What the fuck?

"Dammit, Shelby," Trent hollers as he grabs my ankle and drags me back.

"No. No, no, no!" I scream as he throws me over his shoulder and carries me back down the hall toward the search area. "I hope that crazy madman kills me and you have this on your conscience," I scream and kick. By now, Granny and Marla have shown up at the police station, hopefully trying to post my bail or convince *Detective Crazypants* to let me go.

"Don't worry, Shell," Granny calls. "You've done way more embarrassing things than this before. I bet Detective McHottie will still have sex with you when he's done arresting you!" she shouts. I hear Trent's stupid smirk in his voice, and I move on to glare at Granny. I was wrong; I might not have died today, but there is an old woman I love dearly who is about to!

Trent cannot be swayed even by adorable, meddlesome old women and the thought of my impending death. He carries me into the room with no windows, which is ominous of the horrors that are about to occur. There is another uniformed officer in the room, and I'm about to complain about having a man touch me so intimately when I realize the giant man with a blond mustache is actually a woman named Sally.

She looks as if she brooks no bullshit, so I don't even argue as she instructs me to strip out of my clothes and then does things that I would usually require her to buy me dinner and a movie first, at the very least.

When she's done, I feel the tears burn up my throat and down my cheeks as she hands me a pair of blue hospital scrubs and plain white panties and a sports bra. She slaps a bracelet, which looks similar to the ones used for identification in hospitals, on my wrist, but this one contains my name, booking number, and to my complete horror, my mug shot. *Fuck. My. Life.*

There's a knock at the door, and Sally opens it. Trent is standing there looking as pained as I feel. But I don't give a shit about that. He will never get my sympathy again. I will never forgive him for this. He cuffs me again and leads me down a hall before he buzzes open a door, using a badge and a fingerprint. He walks me down a long, locked hallway. Trent buzzes us in through another door, and this one is a bay full of cells. Trent stops at an empty cell and slides the big, barred door open.

"Shelby . . . ," he says softly.

"Oh, don't quit on me now," I say as I walk into the cell and turn around for him to uncuff me before he locks me in.

"You don't understand," he says, pained.

"Oh, I think I understand just fine," I say, shaking my wrists up and down so he will undo the cuffs that keep him here with me.

"I have to do this," he says as he undoes the cuffs and pockets them. I quickly step forward, deeper into the little cell that is now mine.

"No, you don't, but you are anyway. I hope the department has a good lawyer. You're going to need one," I tell him. I look into his eyes so he can see my tears and the pain he has caused me.

"This is the only way I can protect you," he whispers.

"I don't want your protection, and I definitely don't want you," I say clearly.

"You don't mean that," he says. I see the hurt in his eyes. But I will him to see me. See my hurt. My embarrassment. My humiliation.

"I do," I tell him. Trent closes his eyes for a minute before opening them again.

"I love you, Shelby." At any other time or place, I would have jumped for joy over his declarations, but here and now, I want nothing to do with them.

"I hate you, Trent. I don't ever want to see you again," I tell him firmly. "Please go." And with that, he hangs his head and walks out of the bay, leaving me in a room full of cells of female criminals.

I take stock of my new home for the time being. I have a cot with a folded blanket and pillow that are probably germ-ridden. And a steel sink and toilet. My life is magical. As I slip down to the floor and draw my knees up to my chest, a sob tears free.

I feel like at this juncture in my life, I can cry freely. I can't help but wish I had never met the sexy detective, whom I most definitely love, but also hate. I'm crying so hard that I never notice him look over his shoulder at me, taking in my protective posture and my heartfelt tears. I also never notice his own tears glittering in his bright green eyes.

Chapter TEN

MISS MARPLE AND MARLA

I awake the next morning with a backache and a crick in my neck. Probably because I slept on the cell floor, sitting up with my back against the bars. Last night, things were hopping in downtown San Diego. There were several bar fights in the Gaslamp District and a vice sting went down, so there was an abundance of hookers and johns in the system.

This meant Granny and Marla couldn't post my bail. I'd like to think it was because the station was busy, but I really think it's because Trent is an asshole. And again, my eyes are swollen shut. This is starting to become a habit that begins and ends with Trenton Foyle.

Trent . . . Just thinking about him breaks my heart.

"Breakfast, ladies," a uniformed officer calls out as he slides in a couple of trays. I look up at him. He's brown haired and blue-eyed. Handsome face. Body like a Mack truck. He smiles kindly at me. Everyone who works out of this station now knows the sordid tale of Trent and me.

"No, thanks, Jones." I attempt a smile, but by the look on his face, I've fallen short. Probably because not only does my puffy face resemble a monster but my makeup is no doubt smeared all over my face. Even though Daisy, my cellmate for the duration of my wrongful imprisionment, did her best to clean my face off. "I'm not hungry."

"You gotta eat, doll," Jones, a big man with mountains of muscles and the whitest smile I have ever seen, tells me. If I hadn't just sworn off all police officers, I would definitely be flirting now. "You know Detective Foyle will have my ass if you don't," he tells me, which is a fact I already know.

"Something tells me you could hold your own against the detective," I laugh.

"Yeah, I could, but I would also like to keep my job," he says. "But if he wouldn't kill me or get me busted down, I would surely take you out to dinner." Jones winks at me.

"I'm pretty sure it's not really me you're interested in here," I say softly and smile, patting him on the chest through the bars.

"No, ma'am." He smiles. "Friends?" he asks.

"Of course." I smile at him. "And if you tell the big moron that I'm falling in love with him, I will shoot you myself," I tell him. Then I hear someone clearing their throat from behind Officer Jones, who just smiles sweetly at me. I groan.

"So you do love me," Trent says, not asking.

"I did not say that," I start, but before I can get up a good mad, Daisy jumps into the fray.

Daisy is a fors to be reckoned with. She is one of the alleged prostitutes who were brought in last night. She is a five-foot-ten-inch tall black woman weighing in at about two hundred pounds. She is clad in poison-green leggings, a hot-pink lace bra, and a cropped T-shirt that is cut off at the shoulders so it droops on one side. You would think it is a horrible sight, but she's gorgeous. And her bright hazel eyes twinkle with in-sight.

Also, Daisy definitely won't take anyone's shit. Let alone Trent's. After a good cry last night, I told her my story, and she decided that we were best friends. And Daisy is a good friend to have. And lastly, Officer Jones has been sweet on her for a while but has yet to make his move.

"Are you who I think you are?" Daisy thunders from behind me. A look over my shoulder confirms she's got her hip cocked and a fist resting on it. S he's spoiling for a fight on my behalf. "I know, you're not who I think you are. I *know you are*!"

"What the fuck?" Trent asks.

"You best leave my girl alone. Now. Run along!" she shouts at him.

"Who are you?" Trent asks her.

"Well, I'm Shelby's best friend, and I won't let you treat her badly," she answers without fear.

"It's true," I tell him.

I haven't had friends in a long time. Not since James and I split, so it's nice to have a girlfriend in my corner. Trent just shakes his head.

"Only you, Shell." He smiles at me, his eyes twinkling with mischief.

"What do you want, Trent?" I ask, defeated.

"To see how you are this morning," he says softly.

"Or to gauge your mood and see if you still want to kick him in the nuts," Daisy adds. Jones snorts back a laugh, and Trent glares at him.

"That too," Officer Jones says under his breath.

"Is there something you need, Officer Jones?" Trent asks.

"No, sir. Just enjoying the show." He smiles at him. Interesting.

"He said he'd like to take me to dinner," I tell Trent.

I don't know why. It just popped out. By the sudden widening of Jones's eyes, he did not expect that and is wondering what bombs my statement will set off. By the narrowing of both Trent's and Daisy's eyes, it looks like a lot.

"Well, I gotta go," Jones says as he takes off running. We hear the big door snick closed behind him.

"That man is a mess," Daisy says absentmindedly, sighing to herself.

"You're not really going on a date with him, are you?" Trent asks quietly.

"Would you care?" I ask, just as quiet.

"You know I care, Shelby."

"But you don't want me," I say, my mad gaining steam again. "You care, but you don't want me. You don't want me, but no one else can have me."

"I can't get hurt again, Shell," he says, panicked.

"But you can hurt me?" I question.

"I don't know what to do, Shelby!" he shouts as he pulls at his hair in angry fits.

I hold on to the bars of the cell and rest my head against them with my face tipped down. My tears are flowing freely again.

"I wish you'd hurry up and figure it out because this hurts, Trent. This hurts so bad," I tell him softly.

"I know, baby. It hurts me, too," he says as he strokes my cheek with his palm.

"You can't keep me in this cell forever, Trent," I tell him. "I haven't done anything wrong," I say calmly, hoping he will believe me. At this point, I'm not even sure I believe me. I've never been to jail before.

"I know, baby. I was just so mad," he tells me. "I died a little hearing you cry yourself to sleep from the other side of your door. Kane had to drag me away, baby. I overreacted, but you have to understand that I need to protect you, Shelby. I need it." I look deep into Trent's eyes and nod.

"I know you do," I tell him. "I do. But right now I can't be around you and not be with you," I tell him.

"I don't want to be apart anymore, Shelby. I can't be away from you."

"I just don't know, Trent. It's going to take some time before I can trust you again. I just don't know," I tell him honestly.

"I'm going to prove it to you. I'm going to get you out of here," he promises.

Thank God. I'm still not thrilled with him, but for fuck's sake, I am getting out of this jail. I'm so close to freedom I can almost taste it. Until I don't.

"Detective Foyle! Detective Foyle!" Officer Jones comes running back into the holding area. "Detective Foyle, there's an emergency." He stops just in front of us.

"What is it?" Trent barks. "What's happening?"

"Peaceful Sunset just called. Your grandmother fell down two flights of stairs, sir. She's headed to North Park Memorial," he tells us. Trent doesn't even look back at me as he runs full out to the door.

"I haven't forgotten about the cavity search, you jerk!" I shout at him. If it was my granny, I would have left his ass in the dust, too. "Shit! Now what am I going to do?" I rail against the bars.

"I'm sorry, Miss Shelby. I can't let you go without

Detective Foyle's say-so," he says.

"I know, Jones. It's not your fault," I reassure him.

I don't like being in here. I don't like being stuck anywhere. The walls are closing in on me, and I feel trapped. Trapped. Fuck. I need out of this place. I can't catch my breath. I'm gasping like a fish lying on a dock. I scratch at my chest, trying to free whatever is blocking the air from my lungs, but it's no use. Black spots dance before my eyes. And it's lights out.

"Jones!" I hear Daisy scream from deep within the black. "Jones! Someone! We need help. She's unconscious."

I'm not conscious. I'm dead. Shit, I died in jail. My poor mother will never be able to look her water aerobics group in the face again. Granny will probably think it's bitchin'.

I hear footsteps thunder closer, but the inky blackness is holding me down. It's like being sucked under by a riptide. As hard as I fight, the faster I swim, it only pulls me deeper.

"Oh Lord Jesus, someone do something!" Daisy cries.

"Put her on her side," someone orders. "Get an ambulance in here! Now!"

I can't match the voice with a face, but it's familiar.

The dark waves pull me under again. This time, it pulls me deep. Everything goes completely silent.

I hear beeping, and bright lights burn my eyeballs from the outside and sear my brains. My arms and legs are floating on clouds. My head feels as light as a feather. I try my eyelids, and this time one cracks open.

"Hey, guys," I rasp. Whose voice is that? "What's with the party?" I ask as I see Trent and Kane scowling and Granny and my parents huddled together crying. Sophia is here, too. And George and an older, but no less stunning, brunette that has to be his wife. Standing room only, I guess.

"Shelby—" Trent rasps, his eyes locking on mine. But he's interrupted by my parents, who were on a six-month cruise, celebrating my dad's retirement from the army.

"Baby girl," my dad says lovingly. "What happened?"

I turn my head to look at my dad. I realize now, as tears burn my eyes, how much I have missed him since he's been out of the country. I suck them back; Whitmores are not criers. The sporadic e-mails here and there just weren't enough.

"I don't know, Daddy." My voice is rough. It hurts to talk.

"They had to intubate you on the ride here," Trent

says, moving to my other side.

"Who the actual fuck are you?" my dad booms, not one to mince words. "You're the asshole who hurt my girl? Because you have to realize I won't have that shit. I won't have it!" he says, repeating the same words my granny gave Trent just days ago. I want to laugh at their similarities, but it hurts too much.

"Jack . . ." My granny tries to wade in, but it is no use. My dad is on a roll, and it is best to let him have that moment.

"No, Mom, I'm not playing around. Not when it comes to Shelby. And definitely not after that last asshole put her in the hospital."

"It's not like that, Dad," I say, placing my hand on my dad's. "He didn't hurt me. Not like that. He just put me in jail."

"In jail?" My mom wails into her tissue.

"What the actual fuck?" my dad yells. "Explain yourself, now." And there is no room for any evasion with my dad. It's time for the truth. Trent seems to come to the same realization.

"I just wanted to protect her, sir. I need to protect her," Trent says, looking a bit too much like a little boy for me.

"Why would she need to be protected? Is that asshole back?"

"He was, but he's not the problem," I tell the room.

"So, what now?" Dad asks as he stares Trent and

me down. The CIA should be using him to run terrorist interrogations. I squirm under his gaze. I have never been able to lie to my dad.

"Someone is killing off residents at Granny's place," I tell him. Granny is nodding emphatically.

"Yeah, *God,*" my dad snorts, rolling his eyes.

"Jack!" my mom shouts as she slaps him on the chest.

"What? That place is like the 'Hotel California.' You can check out, but you may never leave." My dad chuckles.

"Usually, I'd say you're right, but someone is helping them along, Dad."

"No shit?" he asks, his laughter stopping dead. No pun intended.

"No shit," I reply

"So why were you in jail?" my dad asks, narrowing his eyes on me.

"Because Trent is a moron," my granny answers. I just nod in agreement. It still hurts to talk.

Kane goes to hand me a glass of water with a straw, and I smile my thanks to him. Trent scowls and then bats Kane's hands away. Trent takes the cup, holds it toward me, and places the straw in my mouth so I can take a sip. I can't help but let my heart soften toward him just a bit while also rolling my eyes at him.

"Well, I think you'd better tell me your name, son," my dad says to Trent on a sigh.

"Trent Foyle, sir," he says, extending a hand over me to my dad. "This is my partner, Kane."

"You care for my daughter?" my dad asks as he shakes his hand.

"Yes, sir, I do." Trent nods.

"Military?" my dad asks.

"Was. Now I'm with the San Diego PD," he says. I roll my eyes.

"What branch?" my dad asks, edging closer to Trent. I hold my breath. Uh-oh. Here we go.

"Army," Trent answers. "Rangers." My dad smiles brightly.

"Trent was just leaving," I tell the room on a growl.

"Now, now," my dad says as he waves me off. "Let's not be hasty," he chastises me.

"Okay. I'll go," I say as I start to sit up and rip off the tape holding my IV tubes to my arms. Alarms are going off all over the place.

"What the hell are you doing?" my dad thunders as he turns back to look at me.

"Leaving!" I harrumph.

"Shell . . . ," Trent starts, but I hold up a hand.

"No," I tell him. *Tell them all.* I'm so freaking tired of everyone telling me what to do and where to be. Who to date. Who not to date. I'm. Freaking. Over it. I get that I'm being irrational, but I don't care. It's been a pretty bad week.

"Goddammit, Shelby," Trent thunders, losing his patience with me once again, and we all stop.

"Son . . . ," my dad says softly, but in warning.

"Do you know why I left New Jersey, Shell?" Trent asks me.

"Miss Marla had a bad fall," I say softly.

"No," he says honestly, The pain raw and bare for all to see. "It was the excuse I needed to leave. But I left because my partner got killed," he says softly. I look to Kane, who nods and tells me with his body language to listen. Really listen to what Trent has to say.

"Trent?" I ask.

"Amy and I were working a big drug bust, but it went bad. She always went off half-cocked. Always. She never thought about the dangers. Never stopped to plan anything out. She just went storming in, guns a-blazing. And I loved it about her. She was wild and unafraid of everything. And it got her killed," he tells me.

But I tip my head toward him in confusion. I don't get it. What do I have to do with this Amy? I've never been in a drug bust. Although, never say never. The room is eerily silent, everyone realizing the other shoe was about to drop right on my head.

"Don't you get it? I loved her and she died. She was wild and reckless, *and she died.* And more than anything, you remind me of her." I gasp.

I'm shocked. Oh, shit. I'm not sure we can come back from that one. And here we are once again, at odd ends with each other. Trent didn't seem like he had demons that big, but I guess everyone has secrets. Just look at my relationship with James.

"Trent . . . ," I start, but I don't know how to finish it.

"When I saw you haul through town like your hair was on fire, I thought I'd died. I realized I fell for the exact same girl and I was going to lose all over again," he tells me. My mad is building again. "But I can't live without you, Shell. And I can protect you better if you're with me as much as possible." That. Fucking. Does it.

"Trent . . . ," I say through clenched teeth. "Becasue I feel for you, my heart breaks for you. No woman wants to hear she is exactly like another woman," I say as quietly and calmly as I can. But really, I want to scream at him. And maybe junk-punch him.

"I can see now that my words were wrong . . ." he says hesitantly. "But you're really not like anyone I have ever met before."

"You got that right," I jump in, ripping the tubes from my arm. Shit! That hurt like a motherfucker. "I am so fucking mad at you right now. You broke up with me because, in a crazy moment, I reminded you of your dead girlfriend. In front of both of our grandmothers."

"Yes."

"In front of both of our grandmothers!" I scream. "I could kill you, you asshole!" I shout as I jump from the bed and fall on my face. I'm overcome with the urge to attack, and Trent and Dad seem to see the sparkle of danger in my eyes. Kane just laughs.

"Son, I know that look," my dad says. "You need to either batten down the hatches or run. You might want to choose the latter. She did get the top honor at scout camp for knife-throwing. Six years in a row."

"Knife-throwing? What the hell kind of scout camp was that?" he screams like a girl as he dodges me.

"Zombie apocalypse camp," I grunt as I give pursuit.

"Jesus!" he shouts.

"Oh, she'll test your mettle," my dad says proudly, as if someone just told him I won the Nobel Peace Prize.

"Dead man walking," Kane says and then laughs.

"Stop saying that!" Trent shouts.

He dodges me again, but I'm getting close.

"Give it up, man. Let her cool off."

"I'm not scared like you, you pussy hockey bastard." Trent yelps as I get close.

"This is almost too embarrassing to watch," Granny says from the corner as she files her nails with an emery board.

"It's like a car crash—you can't help but stop and watch," my dad says, his Mississippi drawl deepening with his amusement.

"Now, Jack. Be nice," my mother says. "She's pushing thirty. Do you ever want grandbabies?" she asks him.

"No, I do not! I know where babies come from," Dad thunders. "Have you touched my daughter, Ranger?" Dad growls, and Trent yelps.

I get close again due to Trent's distraction, but he rallies and gains ahead. Trent wisely stays quiet. I get distracted, and Trent doubles back and pounces on me.

"Rangers Lead the Way!" he shouts as he tackles me to the ground.

I'm flat on my back. And naked. Let's not forget the naked. Apparently, I lost my hospital gown when I was on the crazy train. Trent is on top of me, his hands cradling my head, his hips pressed to mine.

"You didn't answer my question, son. You ever touch my daughter?" Dad growls.

"Oh yeah," Granny says absentmindedly, still filing her nails. "They fuck like bunnies."

"Mom!" Dad shouts.

At the same time my mom shouts, "Verna!"

I just sigh. Kane is laughing his ass off. Trent is smiling at me, a twinkle in his eye just for me.

"I love you, Shelby," he says softly.

"Yeah, me too," I sigh as he plants a soft, sweet kiss on my lips. "But you're still a pain in my ass," I tell him.

"Well, this is embarrassing," my dad says. "I can't

believe you let him double back like that. I thought I raised you better," he harrumphs.

"I was a Ranger, sir," Trent says proudly.

"That's nothing on my Shelby," my dad says proudly.

Trent wilts a little bit at that. But his eyes are still glittering with mischief. And . . . other parts of him still haven't wilted.

"You might want to put that away, Ranger," I whisper in his ear.

"Impossible when you're around," he whispers back. "Ready to blow this popsicle stand?" he asks me as he stands up. I instantly burn red, realizing I'm naked, and try to cover up.

"Still not the most embarrassing thing you've ever done, Shell," Granny says from her spot in the corner.

"I'm going to need to hear this story," Trent says as he unbuttons his baby-blue collared shirt and slips it over my shoulders, pulling it closed. He silently gives me what I need without demanding praise.

"Stories, as in plural, more than one," Granny says. "And anytime." She winks wickedly. I would be mad, but I just love her too much.

"Over your dead body, old woman," I growl as I do up the buttons and Trent rolls the cuffs. I take a look at him now that he is in just a white undershirt and jeans. He's so damn handsome. I smile sweetly.

"Sweet baby Jesus, what in the hell happened in

here?" a nurse demands from the doorway. Looking around, I realize Trent and I really turned up the hospital room in our tussle.

"Whoopsies," I say.

"Family matter," my dad says, leaving no room in his tone for questions. "The matter has been handled."

PUSH AND PULL

"Yeah . . . you're going to need to leave," an older doctor with white hair says.

"Um . . . ," I say. I've never been kicked out of a hospital before. But really, when you think about it, it was only a matter of time.

"We'll be moving along as soon as we can, sir," Trent says, flashing his badge. "We just need to make sure Ms. Whitmore is all set."

"It appears to have been anxiety," the doctor tells us. "Are you under a great deal of stress, dear?" he asks me.

"You could say that," I say, narrowing my eyes on Trent. The jerk. He at least has the decency to look embarrassed. I sigh. I can understand where he was coming from. It doesn't mean it didn't hurt or that I have to like it. But I understand.

"Well, I've prescribed some anxiety medication, and you should take it easy for a few days before resuming your normal schedule. But you're free to go," he tells me. "I'll have the nurse bring in your discharge paperwork."

"Thank you," I say before he walks out the door.

"Well, looks like you'll live, kid," my dad says to me as he kisses my forehead. "And you. You take care of my girl. Or else." He points an angry finger in Trent's direction.

"I'm sorry you cut your trip short for me," I say sadly.

"I would do anything for you, Shell." He smiles down at me. "Plus, it's not every day a man finds out his daughter's new man is a Ranger."

"Dad . . ."

"And it's not every day he gets to watch said daughter get the drop on the Ranger." He shines proudly, puffing up his chest. Trent just smiles.

"Daddy . . ."

"It was a proud moment, Shelby," he whispers against the top of my head. "One I'm glad I didn't miss. Next time, take his ass to the ground, not the other way around." Well, there goes our magical family moment. I sigh.

Without another word, my dad pulls me tight to his side for a crushing hug. It hurts him to see me like this, I know. When he releases me, he walks out the door, pulling my mother along behind him.

Mom is different. She knows how strong I can be. How strong I am. She is, too. So are my grandmothers. There are no wilting violets in this crowd. The Whitmore women could take you out and bake a peach pie all at the same time. And we'd have half a mind to do so if you gave us a reason to. I admit, it's a little odd, but it works for us.

"So, are we going to find out what happened to Marla now?" Granny asks from her perch in the corner. I had actually forgotten she was here. And I am embarrassed to say that I forgot about Marla during my life freak-out.

"She's doing much better now," Trent says from his post beside me. "She re-broke her hip when she fell down the stairs, though."

"No, dummies. I mean are we investigating now that Jack and Mary have gone home. I love my son, but he's a stick-in-the-mud." Jesus, take the wheel. What is she talking about now?

"What investigation?" Trent asks.

"Your grandmother's 'fall,'" she says, making air quotes with her fingers.

"Huh?" I ask.

"You really think she fell?" Granny asks Trent.

"Well, yeah. What else could have happened?" he replies.

"Well, for starters, I think you just fell off the turnip truck because what in the world would a woman with a bad hip be doing walking down five flights of stairs?" she asks. Huh? That one is a head-scratcher. Why *was* she in the stairwell? "Can't come up with anything, can you?" she asks as Trent and I stand there mentally scratching our heads.

"Well, you know how stubborn she can be," Trent says, grasping at straws.

"But not as stubborn as me," Granny declares triumphantly. "And not stupid either."

"It's true. Out of the dynamic duo, your grandmother is usually the voice of reason when I can't be present to rationalize why they should or shouldn't do something," I tell him, placing my hand gently on his forearm.

"Huh?" he says. "She never struck me as overly rational."

"This is true, too," I say. And it is, she's not very fond of holding that role. Marla prefers to be in on the action with Granny.

"You know how much she hated hip rehab with all those old fuddy-duddies," Granny says. "What a bunch of squares. And not a one could hold their tequila."

Trent and I both shudder at the memory of our grandmothers trying to instate Shot Night at the physical therapy facility. Needless to say, neither Marla nor Granny is ever welcomed back.

"That is also true," I tell him. "She wouldn't risk breaking her hip again. You know that," I say softly.

"I do," he sighs. "Fuck! I really don't want you guys to be right."

"We don't know anything yet," I tell him gently. "Look on the bright side—we could still be total fuck-ups. So let's go check on your nana." Trent just nods, and Granny hops up from her chair.

Together we tromp through the hospital. Down the hall, up the elevator to ICU, and back down another hall until we stop at a desk and Trent flashes his badge at the nurse. But before we can make our way to Marla, I hear the obnoxious voice of my nemesis, BBN.

"Trent, baby, how are you doing?" she slithers in. "I'm so sorry about your grandmother. I'll do everything I can to make her more comfortable. But I'd love to do whatever you need to make you more comfortable," she purrs as she trails a bloodred talon down his chest. Trent gently grabs her by the wrist just before she hits no-man's-land. I will cut her.

"I think seeing as how my granddaughter is wearing his shirt, and nothing but his shirt, so help me God, it means your services are no longer needed." My granny smiles her winning smile. "And when I say 'nothing,' I mean *nothing*." She winks. Crazy old woman!

"Yeah, what she said!" Not one of my prouder moments.

Unfortunately, I'm basically functioning off of a lot of stress and life revelations. It's all I have left to work with. Trent just smirks. BBN growls but hits the button under her desk that unlocks the door to the Intensive Care Unit.

As soon as we hear the door's lock click, we all take off like we heard the starting shot at the Kentucky Derby. In single file—Trent, then me, and followed up by Granny—we power walk with a purpose toward Marla's room. We look like that scene from the old *Clue* movie. This time, we're the cast of characters racing from room to room to find the killer. If there even is a killer.

But right now it's looking good—I'm about 87.5 percent sure there really is a killer. But it looks like we are just going to have to wait for Marla to wake up and tell us what happened. If she wakes up. She's going to wake up, right? I'm 75 percent sure she's going to wake up. Well, I'm not a doctor. Or a nurse. We should probably find one of those. Shit.

Trent stops outside of a small fake-pine door, and his shoulders hunch up around his ears. I can see how much it hurts him to see his grandmother like this. It is times like these we remember how little time we may have left with them. It's easy to see their crazy adventures day after day and simply think they will live forever, but that's just not the way life works. And Trent and I have already lost our grandfathers. Marla's accident has brought all of these feelings, these emotions, to the surface. Wow, shit just got really heavy in my head.

Trent opens the door, and we all file in. There are chairs all over. One next to the door we just passed through, one in a corner by the TV, and one next to the hospital bed in which Marla is sleeping. She looks so small and fragile. We can all hear the short, deep breath Trent takes. Granny moves to take the chair in the corner, but Trent stops her.

"Go ahead," he says. "You should sit with her. Gossip like you usually do. I think she would like that," Trent finishes softly.

I don't even try to hold back the hot tear that burns down my cheek. Granny just nods her head in acceptance and pats Trent softly on the chest as she passes him. Trent moves to the chair in the corner as Granny slowly lowers herself into the chair that is pulled up next to the bed. And I gently lower myself into the chair by the door, watching, waiting. For something.

"Did you hear Cheryl has the clap?" Granny takes Marla's hand in hers. "I'd ask where she got it, but we all know Charlie boned that skank from the east wing." Trent's eyes have gone round and are as big as saucers. I would laugh, but it's a somber time.

"She's doing what you asked," I whisper. He locks eyes with me, and it takes a minute before he nods and lets Granny go on with her visit.

"And did you know when Walter died, Karen brought Martha a casserole, and she never returned the pan?" Granny says conspiratorially. "And Karen is fit to be tied. But then again, you already knew she had been having an affair with Walter since her own husband had that last stroke."

I shake my head at Granny. She loves to gossip

with Marla. Lives for it, really. And the things these two find out from their friends in the building is kind of alarming. The NSA and the FBI have nothing on these two. I am wondering what else these two know that we don't when Marla interrupts.

"Tupperware," she rasps.

"No, I believe it was CorningWare," Granny says.

"Nana!" Trent jumps up.

"Marla!" Granny and I say at the same time, all of us realizing that she spoke *something*.

"Tupperware," she rasps again, unseeing.

"Nana, can you hear me?" Trent pleads, and it's heartbreaking to watch.

"I'm going to go get the nurse," I say as I start to run out the door. I'm running as fast as I can to the nurses' station, my bare feet sliding on the waxed linoleum floor.

"Nurse! We need a nurse! Marla Foyle. Room three twenty-five!" I pant, out of breath.

The nurse takes off running back toward Marla's room, and I am in hot pursuit. When we get there, Trent and Granny are shaking Marla. Oh, shit. This does not look good.

"It was *Tupperware*!" Marla screeches right before the worst sound I have ever heard, the alarm on her monitors, erupts through the room,

"Everyone out! Now!" the nurse shouts. Then she hits a button on the wall and screams, "Code blue," into the intercom. The room is now full of medical personnel, and we are shoved out into the hall.

"You all have to leave," another nurse says as she slams the door to the room in our faces. You can hear orders being shouted in the room, but I have no idea what they mean.

"Nana!" Trent shouts before he punches the wall.

"Come on, Trent. Let's go sit in the waiting room," I say softly. "Let them do their job, and we'll be here when she wakes up." I lead us into the waiting room, where we conquer new awful plastic seats.

"What if I lose her?" he asks, broken.

"You won't," Granny says. "At least not yet. But we're all going to go sometime, son. And we're old, so it's sooner than most. But she's still got fight in her."

"That's right. Did you hear her argue about brands of food storage with Granny? She'll be fine. You just wait and see." I cross my fingers behind my back, hoping I'm not writing a check I can't cover.

"She is really particular about her food storage," he says with a laugh.

"She really is." Granny nods her head.

"See? Just catch your breath a minute." I squeeze his hand in mine.

"I'm going to go get us all some coffee," Granny says, standing up and stretching. Her small footsteps echo down the hall. There aren't many others in the waiting room, but it's a pretty somber place. My only hope is that Marla can hang in there.

I wrap my arms around Trent and pull him to me. He rests his head on my shoulder while I give him the silent support that he needs. I haven't been easy on him. At all. And while I'm still not sure where we are going, I will do my best from here on out to try to not make things so difficult for him. I'm not going to change who I am, but I'll try not to be so reckless.

"Whoo-whee, this coffee looks like motor oil," Granny says as she carries a tray with three paper coffee cups on it toward where we're sitting. "This looks like the stuff your pop-pop used to make. He swore coffee only tasted good if you could stand a spoon up in it or drink it in the field."

"He did." I smile softly, missing him.

"My gramps, too. He always said it should put hair on your chest and then burn it back off again," Trent says softly. "I thought that was disgusting until I was coming off of a rough op and was dead on my feet. I got a cup of coffee when I made it back to the tent we were using as mission control. It was so thick that it was like drinking mud, but there in the middle of the jungle, it was the best thing I had ever tasted."

I take a deep breath. It's going to be okay because, well, it just has to. We all sit and sip our coffee even though it has long since run cold. No one says a word. A young woman weeps openly in the corner. There is no good news there. But her family is with her. A TV mounted on the wall in the corner is running some twenty-four-hour news channel that I can't be interested in. Suddenly the doors swing open.

"Detective Foyle," the doctor says as he walks into the waiting room.

"That's me." Trent stands, and Granny and I move with him as he walks up to the doctor. Please let this be good news.

"Detective, your grandmother is going to be all right," he says, letting us all take in the good news. Trent squeezes my hand tight. "She's in and out right now, but as you know, a broken hip and a fall like that take a lot of out someone her age. No matter how wily she might be." Trent smirks.

"Clearly, you know my grandmother." He smiles.

"Yes, I have had the interesting fortune to have met her before." He smiles back. "Anyway, she's stable and doing well. You all go on home, and hopefully, she will be up for visitors in the morning. We have your number on file, so if anything changes during the night, we'll call you right away."

"Thank you," Trent says, shaking his hand.

"Anytime. I love giving good news," he says before making his way back behind the big metal doors that separate the patients from their waiting families.

We quickly collect our belongings and head for the hospital's exit. The doors swing open into the crisp night air, and I realize I'm not wearing any clothes. And I have no car.

"Oh. I don't have a car." I cringe, realizing Trent

will probably throw my ass back in jail. Shit. I really don't want to go back to jail. But I also want to see Daisy and make sure she's okay.

"It's okay," Trent says. "I'm taking you both home."

"And by *home*, you mean *not jail*?" I ask, batting my eyelashes. I lean over a bit to give him a better view of the girls in hopes of enticing him into not cuffing me again.

"I mean home. Not jail. I learned my lesson," he says.

"Yippee!" I cheer.

"He means he wants to get laid," Granny says.

"Yes, that. That exactly," Trent says, and I throw my head back and laugh.

We all pile into Trent's Tahoe and head back toward the retirement condos. Everyone is silent in the car until Trent pulls up into the portico in front of the building. We all get out to walk Granny to the door.

"What do you think Marla meant?" Granny turns back and asks us.

"About what?" I reply.

"Tupperware," she says, shaking her head. "She knows Karen only uses CorningWare."

"I think she's out of her head with pain. It's okay to be confused at a time like this," I say softly.

"Huh. I guess you're right, baby." She pats my cheek. "I've got it from here," she says at the elevator. "You be good to each other," she tells us as the doors close.

Trent and I walk quietly back through the sliding front doors and out to the valet stand, where his SUV is waiting. The whole way, we spoke not one word, and Trent never touched me, but I could feel his heat close at my back. He opens the passenger door for me, and I climb in. Trent slams the door and then walks around the hood to the driver's side and hops in.

Trent heads north, but only for an exit or two, before exiting the highway. He is heading to my little condo, not his ranch home in North County. That's okay. I'm not sure what I'm ready for, but I just figured he wouldn't want to be alone tonight. I definitely don't. I should have stayed with Granny.

Trent parks the Tahoe in a miraculously open spot in the parking lot. He turns the engine off and palms his keys. I unbuckle my seat belt and hop out of the car. Without saying a word, Trent walks me around the complex, to my front door. I have no keys; I have nothing. Just Trent's shirt and nothing else. Pervy Steve walks by and waves. I wave back, and Trent groans.

"You collect all the weirdos, don't you?" he grumbles as he unlocks my door with his own key. Convenient. I didn't realize he had that.

"I collected you, didn't I?" I ask sweetly as I walk past him into my condo. Trent swats me on the ass. Not hard, but enough to sting, and I let out a yip as he laughs quietly and follows me inside.

Trent shuts the front door and locks it before turning back to me and looking into my eyes. I feel a little hypnotized every time I stare into those deep green pools. He stalks toward me, slowly crowding me in. I back up and bump against the wall, stopping my progress. Trent keeps moving until there is little space between our bodies. He lifts a hand to gently brush my hair back from where it's fallen into my face, and then he trails his fingers down to cup my cheek. I close my eyes and lean into his touch.

"Please, Shelby," he rasps. "Don't turn me away tonight," he pleads.

"No," I shake my head. "I won't."

Trent scoops me up like a bride and carries me down the hall to my bedroom. He kicks my door softly closed behind him and places me on my feet in front of him. One by one, he undoes the buttons on the front of his shirt and then gently pushes it wide and down off my shoulders. My breath catches in my throat, and I lower my eyelids. Trent's gaze is burning my skin.

I open my eyes when I feel him trail gentle fingers over my body. Down my shoulder. Over my hips and up my sides. He lifts a hand to the back of his neck and pulls off his T-shirt in that sexy way that men do. He places his badge and gun on the bedside table with a clunk. His belt jangles as he unbuckles it and pulls it free of his jeans. Then it hits the bedroom floor with a purpose.

"Lie back," he says as he slowly lowers his zipper. And I do. I *so* do—I crawl onto the bed without another thought and lie back on my stack of pillows.

Trent drops his pants to the floor and steps out of them. The sight of him standing there in his black boxer briefs makes me bite my lip and groan. He quickly pushes those to the floor and climbs in between my legs, resting his bigger, heavier body on mine. I welcome his weight because I know he needs to give it, and I am willing to take it. To take all of the emotions he has bottled up. For now, at least. That last thought is driven out of my head as Trent slowly pushes his cock into me.

Trent leans into me, clenching his eyes closed. I wrap my arms around his neck and my legs around his waist as he pulls almost all the way out and slides back in. He brings his mouth to mine and kisses me. Not softly. But how he needs to. Trent pulls back and then slams back in. Again. And again. I cling to him. I let him have everything, and he takes it.

He's pumping faster and faster as we cling to each other, and there is a burning in my body that is building higher and higher. I close my eyes and arch my head back, but Trent grabs my hair and pulls me forward, taking my mouth, my screams, as I come. He pounds harder and harder until he comes with a roar, and then there is nothing but silence. Blessed silence where we don't have to worry about anything or anyone because, together, we are drifting off to sleep.

LOVE NOTES

The early morning sunshine is shining in my eyes, and the bed is warm and soft. And also, full of man. One big, sexy detective to be specific. I smile as I stretch my arms overhead and wiggle to work the kinks out of my body. Sleeping in my bed is so much better than sleeping on the floor of a jail cell.

“Morning, baby,” Trent rumbles into my hair as his strong arm snakes around my body, pulling me tight to him. I snuggle in deeper for a minute before trying to wiggle my way out of his grasp. Need coffee. Must. Drink. Coffee.

“No. Coffee,” I say as he turns to get a good look at the alarm clock. It’s early and I’m not usually a morning person, but I’m happy. And I’d like to enjoy the morning. But in order to do that, I need coffee.

“Why are you up so early?” he asks me, but I just

shrug. I'm awake and not going back to sleep. It's okay that he wants to, so I tell him so.

"I'm just up. You go back to sleep, though. I'm going to go make some coffee," I tell him.

"Okay," Trent says as he rolls over and buries his face in his pillows.

I hop out of bed and put a smile on my face as soon as my feet hit the carpet. I grab my silk robe with the lace cuffs off the back of the closet door and wrap it around my body. I take a clip from the drawer in the vanity and twist my unruly red hair up into a messy bun on top of my head.

I start to hum "Heartbeat" by Carrie Underwood as I step out of the bedroom and pad down the hallway. By the time I step into the kitchen, I'm hitting the chorus. I head straight for the coffeemaker, which sits on the countertop under the upper cabinets where I keep all of my coffee and mugs. It's also a long arm's reach to the fridge, where I keep my delicious coffee creamer.

I keep singing, giving my very best Carrie effort. I don't care if I'm horrible and Trent hears me. I love singing. Singing makes me happy. And today, I am very happy. I fill the pot with water and pour it into the coffeemaker. I add the coffee grounds to the top, with a little kick ball change in my step. I replace the pot under the spout and hit the go button.

While my coffee brews, I dance around a little bit—okay, a lot—in front of the cabinet as I pull down a mug and get ready. When the first cup or two have brewed, I pull the pot out, and a drop hits the hot bottom with a hiss as I pour myself a giant mug. I put the pot back and grab the creamer from the fridge, all while singing my heart out.

I press pause on my singing to chug a little coffee and then take a deep breath. Today is a good day. I put the coffee creamer back in the fridge and shut the door as I finish my song on a strong point. I turn around to face the day, like I always do, and stop cold in my tracks. My mug shatters on the kitchen floor as I let out another bloodcurdling scream worthy of a *Halloween* movie.

I'm not sure how long I stand there screaming. All I know is that Trent comes running into the kitchen, naked as the day he was born, with his service weapon, a Smith & Wesson M&P, in his hand. What did you think I meant, pervert? It's times like these that I'm glad he has his priorities in check.

"What? What is it?" he barks, taking in the room. I can't get the words out, so I just point to the sliding glass door that leads to my patio, the one covered in blood. "Stay back," he orders. "Did you touch anything?" I just shake my head.

"No," I rasp. I have to clear my throat because it comes out scratchy and makes me cough. "No. I just came in here and made coffee. I turned around and saw it and screamed," I tell him. Trent seems to take in the spilled coffee and shattered glass and my mostly naked self. I'll give him some professional credit because his man parts only twitched a little when he noticed my near nudity. I know I was looking, too.

"Don't move until I can help you around the glass," he says, checking out the security of the house before unlocking his phone and dialing. "This is Detective Foyle. I need a unit," he barks into his phone before giving them my address and hanging up.

"I'll be okay," I say, starting to step around the mess but wincing when I step on a glass shard. I grab some paper towels off the counter by the sink and start wiping up the mess I made. I have to do something.

"I thought I told you to hold still," Trent growls.

"I have to clean this up," I respond, for lack of anything better to say.

"You're bleeding all over," he says as he scoops me up and sits me on the counter. "Stay here." He calls Kane to let him know what's going on as he stomps down the hall.

He returns moments later wearing a pair of worn jeans and carrying a first aid kit. Trent carefully lifts my foot up by the ankle and plucks the glass from my heel. I yelp and try to pull my foot away, but he only holds me tighter.

Once the glass is out and the cuts are all cleaned, Trent wraps my foot up in a bandage. There is a knock at the door, and he strides away to answer it.

"Look who's out of jail already," Kane says with a chuckle. I just flip him the bird. "Can't stay out of trouble, can you?" he asks me with a smile.

"Nope." I pop the *p* sound. "I guess not," I say softly. I shrug, but my heart isn't really in it. Trent growls from beside me. He doesn't like any of this.

"Does anyone know where the fuck that moron she used to date is?" Trent barks. I cringe.

"I really don't think this is James," I tell him.

"Shelby. Now isn't the time to be stupid." I rear back as if he had slapped me. This guts me. This is everything James used to say to me, all rolled into one fat, disgusting mess and dropped into my lap. Every time he told me I wasn't pretty enough. Smart enough. Skinny enough. Fucking blonde enough—I'm a goddamn redhead! It cut deep. And Trent just proved that all men really are the same.

"Stupid?" I ask.

"Oh, shit," Kane mumbles.

"Yeah, stupid," Trent argues. "I know you love him, or *loved* him. Whatever. I don't care. But now is the time to see that there is a serious threat to you on your patio door."

"You don't care," I say.

"Damn," Kane says, wiping his hands down his face.

"I'm going to need you to leave," I say softly but firmly.

"What?" Trent asks.

"Shell . . . ," Kane starts, but I just hold up my hand to stop him.

"No. No more excuses for him, Kane," I say. "Trent, you don't care. I'm tired of not being taken seriously. This is not James. He's an asshole, but he didn't do this. He's not a killer. Just a self-centered, dumb fuck. Which is apparently my type," I finish darkly.

"What the fuck is that supposed to mean?" Trent growls.

"It means you don't care what I have to say. I have been trying to tell you for days that something serious is going on. Your grandmother is lying in a hospital bed, and you are still not listening. I can't help that. But I can control my own life," I finish strongly.

"Shelby," Kane says firmly, "don't do something you'll regret."

"I regret a lot of things these days, Kane. I regret a lot!" I shout.

I limp my way down the hall to my bedroom, where I do my best to keep my tears at bay. I slip off my robe as I look at the rumpled sheets where I spent hours last night, happy with Trent. I pin my hair up on top of my head and slip on panties and a bra. I throw on some black leggings and a purple tank top under an oversized dove-gray sweater. I slip on my gray Chucks and head for the door.

"Where are you going?" I hear over my shoulder from my spot at the door.

"Out," I say as I grab my purse and my keys.

"The hell you are," Trent grumbles.

"What are you going to do? Arrest me again?" I say sharply.

"Maybe," he growls. "Or maybe I'll just handcuff you to my desk so you can't do anything stupid until I catch that moron."

"Trent, maybe we should let her go and cool off," Kane says softly.

"No. She needs to know that men like James kill their partners every day. That he's dangerous," he barks.

"You think I don't know that?" I growl. "I know that. I know what it's like to be cheated on. I know what it's like to be demeaned, and I know what it feels like when his fist crashes into my face. But these threats? That's not him."

"Then what is it?" he growls.

"What you refuse to see," I tell him. "Someone is killing off a bunch of old people, and our grandmothers are asking too many questions."

"Questions?" he all but shouts. "Nana could barely talk about food storage. What the fuck does that have to do with anything?"

"I don't know. But I'm going to find out," I answer decidedly as I toss my purse over my shoulder and palm my car keys. "If you won't leave, I will," I say as I scoop up Missy into my arms and slam the door behind me.

I stalk down my driveway and unlock my car. I flop

into the driver seat and set my oddly fluffy kitty on the seat next to me before I start my car, never once looking around me. Although I can feel eyes on me, I don't know whose they are or where they are coming from, so I just peel out of the driveway and head for the one place I can just be me.

The drive to Granny's place was fairly quick. I somehow managed to avoid a ton of workday traffic. Or I was so lost in my thoughts I must have driven on autopilot all the way to the retirement condo.

I had exited the freeway and navigated the grid of one-way streets downtown. I'd contemplated stopping at my favorite coffee shop, all too aware that I had missed breakfast. And morning sex. But I just couldn't bring myself to do it. I'll see if my grandmother wants to walk to the café down the block from her place.

I slowly turn into the portico in front of my granny's and remember the not-too-long-ago argument I had with Trent over my reckless ways. I thought we had solved some, if not all, of our issues, but now more than ever, I am sure things will never change. I had so much hope for Trent and me. Probably halfway in love with him already and it hurts to think about.

I scoop up my purse and cat and hand my keys to the kid, who's not much younger than me, working valet and head through the automatic sliding front doors of the building. Without a thought in the world, or at least one worth sharing, I walk to the main desk and sign in as a visitor. If the attendant says hi to me, I don't notice. I walk down the hall with a cloud over my shoulder and stab the call button for the elevator. The ride up is oppressively silent, and I feel the scowl on my face deepen as I ring the doorbell.

"Well, hey, baby." She smiles at me as she answers the door. "I sure didn't expect to see you," she says as she takes in my slumped shoulders and sullen mood.

"Hey, Granny." I try to muster up a smile. And fail. "Can I come in?" I ask her.

"Sure, baby." She opens the door and lets me in.

We both just stand there for a minute, not sure what to say to each other—Granny worrying about Marla and who killed Bitty Sue, and me not knowing how to resolve my feelings for Trent.

"Want some coffee?" she asks me.

"Yeah." I nod. "I dropped mine on the floor when I saw the blood on my door. Things kind of went sideways on me from there," I tell her as I sit down, hugging Missy to my chest.

"Well . . . ," she starts. "Well, the truth is, I'm not quite sure what to say in response to that this morning. So let's get some coffee and sit down, and you can tell Granny what's going on." She squares her shoulders.

"I'm not really sure where to start," I admit weakly.

"You start at the beginning." She looks me square in the eye. "We'll figure it out from there," she says. And she's right. We'll figure it out together. For the first time since I left my condo this morning, I take a deep breath.

Chapter THIRTEEN

DEATH THREATS AND DEVIOUS DAMES

I'm sitting here, in my granny's living room, staring into this tea and wishing for whiskey. How do you tell your beloved yet crazy grandmother that you either have a crazy ex, which is true, who is leaving you death threats, which is unlikely, or that the crazy, cooked-up scheme of someone killing off the old people in their retirement village is more real and less cooked-up crazy than you had originally thought? Oddly, it's more likely than my douche canoe of an ex leaving me morbid gifts. And that is using the term pretty fucking loosely.

"Jesus fucking Christ, Shelby Lynn!" she snaps. "Just say the words. You're scaring me."

"Okay," I say. Granny just nods, waiting for me to begin. "So . . . last night, I ended up with Trent," I start. Granny just sits there and smiles.

"I'm glad you guys worked it all out, baby," she says sweetly. "You scared me there for a minute." She lets out a relieved sigh.

"Well . . . I'm not quite done yet," I say.

She hesitates. "Okay."

"So last night, I ended up with Trent," I start again. "At my house."

"I'm glad you two are back together."

"I didn't say that either," I tell her. "We're . . . what we are is . . . we're the Yalta Conference right now. The war is mostly over, and now there are talks of rebuilding. But we're not sure where to go with that, and we're not even in agreement on which direction to go in. Does that make sense?" I ask.

"No, that does not fucking make sense," Granny snaps. Sheesh, that's a lot of F-bombs for the mid-morning hour.

"Well, Trent wants to pick right back up where we left off . . ."

"And let me guess—you're not so sure?" she growls.

"Um . . . no?"

"Goddamn it, Shelby!" she thunders for such a tiny woman.

"I know. I know. I'm sorry," I say, trying to placate her.

"Well, you damn well should be. You know he's not that limp-dicked little weasel you used to date.

Thank God for that!"

"I know. I know. That's why I let him come home with me," I say.

"Are you sure that's all, or could there be some more lead pipe where that came from? I heard there are about nine inches of pipe . . . ," she hints with a raised brow.

"I am not having this conversation with my grandmother!" I shout back, but I can feel my face burning. And the knowing smile on her face tells me she caught me.

"And why the hell not?" She laughs. "I'm older and wiser and closer to meeting God, so I have all the answers." I sigh.

"I said he came home with me, okay?" I grate. Her forced obtuseness is frustrating this morning.

"No, but it'll do." She smiles.

I know that it's now or never, so I decide the best course of action is to just spit all the rest of it out, kind of like vomit or diarrhea. This is diarrhea of the confessional variety. Yeah, that's it.

"So then, this morning, I got up to make some coffee while Trent was still in bed and I saw a mean message stuck to the slider in blood and screamed and Trent came running naked with a gun and then the cops showed up and he called me stupid so I might have broken up with him again and came right over here. Now you know everything," I say and then take a deep breath. "Whew, I feel much better with that off my chest. Ready to go to lunch?" I ask her.

"Not. So. Fast, young lady." She narrows her eyes at me. My palms and pits start to sweat. My face is burning red. This is not a good sign. "You might have broken up with him?"

"I don't know what you're talking about," I state firmly to the spot just over her left shoulder.

Unfortunately, I have a history with her wooden spoon, and now I'm afraid to lie while looking into her eyes. It's like the eye in the Indiana Jones ride at Disneyland. Don't look into her eyes, or else you'll face certain doom. And death. Can't forget the death part!

"Shelby!"

"Okay! Okay!" I jump. "He freaked out and yelled. I was already freaked out and had yelled. He called me stupid. I told him he was an asshole, and then I left. All right?"

"For now." She smiles. "Now, let's go get some lunch at the café."

I smile as I hold the front door open for my granny. She smiles back at me sweetly, and I think, *Everything just might be okay*, when the moment is broken by my cell phone playing a Rhianna tune. I have no shame in the fact that my music choices tend to reflect my mood. I pull my phone out of my purse and answer.

"Hello?"

"Giirrrrlll," Daisy greets me, loud enough for Granny to overhear. "I'm out! Where you at?"

"Well, I was about to grab a sandwich at the café around the corner from my granny's place and then try to figure out why my life is such a steaming shit show," I tell her.

"You know I love my girl, but you're a red-hot mess," she declares. I nod because, well, it's true.

"Mm-hmm," Granny agrees.

"Hey," I say in my own defense. It's one thing for me to agree in my head, but it's another for all of the people in my life to gang up on me.

"You going to the café in the strip mall?" she asks.

"Yeah," I say, wondering where this is going.

"I'll be there in five." And then she hangs up. What the hell just happened?

"We'd better double-time if we're going to meet your friend there in five," Granny tells me while I just stand there catching flies. "Move, Shelby!"

I squeak and then hustle out the door after my wayward grandmother to go have lunch with her and my new hooker friend. Because that's not at all weird. Well, for normal people it might be, but for us, it's a regular Tuesday.

"I think I like her," Granny says when she sees Daisy jumping up and down and waving at us. Today she is wearing a fluorescent pink pair of leggings and matching sports bra, which is stretched to its max by her ample bosom. Granny and I both look down at our own fairly substantial chests, but in this moment, we both find them sorely lacking.

"I really like her, too," I say as we walk up to the table.

"I already got us waters and bread because you can never go wrong with the bread here, but I didn't know if you were soda or iced tea drinkers. Anyhoo, here are your menus. Now sit down and introduce me to your granny."

"She's awesome," Granny breathes like she just met The Beatles on their first American tour.

"Granny, this is my friend Daisy," I say. "Daisy, this is my granny, Verna."

"I'm really sorry to hear about your friend Marla." She smiles sweetly at Granny.

"Thank you, dear," Granny tells her. "She's going to be just fine as soon as we catch her would-be killer."

Crap.

"Would-be killer? There's a killer on the loose?" she questions me. I kind of just nod. I'm a little scared of how this might go, and Trent and I are already on thin ice with one another.

"Kind of?" I hedge.

"You didn't tell me someone tried to bump off the good detective's granny!" she shouts. "So what are we going to do about it?"

"Catch the bastard!" Granny cheers.

"I'm in," Daisy agrees as if that settles things. I am so fucked.

"Oh, shit," I mumble.

"Don't mumble, dear. It's unattractive," Granny chastises. "Now, where did you two meet?" she asks Daisy and me.

"In the pokey," Daisy says.

"Fantastic! I can't wait to hear all about it." She claps. "So, have you guys tried the french dip here?" she asks as she moves on to her lunch order.

"Shit."

"You already said that, dear."

"What's up, old people? And not-so-old people?" Harmony cheers as she walks into the room.

As it turns out, lunch went so swimmingly that Granny invited Daisy back for some Advanced Senior Yoga. So here we all are in matching shimmery leggings and sports bras—each set, a different color. Daisy in pink, Granny in purple, and me in an emerald green. We are a sight to see.

We slide off our sneakers and sandals and unroll our yoga mats in a row. One by one, we all stand on the edge of our mats, toes pointed forward.

"Let's start off with some deep breathing, friends," Harmony says soothingly as she leads us in breathing exercises with our eyes closed.

I breathe in and out, roll my head around on my shoulders, and feel the weight of the world seep from my shoulders. This is why I love yoga. There is nothing else that makes me feel more relaxed or centered. I tried jogging, but it didn't stick. I mean, with these boobs, there's no way I can jog without getting a black eye.

I take a slow, deep breath in and circle my arms up overhead. I hold in that breath. I'll push it out when I bend forward. This stretch takes the rest of my worries and puts them away for another day. I keep my eyes closed and smile to myself as I arch my back and then straighten up again. I take in another slow, deep breath and repeat the movement. I'm halfway standing when I hear a bunch of wolf whistles and catcalls. The muscles in my back and shoulders immediately tighten back up. That level of old-lady enthusiasm can only be caused by one thing. By one completely annoying man. *Trent,* I think as I clench my teeth.

"Hey now!" I hear him gripe. "No pinching, Mrs. Murphy!" I hang my head and sigh to myself. "Goddammit! Ouch, that hurts!" I hear him whimper.

"Good one, Mrs. Murphy!" Harmony calls out. "I don't tolerate late arrivals to my class, Detective."

"I know, and I am sorry," he apologizes. "I just need to speak with Shelby."

"I'm not so sure about that," she says softly. "Rumor has it you weren't very nice to our Shelby."

You can actually hear Trent grinding his teeth.

"We've had a series of miscommunications," he says diplomatically.

"Okay," she says after a moment of consideration. "You can speak to Shelby here, now, in front of all of us. And if you fuck it up, I'm going to sic the old people on you. And trust me, they can be mean," she says as she nods her head, kind of like a hippieish, pot-smoking mafia don.

We all know that's as good of an option Trent is going to get from her. And damn, who knew Harmony has such a badass side. It must be suppressed by all the yoga and pot.

"Damn, I think I like her." Daisy snickers beside me.

"I know, right?" Granny answers from her other side. I roll my eyes.

"Shush, you two," I admonish.

But it only serves to draw Trent's attention to me. He does a double take when he sees Granny, Daisy, and me in our coordinating outfits and then tries to suppress a grimace.

"Jesus," he mumbles when his eyes coast up and down over my body.

I'm thinking it means he likes what he sees. Mostly. Well, he can keep on looking. I stand up straight and cross my arms over my chest, but it only pushes my breasts up higher. I see his Adam's apple bob. His lack of concentration makes me roll my eyes again.

"Trent." I snap my fingers in front of his face. He shakes off his daze and moves toward me with sure strides of his strong legs. Sexy legs, legs that I've seen naked. Jesus, now who's distracted?

"Shelby," he says when he stops in front of me. "Please don't run off like that again." I want to roll my eyes, but I don't.

"What you said this morning was mean, Trent."

"I know," he says roughly before clearing his throat and running his hand through his dark hair. "When I heard you scream, I lost it. The message, the blood, it scared the shit out of me. And I took it out on you."

"Don't do that."

"I won't," he says quickly. "I promise."

"Don't promise," I say. "Just . . . try your best." I sigh.

"Okay."

"Okay?" I ask.

"Okay," he smiles. "Now come here and kiss me, woman," he demands.

"No," I say as I take a step back.

"Don't. Run," he snaps.

"I would never," I say as I cross my heart and then turn and run. I only make it about three more steps before he swoops me up over his shoulder and swats me on the ass. Hard!

"Eep!" I squeal.

"Good afternoon, all. We'll see you around." He laughs as he strolls through the door.

Just as the door to the gym room where yoga class is held snicks closed, Trent stops his steps and slides me down his body. Slowly. I can feel every dip and ridge as I slither along his body. And there are some pretty good ones.

"Don't be mad at me, baby," he says as he traces my temple with his fingertips. "If I'm guilty of anything, it's of caring too much."

"I know, but don't ever call me stupid," I tell him. I see that he's confused, and I guess I can give him a little piece of me. "When I was a kid, I had a hard time in school. One afternoon, my teacher told my mom, in front of me, that I was hopeless, that I would never amount to anything. She went as far as to call me stupid. And I was devastated. It turned out I'm dyslexic, but that didn't stop her words from hurting. And James would do it too. 'Oh, it's so cute when you say something stupid, babe,' or 'You're just too stupid to understand what I'm telling you.' I hate that shit."

"Honey," he starts.

"No, it's okay. I'm tougher now. But I won't take words like that from you," I tell him honestly.

"It's not okay," he tells me softly. "I keep telling you that I am nothing like that jackass James, and what do I do? I hurt you anyway. I can only promise to be more careful of your feelings in the future."

"Okay," I say.

"Okay." He smiles and inches a little closer.

Our bodies are brushing each other. Life with Trent is a little crazy, but the making-up part is definitely nice. He leans in and puts his mouth on mine. It's gentle and sweet at first, but it quickly picks up in heat.

I gasp, and his tongue slides into my mouth as he skates his thumb over my nipple. I arch into him, and he smiles against my mouth. Trent slides his thigh in between my legs, and I shamelessly rub myself against him.

I wrap my arms around his neck and pull him back down to my mouth. I kiss him greedily. I don't like to fight with him. I groan into his mouth as he pinches my nipple between his thumb and index finger. I grind harder on Trent's thigh. Anyone could be in this hallway, but I just don't care. I'm that close. But Trent eases up, slowing his kisses from passionate to less frenzied to soft and sweet again. His hands come up to cup my face, and his knee falls away.

My brain is foggy, my nipples are hard, and my panties are wet when Trent pulls pack and kisses me on the nose before smiling down at me. Um, what now?

"I'll see you later, babe. I'm glad we had this talk," he says before walking away. Well, this just got awkward.

I shake my head like an Etch A Sketch to clear my

thoughts and then turn around and walk back into the gym room and rejoin the class. Apparently, Trent and I made out in the hallway like a couple of horny teenagers for a while, because the class is half over. Granny and Daisy give me knowing smirks, but I just shrug it off. Why lie? We finish out the class a lot less exciting than last time, not because Trent and I are old news, but because it wasn't Chili Tuesday. Before we know it, class is over and we're all heading back up to Granny's condo to shower and dress for dinner.

After we are all showered and dressed, we walk arm in arm, like the opening credits of *Laverne & Shirley,* into the dining room. We luck out and get another great table by the window overlooking the harbor. It makes me wonder if Granny's got some kind of illegal sports-betting or something going on with the staff who work here.

The wine is flowing greatly, mainly because Granny snuck two extra bottles into the restaurant, in her massive purse. Everyone who works here turns a blind eye. It makes me more and more certain she's selling pot or something on the side. I'll have to ask my mom about this now that she's back home.

Dinner was a fabulous roast chicken and mashed potatoes with chocolate mousse and coffee for dessert. I loved it and I'm stuffed. It's one of the menu secrets I have yet to teach Trent. If you order the roast chicken, you actually get a chicken. But the best part was that no one talked about murder or death threats or even my *whatever this is* with Trent. We just laughed until we cried.

After dessert, I excuse myself to the ladies' room. I study myself in the mirror, and for the first time in a long time, I look happy. Sure, there's still bruising on my face, but it's yellowed enough that I can cover it up with more concealer than a tub of Spackle.

I can't help but feel like maybe Trent is right. Maybe, just maybe, he'll find James and this whole nightmare will be over. Surely, that's it. But why would he hurt Marla or Bitty Sue? I sigh to myself. It just doesn't make any sense. But I'm not about to ruin a lovely evening over things I can't change today.

I resolve to enjoy my evening and then go home to snuggle with my adorable kitty. I walk out of the restroom and turn the corner. Just out of my view are two men talking. They can't see me, and I can't see them except for the sleeve of one of their coats, identifying at least him as a doctor. But I hear them. I flipping hear them. And the words the one speaks make my blood run cold.

"Their deaths are a mercy," he says softly to his companion.

Chapter Fourteen

MERCIES AND BULLSHIT

"Their deaths are a mercy," he says softly to his companion. I cover my mouth with my hand to hide my gasp.

"You can't be serious," the friend says, surprised, voicing my own opinions.

He can't really be serious. I mean, these are people. These people have families who care about them. Well, maybe not the old man in apartment 1215 because he's kind of an asshole and a bigot, but the rest of them are decent people.

"Of course I am." I can hear the censure in his voice toward his friend. "These people are suffering. Every one of them has lived so long that their bodies can't keep up. Just look around you—cancer, Alzheimer's, you name it, it's here. Can you really tell me that it's fair to make them live like that?" he asks.

"No, but still—"

"No buts about it," he interrupts his companion. "I honestly feel like it's the best thing."

In that moment, I see red. This asshole doesn't get to decide for the people who live here. He doesn't get to play God. So I do exactly what I promised Trent I wouldn't do. I launch myself from my hiding spot and onto the good doctor's back.

"What the hell?" his friend shouts.

"You don't get to decide who lives and who dies, asshole," I grunt from behind as I grapple with the big jerk.

"Get off me, you psycho!" he shouts as he tries to pull me over his shoulder.

I wrap my left leg around his waist and my arms around his head, pulling his hair. When he tries to pull me over his shoulder, my right leg wraps around his arm, pinning it away from my body. He slams my back against the wall, and I let out a grunt but still hang on.

"Shelby, what's happening?" Granny shouts as she casually approaches the scene like I attack doctors every day. "I know you're mad at Trent, baby, but this isn't the way to get a date."

"I don't want a date!" I shout, grappling to stay on as the devil doctor swings wildly trying to buck me off of his back. "This is him!"

"Jesus, she's crazy!" the friend shouts.

"She sure is," Granny cheers. "She gets it from

me," she says proudly, jerking a thumb back toward her chest.

"And I'm not dating her!" he shouts as he rams me into the wall again. I let out an *oompf.* "I'm gay!"

"And married!" his friend shouts. "To me!"

"For fuck's sake, someone call the cops!" the doctor shouts.

"Already on the way," someone calls out.

I don't know how long we fight each other. He manages to stay upright, and I manage to stay on his back to the tune of Granny's and Daisy's cheers. One minute, I think I'm gaining the upper hand, and the next, I'm being pulled from the doctor.

"Hey, wait!" I shout.

"How did I know that you would be involved when the call came over dispatch?" Trent sighs. I just hang my head.

"I want to press charges!" the doctor shouts.

"Good luck, buddy." Kane laughs.

"You can't press charges! You're a murderer," I announce, throwing my hands up in the air.

"What?" Granny shouts.

"I overheard him tell his friend that he was killing the residents as a mercy!" I shout to the dining room.

"I did not!" he growls. "I said death was a mercy for the infirm."

"Sure, buddy, sure you did." I nod. "Cuff him,

Trent," I demand, pointing to the doctor.

"I'm not killing people!" He panics, wild-eyed, looking all around the room for anyone who will help him. But the natives are turning savage at the thought that one of their caretakers possibly killing them off.

"Then who is?" I shout, pointing my finger at him.

"God? I don't know, but it isn't me!" he screams.

"Where were you when Bitty Sue died?" I ask.

"At dinner with me," the friend tells me.

"And you are?" I question.

"His husband."

Well, that answers that. I was pretty sure from the previous conversation, but now I know for certain.

"Hey, that means he's—" Granny starts down one of her tangents, and all I can think is, *Oh, fuck*. This is not going to end well if we follow her down the rabbit hole.

"Not now, Granny!" I cut her off, afraid of what might come out of her mouth.

"And when Marla was pushed down the stairs?" I ask quietly. But I'm already losing momentum.

"Why would I push her down the stairs?" He sighs. "Breaking her hip again is causing more suffering, not ending it. If I was mercy-killing, I wouldn't be prolonging their suffering, now would I?"

Shit. I fucked up. *I really, really fucked up.* I look up at the doctor and his husband and see that they both look tired but not angry anymore. I happen a glance at Trent, and he does not share their emotions.

"I'm sorry," I say. "I shouldn't have jumped you like that."

"It's okay. I would be mad, too. My mother-in-law is in the Alzheimer's unit here. We hate that she's suffering, but we live for every last moment we have with her," he says as he pulls his husband close.

"It's why we have dinner here so many nights a week," the husband says. Shit. Now I feel really bad.

"I'm so, so sorry," I say, tears burning my eyes. "I was wrong."

"It's okay. Let's hug it out," they say, and all is forgiven. I smile, about to go back to dinner with Granny and Daisy.

"Not so fast, Shelby," Trent growls. *Uh-oh.*

"Oh, I'll catch you later," I say, trying to evade and escape.

"Yeah, no."

"Tuesday?" I ask. "I can pencil you in." *A quarter to never.*

"Shelby."

"Okay, Wednesday night," I plead. *I'll be in Mexico under an assumed name.*

"Shell."

"March, maybe . . ." *Jesus, take the wheel! I need to get out of here.*

"Now." The way he growls the one word sends shivers down my spine. I'm in trouble with a capital *T*. Dead meat. Dead girl walking. Fuck my life. I sigh. It's over. That's all she wrote. The fat lady sang, and now it's time for me to reap what I sow.

"Okay," I say.

EVADE, ESCAPE, AND HIDE FROM FUCKING TRENT

I drag my feet like a convicted killer on their way to the electric chair as I follow Trent out of the dining room. Granny and Daisy wear expressions of surprise and defeat. Even they know how screwed I am. I can almost picture them kissing their fingers and giving me the *Hunger Games* salute . . . Oh wait, they are.

"Jesus Christ, she's not headed to the gallows," Trent thunders. "And thanks for your vote of confidence, by the way."

"Whoops," I say, wide-eyed.

"Yeah, 'whoops,'" he sighs and then grabs me by the hand and leads me from the room.

Trent guides me through the building, to the elevator, down to the first floor, and through to the portico, where his Tahoe is waiting. He waves to other officers who leaving the building after the misunderstanding.

Trent opens the passenger door for me before gently hoisting me up into the seat and then buckling my seat belt for me. And I find myself nose to nose with the man that drives me crazy in more ways than one.

Coming to some decision, Trent nods once and then shuts my door before walking around to the driver's side and hopping in. The rest of the drive is silent, neither of us willing to give an inch in this moment. That is, until I realize he had passed the exit for my condo and is still heading north on I-15 toward his Escondido home.

"Um, where are you going?" I ask.

"Home," is all I get from him.

"Whose home?" I ask, but he just grunts.

"I really need to be getting back to feed Missy." I grasp at anything to get me out of this awkward moment.

"I already picked her up. She's at home and fed. Happily watching the birds in the yard," he tells me as if he doesn't have a care in the world. Bastard. I see his lips twitch as he watches me.

"I see," I say, folding my arms.

"Don't be mad," he sighs. "I already wanted to spend tonight with you where you couldn't hide, and I like the little creep."

"She's not a creep!"

"She's a little creepy." He shrugs. "At least she didn't claw the shit out of me like she did Kane," he says with a laugh.

"Humph." He just laughs at me.

"We're here," he says as the car pulls to a stop in his driveway.

"Okay," I say, unbuckling my seat belt.

Quietly we walk side by side to the front door. Trent lets us both in, and I feel awkward. I don't really know where we stand, and I hate it. I hate this. I swore to myself that I would never let a man make me feel unsure of myself, not ever again.

"Hey," he says softly, gently touching my cheek with his fingertips. "You're safe here. You'll always be safe with me, Shelby."

"Okay." I nod, my arms crossed over my belly. I'm still unsure. Trent hasn't given me the best show of being safe with him.

"I guess that's not true, is it?" he asks. I tip my head in confusion. "You haven't been safe with me. I let my past and my insecurities hurt you again and again. And that wasn't fair."

"No," I whisper. "It wasn't," I say, clearing my throat.

"I promise that going forward I will do my very best to protect your heart and respect your feelings," he says as he brushes loose hair from my face.

"Okay," I say, looking into his bright green eyes.

Trent is laid bare to me. He's vulnerable to me. And Trent is not a man to be made vulnerable. He is now because he wants to be. For me. Those emotions cut me to the core. If there was ever a man that I could trust again, it would be Trent. But make no mistake, I will not take his shit again.

His eyes close and his nostrils flare at my capitulation. He tips his head back on his shoulders and basks in his triumph for a moment. When he opens his eyes, he drops his lips to mine. My eyes stay open as I watch him watch me.

He releases me only to scoop me up into his arms like a bride. I can't help but feel cherished, loved. Trent walks slowly to his bedroom, where he lays me delicately on his bed before kicking off his shoes. He walks into his closet, and I hear the beeps of the buttons and the tumble of the locks on his safe. When he comes back, Trent is without his sidearm.

I watch him with rapt attention as he drops his wallet and badge onto his dresser before stalking back to me like a lion. He kneels beside me on the bed and traces a delicate hand down the side of my head and over my hair before leaning in to kiss me again. But this time is different. Not a meeting of the mouths, but so much more. I can't help but open up to him.

Trent covers me with his body as he lazily kisses and nips at my mouth. I whimper and moan as he drives my need for him higher and higher, but no prodding can make him go any faster. I grip the back of his T-shirt in my hands and slowly drag it up his body. Trent is forced to break away from my mouth to pull his shirt over his head.

He sits up on his knees and lets me get my fill of looking at his strong chest and chiseled abs. I have to bite my lip to stay still as Trent looks me in the eyes while he unbuckles his leather belt and pulls it free from the loops of his jeans before dropping it to the floor. The clank of the buckle as it hits the hardwood planks makes me groan. Trent smirks at my reaction.

Since the weather had turned cold, I'm wearing black leggings and a chunky gray cowl-neck sweater. The sweater is the first to go as Trent pulls it over my head. His eyes darken when he sees me lying there waiting for him in my black lace bra and leggings, patent leather ballet flats still on my feet.

Trent leans forward and sucks my nipple into his mouth, the lace of my bra abrading the sensitive peak. I tip my head back and close my eyes as I squirm underneath him. Trent lets me go before scooting back on his heels. One by one, he plucks my shoes off of my feet and carelessly tosses them over his shoulder, which makes me laugh.

He reaches for me again and hooks the waistband of both my leggings and my panties in his hands and slowly, oh-so-slowly, pulls them down my legs and tosses them to the floor. All laughter from earlier stops abruptly in my chest.

Trent leans down over my body, his arms caging me in as he slides his cock through my wetness. I gasp as the tip nudges me. I wrap my arms around Trent's neck and pull him down to me, his mouth on mine. I kiss him greedily, deeply, letting my tongue invade his mouth as his cock slowly slides into my center.

I run my hands over the sculpted muscle of Trent's shoulders and back as he glides in and out, back and forth, our mouths never leaving each other's, as he slowly, reverently, makes love to my body and cherishes me.

A climax sneaks up on me, rolling over me like waves, and my mouth breaks free from Trent's so I can cry out. He tosses his head back as he pumps in one more time and follows me over the edge.

Trent rolls us so that he's on his back and I'm lying across his side. Our legs are tangled together. And as our breathing slows, we both drift off to sleep, me surrounded by Trent.

It's still dark out when my eyes open. Just a few hours ago, Trent asked for everything and I happily handed it all over to him. But now that I have a moment to collect my thoughts, I wonder if anything has really changed.

I look at the clock, and it's five in the morning. I'm going to need to get to work, and then I'm also going to have to find a way to covertly help Granny track down a killer. None of these are things I can do with Trent's cock poking me in the ribs.

I gently pull free from his hold and look down at

him as he sleeps. He's so beautiful. And if I'm being honest, I have more than a little fallen for the big bastard. I brush his hair back from his face and smile at him. Too bad I have to trick him.

I throw my clothes on quickly before going into the kitchen to search for a pad and pen. I leave him a quick note next to the coffee pot, which I dutifully fill and set to brew like a nice girlfriend would.

I scoop up my purse and dig my phone out. Missy pads into the kitchen, and I pluck her up and hug her to my chest as I dial the number of the only person I know who will help me out in this situation. It rings twice before the person I'm calling picks up.

"Hey, Daisy. I need you to pick me up and be quick about it," I whisper into the phone before hanging up to wait for our getaway car.

I have Daisy drop Missy and me off at Granny's condo for two reasons: my car is there, and Granny and I need to get serious about getting some concrete evidence because the death threats are getting a little old.

Granny, having always been an early bird, is up when I quietly knock on her door. I can smell the coffee brewing in her kitchen, and I smile at her when she opens the door.

"Everything all right, Shell?" she asks me.

"Yes, Granny, everything is fine." I smile at her. "But we've got to get to work, so I gave Trent the slip this morning."

She just sighs, but then her eyes light up when she realizes we're about to investigate.

"Look out, the Dangerous Dames are on the loose! Let's have breakfast and then call Daisy," she cheers.

Granny and I have showered, dressed, and consumed a large amount of coffee by the time Daisy swings by to pick us up. She takes the turn into the portico on two wheels, and for the first time, it dawns on me that I might be the voice of reason in this outfit . . . or any outfit.

"Get in, bitches! We're going investigating!" she shouts as she rolls down the window and hits the door locks.

"Shuuush!" I growl. "The last thing I want is for it to get around to Trent that we're poking our noses into things we most definitely should not be."

"Where's your sense of adventure, Shelby?" Granny admonishes. I sigh.

"I'm sorry . . . ," I say, but I'm interrupted by my phone ringing. I look at the display. It's Trent calling. "Jesus Christ, he knows!" I shout, dropping the phone as it fumbles from my grasp. My palms are sweating so profusely. I don't think I'm cut out for this shit.

"He doesn't know," Granny says, trying to placate me. "Just act cool." Famous last words.

"Yeah, listen to your granny," Daisy agrees. "Just be cool."

"Okay, act cool. I can act cool," I say to myself before freaking out. "I have never been cool!" I snap.

"We're screwed," they both sigh.

I ignore them and answer my phone. "Hello?"

"Don't do that again," he growls. Shit!

"Do what?" I ask, praying he doesn't have a narc at the old folks' home.

"Leave!" he thunders.

"But I left you a note," I say softly.

"You what?" he asks after a beat.

"I left you a note," I explain calmly.

"Where?" he demands. I'm not quite sure he trusts me yet either.

"I left it in front of the coffeemaker. There's fresh coffee for you, by the way."

"You made me coffee, baby?" His voice is a soft rumble, sexy.

"Yeah," I say with a smile. "How come you didn't see it?"

"I'm still in bed," he says, and I groan.

"Mm-hmm," I purr.

“Yeah, I wish you were here, too,” he says with a chuckle. “I just saw that the bed was empty, and I thought you bolted.”

“I didn’t. I have to work,” I lie. Sort of. I do have obits to write up.

“Okay, well, I’ll let you get to it,” he says.

“You too.” I smile to myself.

“And, Shelby,” he calls me back.

“Yeah, Trent,” I breathe.

“Stay close to Daisy and Verna today. James is in the wind.”

My breath catches in my throat. He’s gone. James is a madman, and they don’t know where he is. I know without a doubt that he will come for me. Maybe Trent is right and it is James threatening me.

“Okay. Let me know when you find him?” I ask.

“Of course, babe.”

“Be safe,” I say to him like I do it every day. And I can already tell that I will. I can hear the smile in his voice when he responds.

“I will. I love you, Shelby.” And then he hangs up.

It’s going on ten in the morning by the time we pull into the parking lot of the hospital after having swung through a Starbucks drive-through. It’s a many-cups-of-coffee kind of a day.

We all file out of Daisy's car. I turn to take a look at it. It's pretty nice, it's new, and it smells good. Maybe I should consider hooking. That probably wouldn't make Trent too happy, though, so I let the thought go.

We go up to Marla's room, and she's awake but on a pretty heavy stream of morphine. I'm not so sure we'll get anything good out of her. Or if we'll be able to use it even if we do.

"Hey, girl. It's me, Verna," Granny says cheerily as she sits down by her side. "I've brought Shelby with me. She and Trent have buried the hatchet." Marla smiles at that.

"Hey, Miss Marla. How are you feeling?" I ask.

"I'm good." She smiles. "How are you at making my grandbabies?" I laugh at her.

"Judging by the way she looked when I picked her up from his house this morning, I'd say she's pretty damn good," Daisy confides.

"This is my friend Daisy," I tell her. "She came to help you feel better."

"And she's a hooker!" Granny claps.

"That's fantastic news." Marla smiles drowsily.

"Y'all are weird, but I like it." Daisy smiles beautifully. "It's a pleasure to meet you."

"We came to ask you some questions about your fall," I say to Marla but regret it when her smile falls from her face.

“Fall?” she asks.

“You fell down the stairs in your building,” I say softly.

“No!” she gasps. “I was pushed.”

You could hear a pin drop in the room. We were all so focused on Marla and her answers, hoping she could give us the ones that we need.

“Pushed?” Granny asks.

“Yes!” she cries, getting herself worked up. “You have to find him.”

“We will, we will,” Granny says, comforting her as she pats her hand.

“Can you tell us who it was that pushed you?” I gently prod.

“Yes! It was Tupperware.” She panics. “He stole my Tupperware,” she says, obviously confused.

It’s just as I thought. The morphine has her too bombed to give us any real answers. For all we know, she really did just have a horrible accident. But one thing is certain: we won’t know anything until the drug-induced fog clears from her brain and she can tell us for sure.

“He stole your Tupperware?” Granny asks, concern evident in her voice.

“No, that’s not right, is it?” she asks, scared as a rabbit.

“It’s okay, honey,” Granny says, soothing her. “You just need some rest, and you’ll feel right as rain.”

"Yes, rest. Okay." She calms as she lies back in her bed.

"Let's go, girls. She needs her rest," Granny orders, and we follow her out to the car. We drive back to her condo, more concerned than ever.

TRAPPED IN THE CLOSET, PART 2

After a somber lunch where no one spoke, we decided to part ways for the rest of the afternoon. Daisy left to go hunt down Jones, claiming that life was too short to wait for him to make a move. Granny was obviously depressed, so I walked her back to her apartment and made her a cup of tea before she told me to go to work. I tried to argue, but she assured me that she was fine.

I have a lot on my mind, so I decide to take the stairs instead of the elevator. I need to clear my head before I can start putting the facts together, so I pop in my earbuds and key up one of my favorite songs, "Ignition" by R. Kelly. It always puts me in a good mood.

I pull the door to the stairwell open and bounce and bop along with the music. One minute, I'm walking down the stairs of the building my granny lives in, singing "Ignition," and I had just gotten to the good part, you know, the "hot and fresh out the kitchen" part—it's the part where I like to mime driving a car, the part after the toots when I pull down my arm like I'm honking the horn on a big rig, right in the middle of my song and dance repertoire—when all of a sudden, I hear one of the doors to the stairwell open and close, which is normal; the nurses and caregivers use these halls to get around faster and not clog up the elevators that the seniors use. The next thing I know, something hits me over the head, and it's lights out. I never even saw the guy. *Or gal.* Who am I to discriminate?

Shit! I blink my eyes open as I come to. I have no idea where I am or how long I've been here, but however long that might be, I find myself awake, with a killer headache. A headache a lot like the one I got when I fell out of my friend's parents' camper in the second grade. My friend who was also named Shelby. Weird, right? Anyway, we were playing after school at her house, and her mom found nothing wrong with our playing in one of those VW vans that were small campers with the part that pops up out of the roof for you to sleep in.

So there we were, playing with our Super Spy Barbies in the pop-up part, when she jumped down to get a clothing change for her doll. Other Shelby was a lot bigger than me. I was the runt of the litter back then. When she went to pull herself back up, dress included, she grabbed the board I was sitting on, and I wasn't big enough to hold the board down, so the other Shelby pulled me and the board down on top of her. We landed in order: borad, then me, then the dolls and their accoutrements. After that, I bounced off of her and out the open sliding door onto the sidewalk, face first.

Next thing I knew, I was coming to, and her mom was running down the driveway with the phone to her ear. A couple of minutes later, my mom and dad pulled up in my mom's old Jeep Cherokee, followed by a fire truck and an ambulance.

As it turned out, I had one mother of a concussion, which we found out while my dad was hanging out with all of the firemen and paramedics that he knew because they all played basketball together at the gym. I spent the night in the emergency room and the next week with the mother of all headaches, which is how I feel right now as I struggle to open my eyes and make them focus.

I look around, and everything is blurry. I blink my eyes a couple of times to clear my vision. It helps a little. I look around me—mops and brooms, shelves of lightbulbs and other various accoutrements and cleaning supplies—when is dawns on me that I am trapped in a utility closet, à la R. Kelly.

I'm sitting on the floor on my butt with my back against some more shelves. My legs are straight out in front of me, and my ankles are tied together with a zip tie. Yippee! I groan out loud when I realize that my hands are bound the same way behind my back.

I could lie down and wait for a psycho to come

back and finish me off, but that's not how my daddy raised me. And if I did die because I was being a big baby, Granny would bring me back to life just to whoop my butt and kill me again. So I wiggle around, trying to find anything I can break these zip ties on. I notice the door has hinges that look like little hooks, and I scoot over to try to hook the tie on my ankles to it. I wiggle and kick my legs like I'm doing a super ab crunch—damn, I need to join a gym—and then I wiggle some more. I guess I should be pretty thankful I keep my biweekly yoga date with my grandmother and her friends.

I hook the zip tie on the bottom door hinge and kick my feet by bending and straightening my knees. "Come on, come on," I chant under my breath as I rub the plastic against the sharp side of the door hinge.

"Yes!" I shout as the tie breaks. I swing to my knees and push up to my feet. My legs shake. Impressive considering there's a polka band playing in my head and I kind of want to puke.

I lean my right shoulder against the shelves and squeeze my eyes tight, hoping to stop the room from spinning before I can find something to undo the tie at my wrists. My eyes pop open at the sudden quiet rattle of the door. I have to squint against the intrusion of the bright light that is immediately switched on. When I open them again, I am face-to-face with the vibrant jade eyes of Trent. I can't help but sigh. I have been avoiding him all day, and here he is, trying to rescue me. Too bad I was in the middle of rescuing myself.

"Jesus, Shelby, you scared the shit out of me!" he booms. I just roll my eyes, which I instantly regret.

"What?" I ask innocently, or as innocently as I can with only one eye open and the other rolling around in my head.

"You just can't help yourself, can you?" he asks.

"I don't understand what you're talking about," I say coyly.

"You just have to stir up trouble, don't you?" he asks, shaking his head.

I don't care to answer, so I don't. It's not like I find myself trapped in a closet every day. Who am I kidding? I may not find trouble, but trouble always has a way of finding me. I sigh. Trent just glares at me.

"I've got her!" he shouts over his shoulder. "She's okay."

"How did you find me?" I ask.

"Funny you should mention it, but an anonymous tip came into the station, warning us that you were getting too close and had to 'be taught a lesson.'" I cringe.

"That doesn't sound so good," I say.

"No, it does not," he agrees, placing a kiss on the tip of my nose.

"I've been thinking, Trent," I tell him as he cuts my arms free, rubbing the circulation back into my hands. "I think you're right. I think it has to be James."

He sighs.

"We found James this morning. He was shacked up with a colleague of Daisy's," he says softly. "I think you were right all along, honey, and I'm so sorry that I didn't listen to you."

Feeling scared and at loose ends, I burst into tears.

"I'm scared, Trent," I tell him. "I'm scared, and I don't know where to look."

"It's okay to be scared, baby," he says sweetly. "Let me take you home. You'll feel better after a big burger and a bubble bath."

"I will. I really will," I agree, nodding my head. Who am I to stop him from providing me with two of my favorite things? Add in my favorite thing in his jeans, and I just might be right as rain.

"Come on. Let's go collect Missy and go home."

And we do just that. It's absolutely perfect. I only wish I had some clue that, in just a few short hours, our lives would change forever. *Irrevocably.*

DANGEROUS WOMAN

The shrill ringing of my cell phone on my nightstand wakes me from a dead sleep. I squeeze my eyes tight before prying them open and wiping the sleep from my eyes. My head aches from the lack of actual sleep. I'm so tired that it feels like I only just fell into bed moments ago, not a few hours ago.

I roll over, and my hand swipes across the empty side of the bed. *Trent.* For someone I tried so hard to get out of my life, I sure do seem to miss the big bastard. I take a second to wonder where he's gone off to. But I guess that's just life with a detective in your bed. *Duty calls.* My phone rings again, and I reach over to grab it.

"Hello," I rasp, my voice still heavy with sleep.

"Shelby, come here right now. I know who it is," my granny whispers into the phone. "And I think they're here right now," she says before hanging up. The disconnect tone blares in my ear and rattles around in my concussion-addled brain.

Without thinking, I am out of bed and tossing the big T-shirt I was sleeping in aside. Trent's T-shirt. One I may or may not have, ahem, stolen from his bag when he was sleeping here regularly. I mean, borrowed . . . I borrowed it. And forgot to return it. I throw on my bra, an old Cal State T-shirt, and a pair of jeans over my panties. I slide my feet into my favorite Chucks and am ready in record time. I would alert Guinness, but I don't have time.

I slip my phone into my jeans pocket, briefly contemplate calling Trent, but nix the idea because he just wouldn't understand. Or worse, he'd call me stupid again. And it might be grade-school chickenshit of me, but I just can't take that again. I toss my long hair up into a messy knot, secure it with one of the many rubber bands I have stashed around my condo, and then head for the door. I grab my purse from the front hall table and my keys from the bowl, stopping one more time to lament the loss of Trent's keys next to mine like a sad, whiny little girl. Missy is still tucked in somewhere for the night, so I don't bother her. Then I head out the door, locking up behind me.

I hop into my car and start her up. I turn off the radio, not wanting to hear more than my thoughts as I race, once again this week, toward my grandmother's house. And my thoughts are plentiful these days. I can't help but think of Mr. Di Francesco and Bitty Sue.

And what they—or at least, their deaths—have to do with Marla's accident. I just can't figure it out.

On paper, it all looks natural. Trent even said it a million times—old people die. Those words echo around and around in my head. And then there's Marla's accident, if it even was one. I am definitely starting to have my doubts. Why would a woman recovering from a broken hip be in the stairwell? The answer is, she wouldn't. My thoughts are interrupted by my phone. This time the tone informs me of an incoming text message.

> GRANNY: THE MEET HAS BEEN COMPROMISED. MEET ME AT THE OLD LUMBERYARD ON PACIFIC HWY

Jesus, I really need to stop letting her watch the military channel. First the ghillie suit she crocheted in macramé class and now her officially worded text messages. I can tell by her message that my dad is back in town and they have been spending a lot of time together. Which is good. He should get some time with her, too, but I can't help feeling a little left out.

The old lumberyard is actually closer to my condo than the retirement home, so it will shave off some of the time it takes to get to Granny. Then she can explain to me all of her cryptic messages. *Cagey old bird.* The actual lumberyard has been abandoned for a few years now. When the economy tanked, the company went out of business. They closed their doors, and that was that. No one ever bought the lot, and most of the lumber and materials are still there, locked behind the chain-link fences.

I park my car in the lot and notice that I'm the only one here. Although, that doesn't surprise me. Granny would have found a way here, and this place hasn't been in business in years, so it stands to reason that I would be the only one in the lot.

I notice the gate is propped open, and like the bimbo in a horror movie, I head on in. I might not be blonde, but I do have big boobs, so anything is possible. I push on the unlatched gate, and it swings open, making an eerie squeak in the dead of night as the rusty hinges announce my arrival. My sneaker-clad feet clomp quietly through the concrete pathways as I search for my grandmother.

I hear a muffled groan and look down an aisle's offshoot. There is Trent, lying on his side, his shirt soaked in blood. He looks up when he hears my approach, his bright eyes, dimmed with the pain, meet mine, and he utters one word that chills me to my bones.

"Run," Trent rasps.

I'm frozen. My brain can't comprehend what is happening. My feet are cemented to the ground. My body won't listen to Trent's command. He closes his eyes tight in defeat just as a voice creeps down my spine.

"I don't think so," an eerily familiar voice says from behind me. I slowly turn and come face-to-face with my worst nightmare.

There stands a wolf in sheep's clothing. The man I thought was trustworthy, the man I never realized was harming the people I care about. And here he stands with a very mean-looking gun, which is pointed at my grandmother.

"Let her go, Ernie," I say as I slowly raise my hands up, palms out. "You don't need her here," I say, trying to buy time.

"You're funny," he says with a laugh. "But no one is leaving. You all owe me this!" he shouts, spittle flying from his weathered lips.

"What do we owe you?" I ask calmly.

"Everything!" he screams.

"I don't understand," I say softly. I see Trent start to move out of the corner of my eye. There's so much blood that it scares me.

"Of course you don't, you stupid girl," he sneers. "Your grandfather took my family from me, so I get to take his."

This man is speaking in riddles I can't begin to understand. My grandfather was the kindest man I knew. He would never have hurt a fly.

"Shelby." Granny's harsh whisper cuts through the night. "He's mad, honey. Bonkers. He can't make sense."

"Do you know what they made us do?" he asks. I just shake my head no, but I see Granny's shoulders slump down. She knows what's coming next. "They said we were cutting LZs in the brush so the choppers could land and bring in troops and supplies. But before we knew it, we were destroying whole fields of crops.

"The government felt that if the poor village people were starving and had no way to feed themselves, they would help our side. Not to mention what the poison did to the bodies of the civilians. *The women and children.* I still have to choke back my vomit when I think about it."

"What poison? What are you talking about? I'm not sure that I understand." I shake my head back and forth, trying to make sense of what he's saying.

God, if only I can keep him talking, maybe I can figure a way out. Or maybe I can convince him to put the gun down and let us go. Shit. I just don't know what to do.

"The war, stupid!"

"The war? You mean Vietnam?" I ask.

That was ages ago. Before I was even born. I never in my wildest dreams thought that a chunk of a history textbook would be what finally took me out. Bad driving on overcrowded California highways? Probably. An atrocious diet consisting of lattes and street tacos? Totally. *Crazy dude wielding a gun and screaming about poison and Vietnam?* Nope, I never would have checked that box.

"Of course Vietnam," he slobbers again. "Bitty Sue's husband was the captain that led us on 'Operation Cherry Picker.' And your grandfather was his henchman!"

"My husband was an honorable soldier!" Granny shouts.

"It's their fault all those men died. *My family.* He made us poison those people!" Ernie screams. Granny just lowers her eyes. It dawns on me now that she knows exactly what he's talking about.

"You knew?" I ask, looking at my grandmother. She nods her head before answering me.

"You have to know, Shell, your grandfather was beside himself," she says softly. "They weren't there to kill the women and children. That was a side effect of the Agent Orange they were using. But everything else he said is true."

"Okay, but what does this have to do with your family?" I ask. "I still don't understand."

"Oh, I'll tell you," he sneers. "My wife was in that village with us. I had to keep her hidden because our affair was forbidden. But everyone in the unit knew. Late one night, we were surrounded by the VC. They were everywhere. We had no chance of defeating them; there were so many. The Captain called for fire on our position, and your grandfather didn't contest it! All the villagers. Our men. *My wife.* We were shelled by our own artillery and bombed by our own airplanes because that call was made!" he screamed.

"He was left with no choice!" Granny yells back. "Without it, you all would have died."

"She's right," Trent says from his place in the corner. His face is now gray, and he is totally slumped over. Shit.

"That's a lie!" he screams again. "I begged him not to do it. I pleaded with him to help me get my wife to safety, but he said there was no time. My wife was pregnant."

"Your wife was a prostitute," Granny grumbles.

Jesus Christ, is she really going to argue with a man holding a gun? Oh, shit. I realize what she's doing. Granny is giving me an opening to run, or fight, which is what any Whitmore worth their salt would do. If I'm going to die tonight, I might as well do it fighting.

"She was not. She was pregnant with my child!" *Oh, shit.* This is escalating fast, much faster than I'm prepared for. The crazed man is gesticulating wildly.

"I doubt it," she huffs.

"Well, I killed them all anyway!" he shouts.

I wonder who it is he's talking about, who he killed. Bitty Sue's husband died in that bombing; we all know it. So who else did he kill? And then it dawns on me.

"You mean Mr. Di Francesco and Bitty Sue?" I ask. "You killed them?"

"Of course." He smiles.

"They recognized you, didn't they?"

"Di Francesco knew who I was the minute I moved into my apartment in the building. Bitty Sue had no idea. One night she was crying over how she still missed her husband, the captain, so I slipped a sleeping pill in her wine and tucked her into bed. I suffocated her with a pillow after she fell asleep."

"Granny and Marla were right," I gasp.

"Marla was. It's why I convinced her to follow me into the stairwell, and then I threw her down them. I didn't expect her to survive it. She's tougher than I thought."

"You did it," I say, reeling for anything to get us out of here. I can't think of how badly Trent is hurt. If I do, Ernie will win while I'm distracted. "You killed them."

"And Whitmore and Foyle," he says, his eyes twinkling with malice.

"What do you mean by 'Whitmore and Foyle'?" I ask. "My grandfather had a heart attack. Trent's grandad died in a car accident."

"He had a heart attack after not taking his heart meds for six months," he says with a laugh. "Although, I do owe a big thank-you to that asshole you dated. When he beat the shit out of you, it sent Whitmore over the edge."

I close my eyes. His death wasn't my fault, but it still was.

"What about Trent's grandfather?" I ask.

"I poked a tiny little hole in his power steering line. It was only a matter of time, and then, BAM! He crashes into a guardrail on the 805. He never did like to wear a seat belt." He smiles. "My only regret was not starting with you two and then moving on to your parents so that they could watch me take everything from them and not be able to do a thing about it," he says, seething.

"I highly doubt that." Granny cackles. "I'm not sure you're smart enough."

Here's my chance. Granny now has his full attention. She's distracting him from me, and it's the opening that I need. After years of watching San Diego's shitty football team with my dad, I spread my arms wide and tip my head down as I run as fast as I can, closing the gap between us. I wrap my arms around his body, pinning his arms to his sides as I take his old-man ass to the mat.

In my head, I thought I could disarm him and call the police. But that is never how it goes. I guess *007* lied to me. While the gun was knocked from his grasp when we hit the ground, I was momentarily distracted as I celebrated that small win. He used that to his advantage by wiggling an arm loose and using it to punch me in the face.

Oh, shit, I think as he flips me to my back, slamming the back of my head against the concrete, making me see stars. This man is not as frail as he led us all to believe. He punches my face again with his fist, and I feel my lip split open, stunning me for a moment. My fingers grab at his shirt as I scratch and rip and claw my way to freedom, my legs kicking anything I can. I manage to get my knee up high enough to kick him in the balls, forcing him to loosen his hold on me.

I flip myself over to my belly and frantically start crawling away. I see the gun lying on the ground, but it is just out of my reach. I look over my shoulder and see that Trent is now unconscious. Fuck, I don't know how much longer he has before he can't be saved. Granny is inching her way toward him, so I have some hope. But all of that is dashed away when I feel a hard hand wrap around my ankle and start dragging me back.

My fingers scratch and claw wildly for anything. For a purchase on something to keep this madman from pulling me back. For escape. For a weapon. I'm too far away from the gun. There's no way I'll be able to reach it with the way Ernie is dragging me backward, laughing the whole time.

My fingernails are clawing at the concrete. I'm desperate for anything I can get my hands on. But there's nothing, absolutely nothing. I'm just about to give up hope and let Ernie finish me off, when suddenly my hand wraps around a piece of wood no longer than a baseball bat. It is rough against my hands and jagged on one end. It must have broken off from a larger piece of lumber.

My potential weapon concealed in the late-night darkness, I almost missed it. Almost. My captor and executioner pulls me back once more, but as he bends down to pull me forward, I turn, swinging my prize. The chunk of wood connects with the side of his head, and the sickening crack echoes through the night. His grip on my body drops immediately as he falls to the ground with less brain matter than he started with.

I fall backward breathing heavily. In my panic, the piece of wood is still clutched in my hands. I see Granny is using Trent's shirt to try to staunch the flow of blood from a bullet wound. I cry out at the sight of him lying there, but I'm unable to get to him. It seems all of the blows to my head this week have caught up to me, and I feel like my body is covered in sandbags.

"Wow, looks like I missed the party," Kane, the dumbass, says as he comes running in with a bunch of other cops.

I'd like to respond with something utterly witty and brilliant, but when I open my mouth, my eyes roll to the back of my head, and everything goes black.

epilogue

As I carry my picnic basket down the hospital hallway, I can't help feeling like a slutty Little Red Riding Hood. But Trent has been here for two days after receiving the gunshot wound and knock on the head courtesy of Ernie the Psycho.

As it turned out, Ernie had gone a little mad with all of the Agent Orange exposure. After his wife died that night so long ago, he had pretended to die with the rest of his unit—only no one questioned it when his body was never recovered.

Ernie happily plotted his revenge while living in the jungles of Vietnam, crazy as a bedbug. That is, until the day Trent, along with a unit of Army Rangers, showed up for training, looking just like the spitting image of his grandfather, Lieutennant Richard Foyle. The knowledge that life went on for the men who survived the bombing that night, when he had nothing to show for it, drove him back to the US under an assumed identity.

Ernie, or Tupperware, as Marla called him, had been acting out his revenge ever since he spotted Trent in the jungle. Mr. Di Francesco was the first to recognize him as the man they all made fun of in the unit. Being given the name "Tupperware," because he always went home with the leftover girl, never getting the first choice, had already broken him down, and for that, our grandfathers paid the ultimate price for the bullying of their youth.

Once we started investigating the death of Bitty Sue, my recounting that Trent and I had seen her with the new guy in the elevator and the fact that he mentioned being with our grandfathers' unit in Mexico in '63 led to Marla putting it all together. Thinking that it was so over-the-top ridiculous and that she needed some serious proof before she went to Trent, her grandson, she followed him, and it almost cost her her life.

I'm happy to report that Marla is recovering quicker than ever. She says it's the prospect of beautiful grandbabies from Trent and me that keep her going. I told her not to hold her breath, but then she hit me with a whammy, saying, "This is what your grandfathers always wanted for you two." And, well, then I was fucked.

I smile as I reach Trent's room. He'd begged me to be with him and had persuaded me with his magical mouth. Who am I to say no to that? So this is our first date since everything shook down.

My palms are sweating. I'm more nervous for this date than I was for homecoming in my sophomore year with Caleb Vanderwhaul. And I had every right to be then. Caleb had seemed just a little too excited when I had accepted his invitation and even more excited when he saw my backless dress with the short, poufy skirt.

We'd had a nice enough time at dinner, being two sixteen-year-olds who didn't know what they were doing in the world and had nothing in common. He'd given me a beautiful corsage with carnations and roses. I felt so grown-up and magical when we walked into the dance at the high school gym.

We laughed and danced with all of our friends in a big circle in the middle of the dance floor. Everyone was watching us, and I knew I was cool. Then poor Caleb got a little too excited; I mean, I could feel his sixteen-year-old excitement poke into me every now and then on the dance floor, but I guess the "Thong Song" put him over the edge.

One minute, I'm "backing that thang up," and the next, I'm wondering what's wet and sticky all over my back. Turns out Caleb blew his load during that dance in front of everyone, and I spent the rest of the night hiding in the bathroom, wiping sixteen-year-old-boy jizz off of my back and calling my dad to come get me.

Dad, the big jerk that he was, loved it and laughed the whole way home—something about my never calling "that douche" Caleb again and how he didn't even have to do anything about it. Thinking on it now, there was a kind of maniacal gleam in his eyes as he drove me home to burn my new dress and take a scorching hot shower while crying over my mortification of everyone seeing what had happened. That's kind of how I feel now as I push open the door to Trent's room, the smile slides right off my face.

"You've got to be fucking kidding me," I growl as I take in a naked Trent receiving a sponge bath from a topless BBN.

"You had to know he'd come back to me, bitch," she sneers. "I can give him so much more than you can. And better, too." She winks as she continues to bathe him.

"It's not what it looks like, Shelby. I swear it!" he pleads.

I sigh because I know she's manipulating the situation. So I do what any normal girl would do when she walks in on her boyfriend receiving a sponge bath from a psycho nurse. I turn around and march back out of the room, Trent's panicked voice shouting my name. Whatever. I have bigger fish to fry.

I stomp to the nurses' station and demand the head nurse. When I tell her what BBN is doing in the room with my boyfriend—okay, I stretched that part a bit—she agrees to follow me back to Trent's room. We walk in on Trent trying to get BBN off of him as she straddles his lap and says that he needs to get over it. Apparently, he'd been trying to call for help, but she disconnected his call button while he was sleeping before she removed her clothing.

"You're fired!" the head nurse roars, gaining everyone's attention in the room.

"You can't fire me!"

"I just did. Get your shit and get out. Don't expect a reference."

"You'll pay for this," she spits at me. I just smile. I defeated a crazy-ass murderer this week; she doesn't scare me.

"You do know I killed a man this week, right?" I ask her.

"Trent, are you going to let her threaten me like that?" she gasps.

"Yep," is all he answers, his eyes sparkling as they lock on mine. I told him I wasn't going to take his shit anymore.

"You can't do this to me!" BBN, who is now spitting mad, shrieks as security officers escorts her out of Trent's room in nothing but her underwear.

"I'll just see to this," the head nurse says. "I'm sorry for the inconvenience, Detective." Trent just nods.

"Soooo . . . on a scale of one to ten, how mad are you right now?" Trent asks.

"Enough. Just enough," I say. His eyes are wide, and I'm kind of enjoying the moment. "But I won't let her ruin our first date," I tell him. Trent smiles wide at me as I unpack our lunch and get down to the business of our first date post serial killer business.

THE END . . . FOR NOW

PLAYLIST

1. Trapped in the Closet — R. Kelly
2. Make You Miss Me — Sam Hunt
3. Speakers — Sam Hunt
4. Ex to See — Sam Hunt
5. Ignition — R. Kelly
6. Run Through the Jungle — Creedence Clearwater Revival
7. Fortunate Son — Creedence Clearwater Revival
8. Dangerous Woman — Ariana Grande
9. Fighter — Christina Aguilera
10. Vandalizer — Sam Hunt

ABOUT THE AUTHOR

Jennifer is a thirty-three-year-old lover of words, all words: the written, the spoken, the sung (even poorly), the sweet, the funny, and also the four-letter variety. She is a native of San Diego, California, where she grew up reading the Brownings and *Rebecca* with her mother, and *Clifford the Big Red Dog* and *The Dog That Glowed in the Dark* with her dad, much to her mother's dismay.

Jennifer is a graduate of California State University San Marcos, where she studied criminology and justice studies. She is also a member of Alpha Xi Delta.

Ten years ago, she was swept off her feet by her very own sailor. Today, they are happily married and are the parents of an eight-year-old and a set of seven-year-old twins. She lives in East Texas and can often be found on the soccer fields, drawing with her children, or reading. Jennifer is convinced that if she puts her Fitbit on one of her dogs, she might finally make her step goals. She loves a great romance, an alpha hero, and lots and lots of laughter.

STALK ME . . .

www.JenniferRebeccaAuthor.com

Facebook.com/JenniferRebeccaAuthor

Twitter: @JenniRLreads

Instagram @JenniRLreads

Pintrest: @Jennigrl83

SnapChat @JennyRLreads

ACKNOWLEDGMENTS

First and foremost, thank you for reading this book. Dead and Buried is so special to me for many reasons, some being that a lot of the little bits and pieces stories about Shelby and Trent's families are a little bit of ours. And second, two years ago, my husband, Sean, and my parents were the only people who knew that I spent my free time writing. I'm fairly shy and intended to keep it that way. Sean had other plans. When my Poppee passed away, my dad asked me to use those skills to write his obituary. The day it published in the San Diego Union Tribune, we laughed and joked that I was finally a published author. Three days later, Shelby was born. Writing this story made me laugh when I didn't think I could so these characters, these stories will always be special to me.

I would like to thank my dad who has no problem telling groups of retired Marines that they should buy my romance novels. It takes a strong man to raise a crazy daughter. And I also want to thank him for talking over plot points with me. We spent an entire weekend working out the plotline of this book. Without him politely pointing out my historical mistakes, the killer would have been about 97 years old. Thank you for being my biggest supporter.

And also, my mom. She thinks this journey is cool. She loves helping pick out cover images and telling all the bloggers we should have chosen "a naked picture." No, mom, you'll never live that down and I wouldn't want you too. You're a dangerous dame through and through, you live your live with joy and love and laughter, and I hope you never change. You have been my editor, my cheerleader, my supporter, and my champion since I was a baby. No one, and I mean no one, believed in me before you did.

Thank you to my strong, brave, brilliant, and beautiful grandmothers. You both are the OG Dangerous Dames. I love you immensely and I hope one day I'm a strong as you are.

I want to thank Alyssa Garcia of Uplifting Designs for such beautiful cover art and interior design, but also for being my friend. Two years ago, we drove together to an EL James signing and talked about Emma killing people with salad, which reminds me I'll stick to pizza or tacos… We also talked about books and in passing I mentioned that I was writing a book. It was this very book and that weekend changed my life.

Together, Alyssa and Stacy, then Christina, welcomed me into their group. They encouraged me and believed in me. Thank you all for everything. You keep me going when I feel burned out and you all inspire me with your kindness and friendship.

Thank you to Shauna Kruse of Kruse Images and Photography and BT Urruela for the amazing cover image. You guys have been wonderful to work with. I appreciate you so much.

Thank you Bethany Pennypacker for being an awesome editor. Not only did you help me make this story the best that it can be, but you loved Shelby. I cannot thank you enough.

I also want to thank Nazarea Andrews and Ink-Slinger PR. You guys have made everything so easy for me and have been a dream to work with. I'm still pinching myself.

Thank you to my sassy minxes who inspire and encourage every day. You guys are the real deal and I look up and love you all. I am so thankful for your friendships.

And last but never least, in life and in my heart, my sweet Sean. Next month is our 10 year wedding anniversary and I swear it feels like yesterday we said I do under the canopy in mom and dad's backyard. I have never not once regretted a single thing where you are concerned. You have given me a beautiful life full of crazy kids, cats, dogs, and now our senior citizens. You're my favorite person to laugh with and the one I want to hold me when I cry. You have such a big heart and a glorious beard. You are my biggest cheerleader and the one who when I think I have figured it all out asks me why? I couldn't have done this journey with with anyone but you because it was only ever you. I knew it that night at Shannon's apartment when I looked into your baby blues, you were going to be a game changer if I let you and I thank God every day that I did...or you sweet talked me into it...semantics. ;) You're my everything- today, tomorrow, and always.

ALSO BY JENNIFER REBECCA

THE FUNERALS AND OBITUARIES MYSTERIES

Dead and Buried

Dead and Gone, TBD

THE CLAIRE GOODNITE THRILLERS

Tell Me a Story

THE SOUTHERN HEARTBEAT SERIES

Stand

Whiskey Lullabye

Mercy (Free on Wattpad)

Just a Dream, coming 2017

Excerpt from...

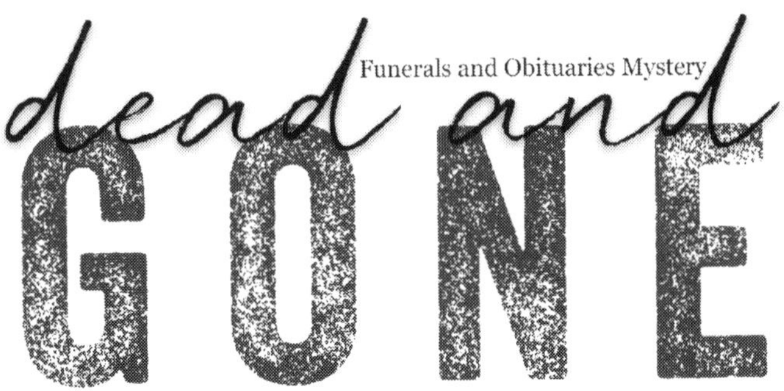

FATAL ATTRACTION

I'm dead meat. Literally. Dead. Meat. Last month, when Trent and I started up again, I promised him that I wouldn't do anything crazy. I wouldn't go off half-cocked. And most importantly, I wouldn't follow our grandmothers down the crazy-ass rabbit hole of Granny Grabbers and Dangerous Dames.

"You're not police officers," he had said.

And I agreed. We're not.

Trent also might have coerced me into agreeing with him in the most despicable way. One minute, my legs were wrapped around his neck, and the next, my eyes were rolled back in my head and I was one more "Oh, yes" away from the Promised Land.

"Shell," he said to me in between licks and kisses. "Promise me you won't do anything crazy." He kissed me again and again.

"Yes." I ignored him as I rocked against his mouth,

moving closer and closer to ecstacy.

"Promise," he commanded as I spiraled closer and closer to the edge.

"Yes!" I cried.

"You promise?" he asked me, but I was too far gone.

"Sweet petunia, yes!"

"I'm so glad we agree. You have no idea how happy this makes me, Shelby." Trent smiled as he slithered up my body like the snake that he is.

Although, I had an idea how happy my climax had made him, as it was currently poking me in the thigh. Before I had a chance to catch my breath or even question what, exactly, Trent and I had agreed on, he slid all the way inside me, and my eyes rolled back in my head.

As it turned out, we had allegedly agreed that I wouldn't go on any more capers with my friend Daisy, the retired hooker, and our grandmothers. Sophia was out; she was at some big figure-skating competition in Chicago.

I still agreed. I mean, what kind of trouble could two widowed senior citizens, a retired hooker, and an obituaries columnist for the local paper get into? I mean, really. Lightning doesn't strike twice. It doesn't, right?

And Trent and I had worked out some kinks. He yelled less. I pretended to listen more. And when I didn't, he used his handsome mouth in better ways than yelling, if you catch my drift. We were officially in the love bubble. The honeymoon stage. I wasn't ready to rock the boat for just anything all willy-nilly.

But Daisy, my sweet, fabulous, eccentrically dressed best friend had a problem. Several of her . . . um . . . colleagues from the old days were missing. Like, really missing, not shacked up with a john. And she was worried. Yes, my thoughtful friend had a problem, and she came to me for help, or advice—I don't really know what. All I know is that that led me to today, sitting handcuffed to the pipes of a bathroom sink in a filthy motel just this side of Mexico and dressed like a cheap hooker. Yep, I'm in trouble, folks. Just like I said . . . Dead. Meat. I guess I should start at the beginning . . .

Excerpt from...

SouthernHeartbeats Vol. 1

Cody

This is it. This is that moment that changes your life. The lynch pin for the life you know you are supposed to live. This moment, this one right here, is mine.

It's the fourth quarter of the biggest game of the year. The biggest game of my life. This is the Super Bowl. My team and I have busted our asses for the last year to be here and we are here. We are mother fucking New York, baby.

My parents and my girl are in the team box watching. My parents, they're proud. I busted my ass as a kid in a small town in Texas to get to the NFL. I'm going to give my ring to my dad, the best guy I know. My girl on the other hand, she's not proud. She gets off on being my fiancée. She's after a different ring and I'm going to give it to her in the off season.

So here I am running to the end zone, fourth quarter

of the biggest game of my life. Timmy, our quarterback and a crazy mother fucker all around waits until the very last moment to snap the ball across the field to me.

I leap up into the air like a mother fucking gazelle. No, they're weak. Like a mother fucking mountain lion on the hunt for my prey. I arch back to grab the ball from the air and see all the flashes. This image. This picture of me is going to be on the front page of every paper in the morning.

My fingers just touch the ball when I'm hit from behind by a Mack truck, or at least that's what it feels like. When my body hits the ground, the ball is in my arms underneath me and the human truck hits me again. I will never forget the sickening crack we all heard before everything went black…

*****

Lights. Lights are bright. And blurry. Where the fuck am I? I blink again, trying to clear my eyes, when I see an angel. From the light up above me comes the most gorgeous girl with bright blue eyes and big, light blonde curls bundled up like my Granny's yarn on top of her head. She smiles a toothpaste commercial smile at me.

"Welcome back." But that's all I hear. Because when I try to ask my angel if I'm dead, everything goes black again. And the last thought I have is what a dumb fucking question to ask an angel. Of course I'm fucking dead. And now, now, I'm also a moron.

*****

When I wake up again, there's a constant beeping that is driving me slowly insane. It's like *Beep...Beep... Beep…* I open my eyes again and this time everything works. I see Kimmy and her perfectly styled red hair. Her gorgeous face marred by an ugly frown. She looks up and realizes I'm awake. I realize that I am in a hospital and that God awful beeping is my heart beating, so that's good, right?

"Oh, good. You're awake," Kimmy says coolly and I can't help but think her first words to me should have been something along the lines of *Yay!!! You're still alive!!!* But who am I to judge. "Look, your parents went to get a cup of coffee, so I'll make this quick."

"Okay," I say but it comes out garbled. Kimmy obviously needs no approval because she just keeps on keepin' on and with the words that come out of her mouth, I think I'd rather get hit by that guy from San Diego that's the size of an elephant again.

"Look, it's not you, it's me."

"What?" I ask.

"This just isn't working out for me anymore," she starts. "I signed on to be a football wife, not the caretaker to an invalid in Nowheresville, Texas," I hear a gasp from the door and see my mom and dad standing there with my angel, who is apparently a nurse. A really hot fucking nurse. But I can't care about that because this crazy person is ripping my heart out. And right in front of my mom, no less.

"I should probably go. I'm going off shift and Jackie will be your nurse if you need anything this evening." And with that my angel leaves me high and dry. I don't even know her name.

"You should probably go," I tell Kimmy. "And you should leave your engagement ring with my mom over there," Kimmy gasps.

"But I love this ring! You know how much I love it," she pleads.

"Funny, I thought you loved me," and with one last pleading look of her big brown eyes, she takes off my ring and stands. Kimmy walks over to my poor, sweet mom and places the ring in her up turned palm. Those eyes, they used to get me. I'd do anything to make her smile. And her puppy dog eyes got me every time. But never again. Brown, green, blue or hazel, I will never fall for another pair of lying eyes from any woman ever again.

Made in the USA
Lexington, KY
01 February 2019